THE CHAOS ARENA

Book 2 of The New Scions

C.L. STEGALL

The Chaos Arena

Copyright © 2026 by C.L. Stegall.

All rights reserved. No part of this book may be used or reproduced in any form whatsoever without written permission except in the case of brief quotations in critical articles or reviews.

This book is a work of fiction. Names, characters, businesses, organizations, places, events and incidents either are the product of the author's imagination or are used fictitiously. Any resemblance to actual persons, living or dead, events, or locales is entirely coincidental.

Printed in the United States of America.

For more information, or to book an event, contact :
(Email & Website)
http://www.CLStegall.com

Book design by C.L. Stegall
Cover design by Safeer Ahmed

ISBN - Paperback: 979-8-9946961-3-2
ISBN - eBook : 979-8-9946961-2-5

First Edition: March 2026

CONTENTS

1 1
2 14
3 26
4 36
5 48
6 56
7 66
8 80
9 87
10 101
11 117
12 128
13 157
14 171
15 181
16 195
17 209
18 228
19 244
20 259
21 273
22 287

ACKNOWLEDGMENTS

We all walk different, sometimes difficult paths.

Hold fast to your convictions.

1

The numbers didn't lie. Alexis Rain wished they would.

Three weeks since Phthonos. Three weeks since she'd watched her half-brother dissolve into cosmic nothingness while their mother, *her* mother, not his, never his, wrapped him in chains of primordial night. Three weeks since the world had confirmed what she'd always suspected: that she was different, dangerous, and very possibly a mistake the universe would eventually correct.

And in those weeks, she hadn't been able to stop thinking about Emerson Greer.

The intelligence center hummed, screens casting blue-white light across workstations that should have been staffed by a full team. At 3:47 AM, Alexis owned the place. Not because she needed the sleep. Two hours a night had been plenty since her abilities manifested, a quirk of primordial inheritance that Keats still complained was cosmically unfair. But this work required solitude. Required secrecy.

Coffee cups formed a small army along the edge of her desk. Seven of them. She'd stopped tasting anything around cup four, but the ritual of brewing and drinking gave her hands something to do while her mind worked.

The data on her screen painted only part of the picture. Emerson Greer: son of Hermes, information broker, the man who'd traded her a god-killing weapon in exchange for saving Keats's life.

She'd made that deal. Odin's Oath, cosmically binding, the kind of agreement that carved itself into the fabric of reality. She'd stolen Hermes's Caduceus from an illegal supernatural auction, handed it to a man she knew was dangerous, and told herself it was worth the cost.

Keats was alive. Phthonos was contained. The Network was operational.

Victory, right?

So why couldn't she stop thinking about what Greer planned to do with the weapon she'd given him?

The Caduceus could kill immortals. Greer had been explicit about that. *In the right hands, with the proper knowledge, it can be used to kill someone who's technically immortal. Someone like a god who's forgotten that divine status doesn't make them untouchable.*

Who did Greer want dead badly enough to bargain for a divine weapon?

The question burrowed into her brain and refused to leave.

Alexis pulled up another database, financial records this time, and let the columns of numbers focus her thoughts. This was how her gift worked best: external data to sharpen the questions, then the inheritance from Nyx to retrieve the answers. If it had been spoken, written down, or transmitted in any form, she could know it. She had to ask the right way.

Why does Emerson Greer want to kill an immortal?

Too broad. The answer came as fragments: rage, loss, decades of planning. Nothing she could use.

She refined the question, let the financial records guide her focus.

What loss drives Emerson Greer?

The answer surfaced like something rising from deep water: *Margaret Greer. Mother. Deceased.*

Alexis pulled up the death certificate through the Network's database, confirmation of what her gift had already told her. Margaret Greer. Age 47. Cause of death: cardiac arrest.

But the date. The date aligned with what her gift was already whispering about.

Was Margaret Greer's death natural?

No.

The knowledge came with certainty that made her stomach clench. Divine intervention. A spike in celestial energy corresponding to retributive justice patterns.

Greer's mother hadn't died of a heart attack. She'd been killed by a goddess.

"Al?"

She'd tracked his footsteps from the moment he entered the corridor. Couldn't help it, the awareness automatic. But her chest clenched anyway. A mixture of relief and guilt that made her hands pause over the keyboard.

Keats stood in the doorway holding two steaming mugs, his brown curls sleep-mussed and those green eyes too observant for 3:47 in the morning. He was wearing the T-shirt she'd stolen from him after Phthonos, some band she'd never heard of, and sweatpants that had seen better days.

"You know," he said, crossing the room, "most people use the extra hours in their day for hobbies. Knitting. Bird watching. Not…" He glanced at her screen. "Whatever this is."

"I don't knit."

"Shocking. Truly." He set one of the mugs on her desk. Hot chocolate. He'd remembered she'd been drinking too much coffee and switched her to something gentler without being asked. "Want to tell me what's actually going on?"

She minimized the window on her screen. Not fast enough to seem suspicious, she hoped, but fast enough that he wouldn't see the death certificate. "Couldn't sleep. Thought I'd get some work done."

"Al. You don't *need* to sleep. Which means you're choosing to be here instead of literally anywhere else." He perched on the edge of the desk beside her, close enough that she could feel the warmth radiating off him. "You've been doing this every night for two weeks. And every time I try to talk to you about it, you change the subject."

"It's nothing. Tying up loose ends from the Phthonos operation."

"And there's the subject change." His voice was soft. Patient. The voice he used when he already knew she was lying and was giving her a chance to course-correct. "Whatever you're carrying, you don't have to carry it alone."

She should tell him. The thought surfaced like a bubble in dark water, urgent and fragile. This was Keats, her best friend since childhood, the person who'd seen her at her worst and chosen to stay anyway. The person she was building something new with, a fragile thing that still felt too precious and uncertain to name.

But if she told him about Greer, she'd have to explain everything. The deal. The weapon. The growing certainty that she'd armed someone who intended to commit divine assassination.

And then he'd want to help. Because that's who Keats was: someone who couldn't stand by while people he cared about carried burdens alone.

She couldn't do that to him. This was her mess. Her deal. Her responsibility.

"I'm fine." She reached for his hand, lacing her fingers through his. The touch grounded her, reminded her that some things had survived the chaos of the past month. "Really. Just processing everything. It's a lot to adjust to."

Keats studied her face with those too-perceptive eyes. For a moment, she thought he was going to push. She saw a flicker in his expression that might have been his new abilities trying to tell him things his conscious mind couldn't grasp yet.

Then he squeezed her hand and nodded. "Okay. But Al? Whatever it is you're not telling me, I'm here. When you're ready."

The guilt twisted sharper. "I know."

"Come to bed? Even if you don't need sleep, you could at least lie down. Keep me company while *I* sleep like a mere mortal."

"Soon. I want to finish one more thing."

He held her gaze for a long moment. Then he leaned down and pressed a kiss to her forehead, gentle, unhurried, carrying a promise she wasn't sure she deserved.

"Don't work too hard. Even primordial goddesses need to take breaks."

"Demi-goddess."

"Semantics." He was smiling as he left, but she could see the worry underneath it.

She watched him go, the sound of his footsteps fading down the corridor. Then she turned back to her screen and pulled up the death certificate again.

Which goddess killed Margaret Greer?

The answer came: *Nemesis*.

* * * *

The pattern emerged quickly once she knew where to look.

Margaret Greer had been proud of her son. Too proud. The kind of pride that ancient Greeks would have recognized immediately, the kind that attracted divine attention.

Hubris.

Alexis pulled up archived records: social media posts, newspaper clippings, interview transcripts. Using them to confirm what her gift was already telling her. The woman had practically announced her son's divine heritage to anyone who would listen. *My Emerson is blessed by the gods themselves. Touched by something greater than human.*

The gods didn't tolerate that kind of arrogance. Never had. The mythology was full of mortals who'd claimed too much, reached too high, spoken too loudly about their connections to the divine. And the goddess who enforced that particular cosmic rule, who punished hubris and restored proper balance, was Nemesis.

Goddess of retribution. Of appropriate revenge. Of making sure mortals remembered their place in the cosmic hierarchy.

Nemesis had killed Margaret Greer. And now her son had a weapon capable of killing immortals.

Alexis's blood ran cold as the implications crystallized.

Greer wasn't planning to kill a god at random. This was personal. This was revenge, the oldest, purest motivation in the divine playbook.

But killing Nemesis herself would be nearly impossible, even with the Caduceus. A primordial concept like retribution couldn't simply be erased. The goddess was too ancient, too essential to cosmic function.

Which meant Greer would do what humans had always done when they couldn't strike at the gods directly.

He'd go after her children.

Does Nemesis have children among the Scions?

One.

The name came with a rush of associated information: Finola Cavanagh. Age 26. Last known location: Portland, Maine. Status: Inactive/Non-cooperative.

Alexis pulled up the Scion Registry to confirm, databases and gift working in tandem, the way she'd always done it. The file was sparse, but the photo showed a woman of average height with sandy brown hair and light brown eyes that seemed to look straight through the camera. Her expression suggested she was measuring the photographer and finding them wanting.

Occupation: Paralegal.

Ability: Truth detection.

Notes: Subject discovered divine heritage three years ago. Rejected all Network contact. Specifically requested to be removed from active roster. Subject wishes no involvement with divine affairs and has taken deliberate steps to remain untraceable.

Alexis stared at the file, her stomach twisting into knots.

Finola Cavanagh had done everything right. She'd learned she was half-divine, looked at the chaos and violence that came with that heritage, and walked away. She'd built a normal life as a paralegal in a coastal Maine town, deliberately disconnecting from a world she wanted no part of.

And now that world was hunting her anyway.

Because Alexis had given Emerson Greer the means to kill her.

The guilt she'd been carrying since Ontario crystallized into something harder, sharper. This wasn't abstract anymore. This wasn't *someone might get hurt*. This was a specific woman with a name and a face and a life she'd chosen, a woman who would die because Alexis Rain had made a deal to save someone she loved.

She thought of Keats's face when he'd brought her hot chocolate. The way he'd looked at her, knowing she was hiding something, choosing to trust her anyway.

She couldn't tell him. Not this. Not yet.

Because if she told him, he'd insist they bring in the Network. Make it an official operation. And then everyone would know what she'd done. The deal she'd made. The weapon she'd handed over.

This was her mistake. She had to fix it herself.

* * * *

Finding Finola Cavanagh proved exactly as difficult as the Registry notes had suggested.

Where is Finola Cavanagh now?

The answer came vague: *Coastal Maine. Moving. Hiding.*

Alexis tried again, refining her questions, using the Network databases to help focus her gift. The Portland address in the file was two years old. The apartment had been rented to someone else for eighteen months. Her former employer reported that Ms. Cavanagh had resigned "for personal reasons" and left no forwarding information.

Finola knew how to disappear. Three years of wanting nothing to do with the divine world had made her an expert at avoiding attention.

Which made sense, given her ability. A woman who could detect lies would know exactly how many people weren't telling the truth. Would understand, on a visceral level, how little she could trust anyone who approached her with friendly intentions and hidden agendas.

Including, Alexis realized with a sinking feeling, anyone who showed up claiming to want to protect her.

She was deep in a search of shipping manifests, trying to narrow her questions, find the right angle, when a notification flashed across her secondary monitor.

NEW INCIDENT REPORT — Priority: Medium

Alexis glanced at it, her attention still mostly focused on Finola. Artifact theft. Another one. The Network had been tracking a pattern of these for weeks now, minor divine items going missing from temples and sacred sites across multiple pantheons.

She opened the report anyway.

Location: Protected shrine, Corinth, Greece

Item: Iris's Rainbow Prism

Method: Unknown. No alarms triggered. No witnesses. Security footage shows artifact in place at 23:47 local time, missing at 23:52. No visible entry or exit.

Assessment: Professional extraction. Perpetrator demonstrates intimate knowledge of divine security protocols.

Iris's Rainbow Prism. A communication artifact, the kind of divine tool that facilitated messages between the gods and their mortal connections.

Alexis flagged the report for follow-up and returned to her search for Finola.

Someone else could look into the artifact theft. Aaron's team was already tracking the pattern. They'd add this to the list, analyze it, try to identify whoever was systematically targeting divine items.

She had a more immediate problem.

The Iris report slid to the back of her mind, filed under "later" alongside a dozen other Network concerns that didn't involve preventing the murder she'd made possible. Another data point in a pattern she wasn't looking at closely enough.

* * * *

The breakthrough came at 6:23 AM, when dawn was beginning to lighten the sky outside.

Has Finola Cavanagh made any traceable purchases recently?

The answer bloomed in her mind: *Grocery store. $47.83. Yesterday. Card linked to alias 'Fiona Walsh.' Kennebunkport, Maine.*

Alexis pulled up the financial records to confirm. There it was, exactly as her gift had revealed. A small purchase, the kind someone trying to stay invisible might make without thinking, using a backup identity they'd almost forgotten they had.

Kennebunkport. A coastal town about forty minutes south of Portland.

She could bring this to Lily. Could coordinate a team, run surveillance, approach Finola through official Network channels.

Or she could go herself. Now. Before anyone else woke up and asked questions she didn't want to answer.

The decision wasn't really a decision at all. She'd made it weeks ago, the moment she'd started researching Greer in secret instead of bringing her concerns to the team.

Alexis erased her search history. Cleared the files from her workstation. Removed any trace of her investigation from the Network's systems.

This was her mess. Her deal. Her responsibility.

She wrote a note for Lily, quick and vague, the kind of message that would buy her a few hours before anyone started asking questions. *Following a lead. Back soon.*

Before she left, she paused at the doorway. The intelligence center had been her sanctuary since everything changed, the place where she'd processed guilt and fear while everyone else went about their lives. The screens still glowed with data streams, overnight reports scrolling past.

Prayer response rates down 12% across three continents.

Divine inspiration incidents at historic lows.

Another artifact theft pending verification.

The world was fraying at the edges. Divine connections weakening. A threat building in the background while she focused on her personal guilt.

She pushed the thought aside. One problem at a time. Right now, the problem was Finola Cavanagh.

Her gaze fell on the chair where Keats sometimes sat during her late sessions, keeping her company without demanding anything in return. The memory of his kiss on her forehead, gentle, trusting, patient, twisted a knot in her chest.

She was lying to him. Hiding things. Building walls when she should have been building bridges.

But she couldn't see another way. The guilt was hers. The responsibility was hers. Dragging Keats into it, dragging *anyone* into it, would mean more people carrying weight that belonged on her shoulders alone.

That was what she told herself as she reached for the ether.

That was what she believed as the shadows wrapped around her, responding to the primordial inheritance that connected her to Nyx, to darkness, to the spaces between spaces. The ether opened for her the way it always did, the way it opened for no one else.

That protecting people meant carrying everything alone.

She stepped into the void, hunting a killer she'd created.

And somewhere in the White Mountains compound, Jamie Keats woke to an empty bed and a feeling in his gut that something had gone terribly wrong.

2

Jamie Keats was still getting used to the visions.

Three weeks since he'd learned Apollo was his father. Three weeks since the Oneiros Device had cracked open his mind and poured in knowledge he was still struggling to process. The device had given him understanding, *how* oracle abilities worked, *what* they could do, but actually using them was something else entirely.

Like being handed the keys to a race car when you'd only ever ridden a bicycle.

He sat cross-legged on the meditation platform overlooking the White Mountains compound, the morning sun warm on his face. The view stretched for miles, forested slopes giving way to distant peaks still capped with late-spring snow, but Keats wasn't seeing any of it. His attention was turned inward, reaching for the golden light that connected him to his father's domain.

The light came. It usually did, when he concentrated hard enough. But today, instead of glimpses of possible futures, fragmentary images he was still learning to interpret, he found only static.

Broken pieces flickered through his mind's eye. A woman with sandy brown hair, running. Shadows that moved wrong. A vast structure built for combat. Alexis, her face twisted with pain, reaching for something he couldn't see.

None of it connected. The images stuttered and jumped like a damaged film reel, refusing to coalesce into anything meaningful.

And underneath it all, something else. A presence at the edge of his perception, vast and old, deliberately hiding.

Was that real? Or was he doing it wrong?

Keats opened his eyes and let out a frustrated breath. That was the problem with being new at this. He had no baseline for *normal*. No way to tell if the static was external interference or his own inexperience. The Oneiros Device had shoved a lifetime of knowledge into his head, but knowledge and skill weren't the same thing.

"Looking a little rough there, Keats."

Lily Abrams stood at the edge of the platform, two water bottles in hand. She was still in her running gear, her red hair pulled back in a ponytail that had seen better days, and there was something off about her expression.

"Trying to make sense of all this." He gestured vaguely at his own head as he accepted the water bottle she tossed his way. "The visions aren't cooperating."

"Cooperating?" She raised an eyebrow. "They're supposed to do what you tell them?"

"Ideally, yes. According to the knowledge the Device crammed into my skull, I should be able to focus on a question and get...

possibilities. Futures." He took a long drink of water. "Instead I'm getting snow on the television screen. Maybe I'm bad at this."

"Or maybe the cosmic cable company is having an outage." Lily dropped onto the bench beside the platform, but instead of her usual easy sprawl, she was rubbing her calves like they'd betrayed her. "Join the club of weird, by the way."

"What do you mean?"

"I felt slow this morning. Like running through water." She scowled at her legs. "My times were off by almost eight percent. Eight percent, Keats. That's not a bad day. That's…"

"You don't *do* slow. You're literally the daughter of the speed god."

"I know, right?" She shook her head, red hair catching the morning light. "Probably nothing. Maybe I'm coming down with something."

"Since when do Scions get sick?"

"Since when do oracle newbies get static instead of visions?" She shot back with a grin. "We're both off our game. Probably residual weirdness from the Phthonos situation. Cosmic dust settling or whatever."

"Yeah." Keats tried to sound convinced. "Probably."

They sat in silence for a moment, the mountain air crisp and clean around them. Then Lily asked the question he'd been dreading.

"Where's Alexis?"

The question landed like a stone in his stomach.

He'd woken to an empty bed and a vague note that explained nothing. *Following a lead. Back soon.* No details about what lead. No indication of where she'd gone or when she'd left. Absence where there should have been warmth.

"Following a lead," he said, keeping his voice neutral. "She left a note."

Lily's expression shifted into something careful. "A lead on what?"

"She didn't say."

"That's helpful." The snark was gentle, more worried than sharp. "She's been weird lately, hasn't she? In the intel center every night. Jumping at questions. Looking like she's carrying the weight of about six worlds on her shoulders."

"She's dealing with a lot," Keats said. But even as the words left his mouth, he knew they weren't true. Alexis was *hiding* a lot. There was a difference. "We all are."

He tried to reach for a vision. A glimpse of where she was, whether she was safe.

Static. Shadows. That vast presence again, watching from beyond his perception.

Was something blocking him? Or was he not skilled enough yet to see what he needed to see?

"Keats?" Lily was studying him with concern. "You okay?"

"Fine." He forced a smile. "Frustrated. These abilities came with knowledge but no instruction manual. I know *what* I should be able to do. I can't actually do it yet."

"Welcome to being a Scion. We're all making it up as we go." She stood, offering him a hand up. "Come on. Briefing in twenty. Maybe Aaron's got something useful."

The ether stretched around Alexis like an infinite gray sea.

She'd been using this space for months now, the dimension between dimensions, the void that existed in the gaps between reality. Her connection to Nyx gave her access in ways no other Scion could match. Hereditary privilege, passed down from a primordial goddess to her half-human daughter.

It should have felt like a gift. Most days, it felt like another thing that set her apart from everyone else.

Where is Emerson Greer?

The answer came with her gift's usual certainty: *Kennebunkport. Watching. Waiting.*

He'd found Finola. She was sure of that now. But he wasn't rushing in. Greer was cautious, patient. The kind of man who'd spent years planning revenge and wasn't about to ruin it with impatience.

Which meant she still had time.

Alexis pushed through the gray void toward the exit point nearest Kennebunkport. The ether responded to her movement, currents shifting around her presence like water around a stone. She'd never seen anyone else in here. Had never expected to. This was her private highway, her shortcut through the spaces between.

A shift at the edge of her perception.

She froze, every sense straining. The ether was supposed to be empty, a transit space, nothing more. But for a moment, she'd felt something else. Something watching. Old and patient and curious.

Interesting.

The word wasn't spoken. It was more like a thought that wasn't hers, pressed gently against the edges of her awareness. Then it was gone, leaving only silence and gray.

Alexis shook off the unease. She didn't have time for paranoia. Finola Cavanagh was in danger, and every minute she spent jumping at shadows was a minute Greer could be using to get closer to his target.

She found the exit point and stepped through.

* * * *

The briefing room felt emptier than usual without Alexis.

Keats sat near the back, nursing a coffee he didn't want while Aaron Richardson walked the assembled team through the morning's intelligence updates. The room held maybe a dozen people: Network operatives, analysts, a handful of Scions who'd found their way to the White Mountains compound looking for safety and purpose.

Aaron stood at the front, data displays flickering behind him as he pulled up the latest reports. The son of Ares had a military bearing that made everything feel like a strategic briefing, even when he was reviewing overnight communications.

"Prayer response rates continue to decline," Aaron was saying. "Down another four percent since yesterday across the Greek pantheon alone. We're seeing similar drops in Norse, Egyptian, and Japanese divine connections. Apollo's communications office has flagged it as a priority concern."

"Any explanation?" someone asked.

"Nothing definitive. The running theory is residual effects from the Phthonos situation. Cosmic disruption takes time to heal." Aaron didn't sound convinced by his own explanation. "But the pattern is concerning. Instead of improving, the connections are getting weaker."

He pulled up a new display, a map dotted with red markers.

"More immediately relevant: another artifact theft overnight. Thoth's Palette, taken from a protected archive in Alexandria."

Keats straightened. That made ten thefts in three weeks. He'd been tracking them loosely, though the artifact situation had taken a back seat to his concerns about Alexis.

"Same pattern as the others?" Lily asked from her position near the door.

"Identical. No alarms triggered. No witnesses. Security footage shows the item in place one moment, gone the next. Whoever's doing this has intimate knowledge of divine security protocols." Aaron's jaw tightened. "And access to spaces that should be impossible to breach."

"So we're looking for someone with serious connections," Lily said. "Someone who knows things they shouldn't."

"Or someone with help from someone who does." Aaron pulled up another slide. "The only commonality we've found is that every stolen item is what we'd classify as a 'connection artifact,' objects that facilitate interaction between divine and mortal realms."

Keats filed the information away, his mind trying to draw connections he wasn't sure were real. Prayer response rates declining. Divine abilities flickering. Artifacts that connected gods and mortals going missing.

Was there a pattern there? Something he would have seen clearly if his visions weren't acting like a broken compass?

He tried one more time to reach for clarity. The thefts felt important, felt like the universe was trying to tell him something his conscious mind couldn't grasp.

Static. Shadows. That vast presence again, watching from somewhere he couldn't see.

He gave up and focused on the briefing.

"Keep me updated," Lily was saying, her tone suggesting the matter was being shelved rather than prioritized. "Right now we've got more immediate concerns. The Cairo situation needs attention, and we're still waiting on confirmation from the London cell about…"

The briefing continued, moving on to operational matters that demanded immediate action. The artifact thefts were noted, filed, added to a growing list of concerns that no one had time to properly investigate.

Whatever was happening with the artifacts, someone else would have to figure it out. Keats had his own problems: a girlfriend who was hiding something, abilities that weren't working right, and the growing certainty that things were about to go very wrong.

* * * *

The Maine coast hit Alexis with salt air and morning chill as she emerged from the ether.

She materialized in the shadow of a boathouse, the weathered wood providing cover while she oriented herself. Kennebunkport spread before her, a picturesque coastal town that looked like it belonged on a postcard. Fishing boats bobbed in the harbor. Tourists wandered the main street. Seagulls wheeled overhead, their cries mixing with the distant sound of lobster traps being hauled.

Normal. Peaceful. The kind of place someone would choose if they wanted to disappear from a world of gods and monsters.

Alexis stretched and started walking. The grocery store purchase had been made three blocks from the harbor. If Finola was living nearby, she'd probably be within walking distance of supplies and employment.

A paralegal could work remotely these days. Finola might not even need to leave her apartment except for essentials.

Which would make her harder to find, but also harder for Greer to reach.

Alexis was considering her next move when she felt it: the subtle awareness of another Scion nearby. The sensation was uncertain, requiring focus. Not like the unmistakable tingling that announced a god's presence, but something vaguer. A recognition of shared heritage that some Scions sensed more easily than others.

She concentrated, trying to pin down the source.

Not Finola. The daughter of Nemesis would feel different, tinged with the cosmic weight of justice and retribution. This felt like Hermes's heritage. Speed. Cunning. The god of travelers and thieves.

Greer.

He was here. In this town. Close enough that she could feel the edges of his presence.

Alexis slipped into the shadow of a nearby building, reaching for her connection to the primordial dark. She needed to find him before he found Finola. Needed to stop whatever he was planning before an innocent woman paid the price for Alexis's deal.

But she couldn't attack him here. Not in broad daylight, surrounded by tourists and locals who had no idea that demigods walked among them. A fight between two Scions would draw attention, the kind of attention that got innocent people killed.

She needed to find Finola first. Warn her. Get her to safety before Greer could...

"Alexis Rain."

The voice came from behind her. Smooth, cultured, carrying the easy confidence of someone who'd been controlling conversations for a very long time.

She turned slowly.

Emerson Greer stood ten feet away, looking exactly as she remembered: silver-blonde hair, California tan, expensive suit. He held himself with the casual arrogance of divine heritage, but his eyes were sharp. Calculating. Already three moves ahead in whatever game he thought they were playing.

"I wondered when you'd show up," he said. "Though I confess I didn't expect you to find me this quickly. You've been busy."

"I know why you're here." Alexis kept her voice steady, her stance balanced. Ready. "I know about your mother. About Nemesis."

Pain flickered in Greer's expression, old and deep, quickly buried beneath practiced control. "Then you understand why this has to happen."

"I understand that you want revenge. That doesn't make it right."

"Right?" His laugh was sharp and humorless. "My mother was killed for loving me too publicly. For being proud of what I am. Nemesis destroyed her because she dared to acknowledge that her son was touched by the divine." He took a step closer. "Where was your concern for 'right' when you handed me the weapon to do something about it?"

The guilt twisted in her chest, sharp and familiar.

"I didn't know," she said. "When I made that deal…"

"You knew I intended to kill a god. You didn't care which one, as long as you got what you wanted." Greer's smile was thin and cold. "We're not so different, you and I. We both make deals. We both live with the consequences."

"Finola Cavanagh didn't make any deals. She walked away from this world. She wants to be normal."

"And my mother wanted to be proud of her son." The coldness in his voice could have frozen the harbor. "We don't always get what we want."

Alexis felt power building under her skin, shadows responding to her emotional state. She could fight him here. Should, probably. The Caduceus made him dangerous, but she was the daughter of a primordial goddess. She had advantages he couldn't anticipate.

But there were people everywhere. Tourists. Families. Children eating ice cream on the pier.

"This isn't over," she said.

"No." Greer's smile widened. "It isn't. But I've been planning this for a very long time, Ms. Rain. Longer than you've been alive. One

Scion with a guilty conscience isn't going to stop me, no matter whose daughter she is."

He stepped back, shadows gathering around him. Not the ether, which he couldn't access, but the ordinary darkness of alleyways and overhangs. Hermes's children could slip between spaces in the mortal realm, move unseen through the gaps in perception. It wasn't the same as her ability, but it was enough.

"Find her if you can," he said as the darkness swallowed him. "Warn her. It won't matter. Some debts can only be paid in blood."

And then he was gone, leaving Alexis alone on the Kennebunkport waterfront with the taste of failure in her mouth and the certainty that she was running out of time.

Finola was close. Greer was closer.

And somewhere in the White Mountains, Keats was trying to see a future that something was deliberately hiding from him. Though whether the block was external or his own inexperience, he couldn't say.

None of them saw the pattern yet.

None of them understood that their individual problems were threads in a web they couldn't perceive, a scheme set in motion by someone powerful.

The peculiar events continued to pile up, each one dismissed as coincidence or fatigue or bad luck.

The reckoning would come later.

3

Alexis found Finola Cavanagh forty-three minutes after Greer vanished.

Where is Finola Cavanagh's current residence?

She'd had to ask the question a dozen different ways to get to this point. The universe was being problematic around this Finola.

The answer finally came crisp and certain: *Third floor apartment, 847 Harbor Street. Blue door. Living under the name Fiona Walsh.*

The building was a converted Victorian, the kind of place that had probably been a single-family home a hundred years ago before someone carved it into rental units. Alexis stood across the street, watching the blue door on the third-floor landing, trying to figure out how to approach a woman who could detect lies on contact.

Hi, I'm the person who armed the man trying to kill you. Want some help?

Yeah. That would go over well.

The truth was, she had no good options. She couldn't lie to Finola. The woman would know instantly. She couldn't hide her involvement in Greer's vendetta. Finola would sense the deception the moment Alexis tried to downplay it. The only thing she could offer was the truth, and the truth made her look like exactly what she was: someone whose mistakes had put an innocent woman in danger.

She was still working through her approach when the blue door opened.

Finola Cavanagh stepped onto the landing, grocery bag in hand, keys already out. She was smaller than her photo suggested, compact and watchful, with sandy brown hair pulled back in a practical ponytail. Her light brown eyes scanned the street with the automatic wariness of someone who'd spent three years looking over her shoulder.

Those eyes found Alexis. Held.

Even from across the street, Alexis felt the weight of that gaze. Measuring. Assessing. A truth-detector sizing up a stranger who'd been watching her apartment.

Finola's expression shifted. Recognition of what Alexis was, if not who. One Scion sensing another.

She turned and ran.

"Wait—" Alexis started across the street, but Finola was already through the door, footsteps pounding up the interior stairs. "I'm not here to hurt you!"

The words probably didn't help. A strange Scion shouting reassurances while chasing you was exactly the kind of thing Finola had spent three years trying to avoid.

Alexis reached for the shadows…

Something hit her from behind. Hard.

She went sprawling across the sidewalk, the impact driving the breath from her lungs, her palms scraping against concrete as she tried to break her fall. She rolled and came up in a defensive crouch, instincts screaming. Greer stood where she'd been a moment before, the Caduceus gleaming in his hand. The twin serpents coiled around the staff seemed almost alive, their golden eyes glinting with ancient malevolence.

The staff she had given him. The weapon she had placed in his hands because she'd been too desperate, too shortsighted, too convinced that helping him was the right thing to do.

You did this, whispered the guilt in her chest. *You armed him.*

"Predictable," he said. "I knew you'd find her. I just had to wait."

He'd used her. Let her do the work of tracking Finola while he watched, patient as a spider waiting for the web to vibrate.

"Greer, don't do this." Alexis rose, power building under her skin. Shadows gathered at the edges of her vision, responding to her emotional state. "She's innocent. She walked away from all of this."

"So was my mother." He raised the Caduceus, her gift, her mistake, her weapon turned against everything she cared about. "And now you're going to watch what happens when someone takes away the thing you care about."

He moved. Faster than she'd expected. Hermes's blood singing through his veins, lending him speed that bordered on supernatural. The staff swept toward her head in a killing arc.

Alexis dissolved into shadow.

The staff passed through darkness where she'd been. She reformed three feet to his left, driving an elbow toward his kidney. He twisted, impossibly fast, and the Caduceus came around in a tight spiral that forced her back.

They circled each other on the quiet street. Somewhere above, Finola was running. Alexis could feel the woman's panic like a distant heartbeat, one Scion's awareness of another.

"You can't protect her." Greer's voice was almost conversational. "You can barely protect yourself. That shadow trick is impressive, but the Caduceus has killed gods, Ms. Rain. Do you think you can stand against it?"

"I don't have to beat you." Alexis pulled darkness around her like armor, feeling Nyx's power respond to her need. "I just have to keep you busy long enough for her to get away."

"Noble." His smile was cold. "Stupid, but noble."

He attacked.

* * * *

The fight moved through Kennebunkport like a storm.

They crashed through an alley behind the Victorian, Greer's speed countered by Alexis's ability to slip between shadows. She couldn't match him in direct combat. The Caduceus gave him reach, and his Hermes blood gave him reflexes that made her feel slow and clumsy. But she could keep dissolving, keep reforming, keep staying out of reach of that deadly staff.

The alley was narrow, brick walls pressing close on either side, the ground littered with trash cans and wooden crates from the restaurant that backed onto it. Greer swung the staff in a horizontal arc that would have taken her head off. She dropped into shadow and came up behind a dumpster, using the brief cover to catch her breath.

He was on her in an instant, vaulting the dumpster with inhuman grace. The staff drove down like a spear, and Alexis barely rolled clear, feeling the impact through the concrete as the Caduceus punched a crater where her chest had been.

Too fast, she thought. *He's too fast and I'm too slow and the weapon I gave him is going to kill me.*

The guilt fueled her fear, which fueled her power. She grabbed the dumpster with tendrils of shadow and heaved it toward him, a desperate move, buying seconds. Greer batted it aside with the Caduceus, but those seconds were enough. She dissolved again, reforming twenty feet back, at the alley's mouth.

The alley opened onto a small parking lot behind a seafood restaurant. The smell of fried clams and salt air mixed with her own fear-sweat. Alexis emerged from shadow behind a delivery truck, breathing hard. Her power was holding, but each transition took something out of her. She couldn't keep this up forever.

Greer appeared at the alley mouth, not even winded. "Running won't save her. Running won't save you."

"I'm not running." She reached for the connection to Nyx's domain, drawing deeper than she had before. Shadows erupted from every corner of the parking lot: from beneath cars, from behind dumpsters, from the narrow gaps between buildings. They coiled around Greer like living things, wrapping his arms, his legs, trying to pin him in place.

For a moment, it worked. He struggled against the darkness, the Caduceus flaring with golden light as he tried to burn through her bindings.

Then the staff pulsed with power older than anything Alexis had ever felt.

Her shadows shattered. The backlash hit her like a physical blow, driving her to her knees on the asphalt. For a terrifying moment, she couldn't feel her connection to Nyx at all. Emptiness where her mother's power should have been. Her ears rang. Her vision grayed at the edges. Blood trickled from her nose. The Caduceus had done more than break her shadows. It had wounded something inside her.

"The Caduceus was forged in cosmic power by the most adept smiths the world has ever known," Greer said, advancing on her. "Did you think primordial darkness would be enough to stop it?"

Alexis forced herself upright. The connection was coming back, slowly, painfully, like feeling returning to a limb that had fallen asleep. But she needed time she didn't have.

She ran.

Not away from Finola. Toward her. If she couldn't beat Greer, she could at least draw him away from his target. Lead him somewhere that civilians wouldn't get caught in the crossfire.

She burst out of the parking lot onto the main street, tourists scattering as she sprinted past. A woman screamed. A man dropped his ice cream cone. Someone shouted about calling the police. Greer was right behind her. She could feel him, that Hermes-quick presence closing the distance with every step.

The harbor. She needed to reach the harbor.

Is Finola still in the building?

No. Running. Heading north on foot.

Good. As long as Finola kept moving, as long as Alexis kept Greer focused on her instead…

The Caduceus caught her across the shoulders.

She went down hard on the wooden planks of the harbor pier, the impact driving the breath from her lungs. Her chin cracked against the wood, and she tasted blood where she'd bitten her tongue. Pain exploded through her back. Not physical pain, but something deeper. The staff's divine power burning against her skin, trying to sever her connection to Nyx entirely.

She could smell salt and fish and the diesel of boat engines. Could hear gulls crying overhead, oblivious to the violence happening on the pier below them. Could feel the wood rough against her palms as she tried to push herself up and failed.

"Enough games." Greer stood over her, the Caduceus raised for a killing blow. Around them, people were screaming, running, pulling out phones to call 911. None of it mattered. None of them could see what was happening: a man with a strange staff standing over a fallen woman.

"I'm going to kill her," Greer said. "And then I'm going to find Nemesis herself and show her what it feels like to lose a child. But first…" He smiled, and there was nothing human in it. "First, I'm going to kill you. Consider it a thank you for making all of this possible."

For making all of this possible. The words cut deeper than the Caduceus had. Because he was right. She had made this possible. Had put the weapon in his hand, had trusted his story of vengeance and loss, had been too desperate to see the monster behind the grieving son.

The Caduceus came down.

Alexis reached for the only place she could go.

* * * *

The ether.

She'd only ever pulled someone else through once, and that was Keats. Hadn't known if it was possible with Greer. But desperation made everything possible, and in the moment between the Caduceus falling and her own death, she'd grabbed Greer's arm and *pulled*.

The gray void swallowed them both.

Greer screamed.

The sound was wrong in this place, distorted, stretched, like something being played at the wrong speed. He was on his knees in the endless gray, the Caduceus still clutched in his hands, but his form was flickering. Unstable. The edges of his body rippling like heat shimmer off summer asphalt.

"What—" He looked around wildly, eyes wide with something Alexis had never seen in him before: fear. "What is this place? What did you do?"

"The ether." Alexis rose, feeling her own connection to this space stabilize as Greer's unraveled. Here, she was whole. Here, she was home. "And you're not supposed to be here."

"Get me out." He tried to stand and failed, his legs refusing to solidify properly. The flickering was getting worse, his hands translucent one moment, solid the next. "Get me out of here!"

"I don't think I can." The realization hit her even as she spoke. She'd dragged him in, yes, but she'd never tried to take someone out. Didn't know if it was possible. And even if it was, even if she could somehow carry him back to the mortal world...

He'd try to kill her again. Try to kill Finola. The Caduceus was still in his hands, and as long as he had it, he'd never stop.

"Please." Greer's voice cracked. The arrogance was gone, the cold calculation stripped away. What was left was a man, a son who'd lost his mother and spent decades drowning in rage. "Please, I don't want to die here. Not like this."

The guilt that had been sitting in Alexis's chest for weeks turned to ice.

She'd made this. All of it. The deal, the weapon, the hunt for Finola, and now this: a man dissolving in a void because she'd been desperate enough to drag him somewhere he couldn't survive.

But Finola was innocent. Finola had walked away from everything divine, built a normal life, wanted to be left alone. And Greer would have killed her. Would still kill her, if Alexis found a way to get him out.

"I'm sorry," she said. And meant it.

"Sorry doesn't—" Greer's voice cut off as another ripple passed through him. Larger this time. His grip on the Caduceus loosened, the staff beginning to drift away from fingers that couldn't hold it anymore.

The Chaos Arena

4

Time didn't work properly in the ether.

Alexis had been walking for what felt like hours. Or days. Or possibly minutes. Her internal sense of time had abandoned her somewhere between the third identical stretch of gray void and the fourth. The Caduceus was heavy in her hands, a constant reminder of what she'd done to get here.

What she'd done to Greer.

She just loved me. That's all she did.

She pushed the thought away. Guilt could wait. Survival couldn't.

How do I exit the ether?

Silence. Her gift, usually so reliable, returned nothing. Either the information didn't exist, or something was blocking her access to it.

Neither option was comforting.

The void stretched endlessly in every direction. No landmarks, no variations, nothing to distinguish one patch of gray from another. She might have been walking in circles. She might have been standing still while the ether shifted around her. There was no way to know.

"This is fine," she muttered to herself. "Trapped in an infinite void with a god-killing weapon and no way home. Totally fine."

The Caduceus pulsed faintly in her grip, as if responding to her frustration. The twin serpents had gone still since Greer's dissolution, their golden eyes dim. Even they seemed unsettled by this place.

Alexis stopped walking. Took a breath. Tried to think.

She'd been using the ether for months without understanding what it really was. A shortcut. A transit space. Her personal highway through the gaps between reality. She'd never stopped to wonder *why* she could access it when no one else could. Never questioned the gift beyond being grateful it existed.

Stupid. Careless. The kind of assumption that got people killed.

"Okay," she said aloud, because the silence was starting to feel hostile. "If I can't find an exit, maybe I can find someone. Whoever owns this space."

The ether belonged to someone. Everything did, at the cosmic level. And whoever owned this space had been watching her. She'd felt that presence before, in the moments before she'd dragged Greer through. Ancient. Curious. Deliberately hidden.

Maybe it was time to stop running and start demanding answers.

"Hey!" Her voice was swallowed by the void, absorbed into gray. "I know you're there. I know you've been watching. So how about you stop hiding and tell me how the hell to get out of here?"

Nothing.

"I'm not going to beg," she continued, louder now. "And I'm not going to wander around this nothing-space forever. So either show yourself, or I start breaking things."

She raised the Caduceus. The serpents stirred, sensing her intent.

"This thing killed gods. Maybe it can put a dent in your pretty gray void too."

Silence stretched. Alexis tightened her grip on the staff, power building...

A path appeared.

Not gradually. One moment there was nothing, the next there was a ribbon of darker gray cutting through the void, leading toward a point on the horizon that hadn't existed a heartbeat before.

Interesting, a presence whispered. The same not-voice she'd felt before. *Most who find themselves here weep. Plead. Bargain. You threaten.*

"Crying seemed unproductive," Alexis said. "Are you going to show yourself, or do I have to follow the creepy path first?"

Follow. The whisper carried what might have been amusement. *If you dare.*

"Was that supposed to be ominous? Because I've had a long day, and my tolerance for dramatic pauses is running low."

The whisper didn't respond. The path waited.

Alexis walked.

* * * *

The path led to a place that shouldn't exist.

After an unknowable span of walking, the void gave way to... a space. Not a room. There were no walls, no ceiling. But there was ground beneath her feet now, solid and dark. There was depth, a sense of dimension that had been absent in the endless gray. And there was light, of a sort. A soft luminescence that seemed to emanate from everywhere and nowhere.

At the center of it all, a being waited.

Alexis had met divine beings before. Her mother, Nyx, primordial goddess of night. Apollo, radiant and powerful. Even Phthonos, twisted and hateful. Each had carried a presence that marked them as other, as beyond the scope of mortal experience.

This was different.

This was *before*.

The being before her had no fixed form. It shifted constantly. Now a vaguely humanoid shape of swirling gray and silver, now a vastness her mind refused to fully process. Stars flickered in its depths. Galaxies swirled where eyes might have been. The sense of age radiating from it was so profound that Alexis felt her knees want to buckle, her body instinctively trying to prostrate itself before a force so fundamentally ancient.

She could feel its attention like physical pressure. Like standing at the bottom of an ocean, compressed by the weight of all the water above. Her lungs labored for breath that had nothing to do with atmosphere. Her heart hammered against ribs that suddenly felt too fragile to contain it. Every instinct she possessed screamed at her to kneel, to bow, to make herself as small as possible before a being that could unmake her without noticing.

The form shifted again, and for a moment she saw, or thought she saw, the echo of everything that had ever existed. Every star that had ever burned. Every life that had ever flickered into being. Every thought, every dream, every moment of love and loss and longing that had occurred since time began. All of it flowing from this single point. All of it returning here in the end.

She locked her knees and stayed standing.

"Let me guess," she said, and was proud that her voice barely shook. "Chaos."

The being's attention focused on her. A weight that made her skin prickle. Her shadow, cast by light that came from nowhere, seemed to darken, deepen, as if reaching toward its source.

You know me. The voice was everywhere and nowhere, resonating in her bones. Not words exactly, but meaning translated directly into her consciousness. Each syllable carried the weight of eons. Each pause held the silence between stars. *How curious. Most mortals have forgotten my name.*

"I'm not most mortals."

No. Amusement rippled through the space. She felt it as a shifting in the light, a slight warming of the impossible air. *You are not. You are Nyx's daughter. My granddaughter, after a fashion. The first of her line to be born in... oh, a very long time.*

"Granddaughter." Alexis tested the word. It felt strange applied to something so utterly inhuman. "Is that why I can use the ether? Family privilege?"

In part. Chaos drifted closer. Or she drifted closer to Chaos; direction was meaningless here. The being's form resolved into something almost humanoid, and she caught glimpses of features that shifted too quickly to track. A face that might have been ancient or might have been new, eyes that held galaxies one moment and were dark the next. *Nyx was born from me, in the time before time had meaning. Her children have always been able to touch the spaces I inhabit. But you...*

The swirling form paused. *You have used this realm freely. Casually. As if it were yours to command.*

"I didn't know it belonged to anyone. No one told me I needed permission."

And if you had known? Would you have asked?

Alexis considered lying. Dismissed the idea immediately. This being would know. Would probably find it insulting.

"Probably not," she admitted. "I would have used it anyway and hoped you didn't notice."

Honest. The amusement was stronger now. She could almost see a smile forming in the chaos of shifting features. *Defiant. Stubborn. You have your mother's fire, child. She was always the most... intriguing of my offspring.*

"Is that why you let me use the ether? Because I'm intriguing?"

I let you use the ether because I was curious what you would do with it. Chaos's form shifted, galaxies rearranging themselves into something almost like a smile. *I have existed since before existence itself. Do you have any idea how rare it is to encounter the genuinely unexpected?*

"Happy to entertain." The words came out sharper than she intended. Fear and frustration making her reckless. "Now can you tell me how to get out of here? I have people waiting for me."

The boy. Chaos's attention intensified, and Alexis felt her skin prickle. The sensation of being seen not just physically but deeper, down to the molecular level, down to the level of thought and feeling. *Apollo's son. The one you love.*

"Stay out of my head."

I am not in your head, child. I am simply aware. Everything that exists emerged from me. Every thought, every feeling, every moment of connection between beings. All of it carries my echo. The form drifted back. *Your love for him is genuine. Fierce. Somewhat terrifying in its intensity. He is fortunate.*

Alexis didn't know how to respond to that. A primordial being commenting on her love life wasn't something she'd prepared for.

"The exit," she said instead. "Please."

Ah. Chaos seemed to settle, the constant shifting slowing to something almost still. The being's form solidified. Not human, never that, but something her eyes could rest on without sliding away. *Now we come to it. You want to leave. I want... compensation.*

"Compensation." Alexis's grip tightened on the Caduceus. "For what?"

For months of trespass. For treating my realm as your personal thoroughfare. For bringing that... a flicker directed at the staff in her hands, distaste or acknowledgment *...into a space where it does not belong. And for the entertainment, I suppose. I should pay you for that, honestly. But tradition must be observed.*

"What kind of compensation?"

A boon. The word carried weight. Cosmic weight, the kind that pressed against reality itself. Alexis felt it settle onto her consciousness like a brand. *A favor owed. Undefined. Callable at any time. Impossible to refuse.*

Alexis's blood went cold. "You want me to owe you a favor without knowing what it is?"

That is traditionally how boons work, yes.

"And if I refuse?"

Then you remain here. Chaos's voice carried no threat, no malice. Just fact. *I have no desire to harm you, granddaughter. You are far too entertaining for that. But neither will I allow you to leave without settling the debt between us. The universe runs on balance. Even I must respect that.*

"So I either agree to owe you anything, or I stay trapped in this void forever?"

Forever is such a mortal concept. Amusement again. *But essentially, yes.*

Alexis wanted to scream. Wanted to rage against the unfairness of it. She'd been trying to save someone, trying to fix a mistake she'd made, and now she was being extorted by a primordial deity for the privilege of going home.

But screaming wouldn't help. And rage was just fear wearing a different mask.

She made herself stop. Made herself think. This was like any negotiation. There had to be limits, had to be boundaries, even if Chaos claimed otherwise. She had to find them.

"What kind of favor?" she asked, forcing her voice to stay level. "What are the limits?"

Limits? Chaos seemed genuinely puzzled. *Why would there be limits?*

"Because I'm not agreeing to hurt the people I love. I'm not agreeing to betray my friends or destroy the Network or—"

Child. Chaos's voice was gentle now, almost kind. *I am Chaos. I am the void from which everything emerged and to which everything will eventually return. Do you truly think I have any interest in your Network? In your mortal politics? In the petty squabbles of gods and demigods?*

"Then what *do* you want?"

I told you. I find you intriguing. The galaxies in Chaos's form swirled faster for a moment. *When I call in this boon, if I ever call it in, it will be because I want something only you can provide. Something that entertains me. Something unexpected.*

"That's not reassuring."

It's not meant to be. It's meant to be honest. Chaos drifted closer again, and this time Alexis felt the full weight of that ancient attention pressing against her soul. Not hostile. Never hostile. But overwhelming. Like being seen by something that had watched the birth of stars and would watch their death. Like having her entire existence weighed and measured against scales that measured in eons. *You have a choice, Alexis Rain. You always have a choice. That's what makes you interesting. You can refuse my terms and stay here. Many would consider that the noble option. Or you can agree, return to your life and your love and your battles, and carry the weight of an undefined debt. Neither option is wrong. Both have consequences.*

Alexis thought of Keats. Waking up to find her gone. Waiting. Worrying. Not knowing if she was alive or dead. She thought of his face. That crooked grin she loved, the way his eyes went gold at the edges when he was trying to see beyond his oracle sight. She thought of how he'd looked at her the last time they'd been together, like she was precious, worth protecting.

She thought of Lily, dealing with Network operations alone. Aaron, tracking artifact thefts without backup. The compound full of Scions who were counting on her to come back.

She thought of the Caduceus in her hands. A weapon that needed to be destroyed before anyone else could use it. A weapon she had given to the wrong person, that had nearly killed her, that would kill again if she didn't stop it.

She thought of Greer. *She just loved me. That's all she did.* The weight of his death, still fresh, still bleeding somewhere inside her where guilt lived.

If she stayed here, no one would know what happened. No one would be able to find the Caduceus, destroy it, prevent whatever came next. She'd have made her stand on principle and accomplished nothing but her own erasure.

If she agreed...

If she agreed, she'd be binding herself to something vast and incomprehensible. Carrying a debt that could be called in at any moment, for any purpose. Living with that weight pressing against her soul for the rest of her life. Or, at least, until Chaos called the debt.

But she'd be living. She'd be home. She'd be with Keats, and Lily, and everyone else who mattered.

What would Keats do? she asked herself. And knew the answer immediately. He'd tell her to come home. He'd tell her that carrying a debt was better than being dead. He'd tell her that they'd figure it out together, whatever came.

He'd tell her to trust herself. To make the choice and live with it.

"Fine," she said. "I agree. One boon. One favor. Callable whenever you want."

And impossible to refuse. Chaos pressed. *Say it.*

Alexis gritted her teeth. "Impossible to refuse."

The words left her mouth and she felt a shift. Not in the space around her, but in herself. A weight settling onto her soul. A thread connecting her to the primordial being before her, invisible but unbreakable. It felt like a second heartbeat, like an awareness that would never sleep.

Done. Chaos's voice carried satisfaction and something softer. Affection, maybe, or as close to it as a primordial being could feel. *The debt is struck. The boon is owed. And you, granddaughter, are free to go.*

An exit appeared beside her. A tear in the gray void that showed glimpses of the mortal world beyond. Blue sky. Green trees. The White Mountains compound, exactly where she needed to be.

Alexis turned toward it, then stopped. Looked back at the swirling form of her grandfather.

"Why me?" she asked. "You've got other grandchildren. Other descendants. Why am I so interesting?"

Because you should not exist. Chaos's voice was thoughtful now, contemplative. *Nyx has not taken a mortal lover in millennia. Has not produced a half-human child since the world was young. And yet here you are. Proof that even the most ancient patterns can be broken. That even cosmic certainties can surprise.*

The being drifted closer one last time.

You are unexpected, Alexis Rain. And in a universe this old, the unexpected is precious beyond measure.

"I'll try to take that as a compliment."

You should. Now go. Your boy is worried about you. And you have a weapon to deal with. A pause. *I would suggest fire. Hephaestus's forge, if you can reach it. Mortal flames won't be enough.*

Alexis nodded, not trusting herself to speak. She stepped toward the exit, the Caduceus heavy in her hands...

One more thing.

She stopped.

Be careful, granddaughter. There are others of my children who do not share my... appreciation for the unexpected. Others who see your existence as a violation of the natural order. The galaxies in Chaos's form dimmed. *Darkness has many faces. Not all of them are as fond of you as I am.*

A warning. Cryptic and unsettling, like everything else about this encounter.

"Thanks for the heads up," Alexis said. "I'll add it to the list of things trying to kill me."

That fire. That defiance. Chaos sounded almost proud. *Never lose it, child. It may be the only thing that saves you.*

Alexis stepped through the exit and left the void behind.

The weight of the boon stayed with her.

It would stay with her forever.

5

Less than an hour.

That's how long she'd been gone. Alexis had spent what felt like an eternity wandering the gray void, negotiating with a primordial being, carrying the weight of a cosmic debt, and in the mortal world, less than an hour had passed since she'd left the Kennebunkport pier.

Time moved differently in Chaos's realm. She understood that now, in a way she hadn't before.

The White Mountains compound materialized around her as she stepped out of the ether. The familiar grounds, the morning light filtering through pine trees, the distant hum of activity from the main building. The compound sprawled across the mountainside the way it always had. Part military installation, part university campus, part sanctuary for beings who existed between worlds. The main lodge anchored everything, its converted great room visible through windows that caught the morning light. Smaller buildings clustered around it like satellites: the training barn with its weathered red siding, the dormitory wings where Scions who'd lost everything could rebuild, the medical center that never seemed to close. Smoke rose from the kitchen chimney, carrying the smell of coffee and bacon. Someone was already awake, already working, already holding the line.

It wasn't much. But it was theirs.

The Caduceus was still in her hands. She needed to hide it. Destroy it.

Later. She'd deal with it later.

"Alexis!"

Keats's voice hit her like a wave. Relief and fear and anger all tangled together. He was running toward her from the main building, and even from this distance she could see how pale he was. How wild his eyes looked.

He'd been terrified. For her.

The guilt that was becoming her constant companion twisted sharper.

"I'm okay," she called back, but he was already there. Pulling her into his arms so tightly she could barely breathe. She let the Caduceus drop to the ground and held on, burying her face against his shoulder.

"You *vanished*," he said into her hair. "I felt... something. My abilities are still garbage, but I felt *something*, and then I saw your note and you were gone and we couldn't find—" His voice cracked. "Where *were* you?"

"Kennebunkport." It wasn't a lie. Not technically. "There was someone I needed to find. Someone in danger."

"And?" Keats pulled back enough to look at her face. His green eyes were searching, desperate for answers.

"She's safe. The threat is... handled."

"Handled how?"

Greer's face flickered through her mind. The fear, the humanity, the moment he'd dissolved into nothing. *She just... loved me. That's all she did.*

"He won't be a problem anymore," she said. "That's what matters."

Keats's expression shifted. He knew she wasn't telling him everything. She could see it in the way his jaw tightened, the slight narrowing of his eyes. Three weeks of her lying by omission had taught him to recognize the signs.

But before he could push, Lily appeared around the corner of the building, red hair flying behind her as she sprinted toward them.

"Oh thank the gods." Lily skidded to a stop, breathing hard. "When Keats said he felt something through whatever half-functioning oracle connection he's got, I thought—" She shook her head. "Never mind what I thought. You're okay?"

"I'm fine."

Lily's gaze dropped to the Caduceus on the ground. Her eyes went wide.

"Is that—"

"Hermes's Caduceus. Yes." Alexis bent to retrieve it, the serpents cool against her palm. "I need to hide it or destroy it. But apparently mortal flames won't be enough."

"How do you know that?" Keats asked.

The question hung in the air. Alexis felt the weight of the boon pressing against her soul. That invisible thread connecting her to something ancient and vast.

Tell them, a voice in her head whispered. *Tell them about Chaos. About the deal you made. They're your team. Your family. They deserve to know.*

But if she told them, they'd want to help. They'd try to find a way to break the boon, to free her from the cosmic debt. And Chaos had been clear: impossible to refuse. There was no breaking it. There was only carrying it.

Alone.

"Research," she said. "I've been looking into artifact destruction methods. Hephaestus's forge is the only thing powerful enough to unmake something like this."

It wasn't entirely a lie. She *had* been researching. Not in the way they'd assume.

"We can work on that," Lily said. "But first, what happened? Who was the threat? Keats said you left a note about a lead, but you didn't tell anyone what you were doing."

"It was personal." Alexis met Lily's eyes, hoping her friend would understand. "Something I needed to handle myself."

"Personal." Lily's tone flattened. "You disappeared for an hour, came back with a literal god-killing weapon, and it's *personal?*"

"Yes."

The silence stretched between them. Alexis could feel both of them waiting. Wanting more, deserving more. She could feel Keats's hurt like a physical thing, radiating off him in waves.

"Fine," Lily said finally. "When you're ready to talk about it, you know where to find me." She turned and walked back toward the main building, her posture stiff with frustration.

Keats didn't move.

"Al." His voice was quiet. Careful. "Something's different about you."

Her heart stuttered. "What do you mean?"

"I don't know. I can't—" He ran a hand through his curls, frustration bleeding through. "My abilities are still a mess. Half the time I can't see anything, and the other half it's static and shadows. But when I look at you now, there's…" He trailed off, searching for words. "There's something else. Something connected to you that wasn't there before. Something big."

The boon. He was sensing the boon.

Alexis forced herself to meet his eyes. "I'm fine, Keats. It was a rough morning, but I'm okay now."

"You keep saying that." He took a step closer, and she could see the conflict in his face. The desire to push warring with the desire to trust her. "You've been saying that for three weeks. And every time you say it, I believe you a little less."

The words hit harder than they should have. Because he was right. She *was* lying to him. Had been lying since the night she'd started researching Greer. And now she was adding another secret to the pile, another wall between them.

"I'm sorry," she said. "I know I've been… distant. I'm trying to figure things out. There's a lot happening right now."

"Then let me help." He reached for her hand, his fingers warm around hers. "That's what I'm here for. That's what *this* is for." He gestured between them. "You don't have to carry everything alone."

Yes I do, she thought. *That's exactly what I have to do.*

"I know," she said instead. "And I promise, when I'm ready to talk about it, you'll be the first person I come to."

It wasn't a lie. When she was ready. If she was ever ready.

Keats studied her face for a long moment. Then he sighed, and she saw him make a choice. To step back, to give her space, to trust her even though she was giving him no reason to.

"Okay," he said. "But Al? This can't keep going on. Whatever you're carrying, it's going to break you if you don't let someone help."

"I know."

She didn't know if she believed it. But she said it anyway, because it was what he needed to hear.

* * * *

The rest of the day passed in a blur of activity.

Alexis secured the Caduceus in the compound's vault. A temporary measure until she could figure out how to get it to Hephaestus's forge. She sat through a briefing with Aaron about the latest artifact thefts, nodding in the right places while her mind drifted elsewhere. She ate dinner with the team, laughed at Lily's jokes, touched Keats's hand under the table.

Normal. Everything was normal. She was fine.

The weight of the boon pressed against her soul with every breath.

That night, after Keats had fallen asleep beside her, his arm draped protectively over her waist, his breathing slow and even, Alexis lay awake in the darkness and stared at the ceiling.

She didn't need to sleep. Two hours a night was plenty, and she'd been running on less than that for weeks. But usually she stayed in bed anyway, enjoying the warmth, the closeness, the simple comfort of being next to someone she loved.

Tonight, the closeness felt like a lie.

Carefully, she slipped out from under Keats's arm and padded to the window. The White Mountains stretched beyond the glass, silver-blue in the moonlight. Beautiful. Peaceful. A sanctuary she was helping to build, to protect, filled with people who trusted her.

People she was lying to.

It doesn't matter, she told herself. *The boon is a possibility. Chaos might never call it in. He said I was interesting. Maybe watching me is enough. Maybe he'll leave me alone.*

Even in her own head, the words rang hollow.

She thought about what Chaos had said. *There are others of my children who do not share my appreciation for the unexpected. Others who see your existence as a violation of the natural order.*

Darkness has many faces.

What did that mean? Chaos's other children. Other primordial beings, entities as old as creation itself. Was one of them watching her? Planning something? Was that why Keats's visions had been blocked, why Lily's speed had faltered?

Or was she being paranoid, looking for patterns that weren't there?

Stop, she commanded herself. *You dealt with Greer. Finola is safe. The Caduceus is stored away. That's enough for one day. That's enough for one lifetime.*

She could forget about the boon. Push it to the back of her mind and go on with her life. Help lead the Network. Love Keats. Be the person everyone needed her to be.

The boon didn't have to define her. It was a debt. A favor owed. It didn't change who she was or what she was fighting for.

It doesn't matter, she told herself again. *It doesn't matter. It doesn't matter.*

If she repeated it enough times, maybe she'd believe it.

Behind her, Keats stirred in his sleep. "Al?" His voice was groggy, concerned. "You okay?"

"Fine." She turned away from the window, away from the moonlit mountains, away from all the questions she couldn't answer. "Couldn't sleep."

"Come back to bed."

She went. Slid under the covers and let him pull her close. His heartbeat was steady against her back, his warmth surrounding her like armor.

"Love you," he murmured, already half-asleep again.

"Love you too."

That, at least, wasn't a lie.

But as she lay there in the darkness, listening to Keats breathe, she couldn't shake the feeling that something was coming. Something big. Something she couldn't run from, couldn't hide from, couldn't handle alone no matter how much she tried.

The boon sat heavy on her soul.

And somewhere in the cosmic dark, she could almost feel Chaos watching.

Waiting.

Interested.

6

The emergency klaxon shattered Alexis's attempt at normalcy before breakfast.

She was in the compound's kitchen, hands wrapped around a mug of coffee that had gone lukewarm while she stared at nothing. The ceramic was smooth against her palms, the smell of dark roast mixing with the pine-scented morning air drifting through the open window. Keats sat across from her, picking at scrambled eggs he wasn't eating, the scrape of his fork against the plate the only sound between them.

They hadn't talked about last night. About her standing at the window. About all the things she wasn't saying.

Then the alarm screamed through the building. Three sharp blasts that meant *emergency briefing, all hands*. And the silence between them became irrelevant.

Keats was on his feet before the third blast faded, his chair scraping against the hardwood floor. Alexis abandoned her coffee and followed, the weight of her choices pressing against her soul like a stone in her chest as they jogged through corridors that smelled of fresh paint and old wood.

The briefing room was already filling when they arrived. A dozen Network operatives crowded around the central table, their faces lit blue-white by the holographic displays flickering to life above its surface. The air was thick with tension. Alexis could taste it, metallic and sharp, like the moments before a thunderstorm.

The intelligence center had grown since she'd first arrived. More screens, more workstations, more evidence of the Network expanding to meet threats that multiplied faster than they could track. The lodge's original stone fireplace still dominated one wall, incongruous against the banks of monitors, a reminder that this had once been a place where families gathered for summer vacations. Now it gathered Scions, and the fire that burned in it was purely metaphorical.

Aaron stood at the head of the table, his jaw tight and his posture rigid in a way that made him look more like a soldier than usual. Lily was beside him, her red hair still damp from a shower she'd clearly cut short. She caught Alexis's eye and shook her head. *I don't know either.*

"Close the doors," Aaron said. His voice carried the clipped precision of someone delivering bad news. "What I'm about to show you doesn't leave this room."

The heavy oak doors swung shut with a sound like a coffin closing. Alexis found a spot along the wall, Keats pressing close beside her. His shoulder was warm against hers, solid and grounding.

Aaron tapped the table's surface, and the holographic display expanded into a global map studded with red markers. Dozens of them. Scattered across every continent, clustering in patterns that made Alexis's stomach clench.

"Overnight, we received reports from seventeen different cells." Aaron's voice was flat, controlled. The voice of someone trying hard not to panic. "Scion abilities failing. Powers flickering or gone entirely. Divine connections severed without warning."

Murmurs rippled through the room. Alexis felt Keats stiffen beside her.

"That's not all." Aaron pulled up another layer of data. Prayer response rates, divine intervention statistics, communication logs between the mortal and divine realms. All of them trending sharply downward, the lines on the graphs plummeting like stones dropped from a height. "The failures aren't random. They correspond exactly, *exactly*, to the locations and timing of artifact thefts over the past month."

He zoomed in on Greece. A red marker pulsed over Corinth.

"Iris's Rainbow Prism. Stolen three days ago. Within twenty-four hours, every Scion in a two-hundred-mile radius reported difficulty communicating with their divine parents. Prayers going unanswered. Visions failing."

Egypt. Another marker, this one over Alexandria.

"Thoth's Palette. Gone yesterday. This morning, three Egyptian Scions woke up unable to access their abilities at all. One of them—" Aaron's voice caught. "One of them tried to heal a child with a fever. The power wasn't there."

The room had gone quiet. Alexis could hear the hum of the compound's electrical systems, the distant cry of a hawk outside, the ragged breathing of the operative standing nearest to her.

"Someone is systematically destroying the connection between divine and mortal realms," Aaron said. "And they're using the artifacts to do it."

* * * *

The questions came fast after that. Alexis let them wash over her, her mind racing through implications she didn't want to face.

This was bigger than Greer. Bigger than her guilt, her secrets, the boon weighing on her soul. Someone was dismantling the infrastructure that connected gods to mortals, and they were doing it with surgical precision.

"How many artifacts total?" Lily asked. She was leaning forward, her fingers drumming against the table's edge. A nervous habit Alexis had noticed before. Today, the rhythm was faster. More erratic.

"Confirmed stolen? Twelve." Aaron pulled up a list that floated in the air between them, glowing text cataloguing divine losses. "Apollo's Lyre. Demeter's Seeds. Thor's Járngreipr, the iron gloves he needed to wield Mjolnir. Amaterasu's Mirror. The list goes on."

"All connection artifacts," someone said from the back of the room.

"Every single one." Aaron nodded grimly. "Whoever's doing this knows exactly what they're targeting. These aren't random thefts. They're strategic strikes against the divine-mortal bond itself."

Keats shifted beside Alexis. She glanced at him and saw his face had gone pale, his green eyes distant in the way that meant he was trying to reach for a vision.

Static, probably. Shadows where there should be clarity. Whatever was blocking his abilities was still at work.

"The peculiar events," Lily said slowly. "My speed being off. Keats's visions failing. That wasn't us being tired."

"No." Aaron's jaw tightened. "You're both affected. As of this morning, our divine connections are operating at roughly sixty percent capacity. And that number is dropping."

The words hit like a physical blow. Alexis saw Lily's hand clench into a fist, saw Keats's shoulders go rigid with tension.

"What about Alexis?" Keats asked. His voice was rough. "Her connection to Nyx. Is that affected too?"

Aaron hesitated. "We haven't been able to measure it directly. Primordial connections don't follow the same patterns as Olympian ones. But..." He looked at Alexis, something careful in his expression. "Have you noticed any changes? Any weakness in your abilities?"

She thought about the ether. About how easily she'd moved through it yesterday, how her shadows had responded to her will even when everything else was falling apart.

"No," she said. "Nothing's changed."

But even as she said it, she wondered. The boon connected her to Chaos, to the primordial void that had birthed everything, including whatever was doing this. Was that connection protecting her? Or was it something else?

"We need more data," Aaron continued. "Which brings me to our next piece of business." He gestured toward a corner of the room. "Cerval, if you would?"

A figure stepped forward from the shadows near the door, and Alexis realized with a start that she hadn't noticed him there. He was tall and lean, with dark hair cut close to his scalp and features that were handsome in a forgettable way. His clothes were nondescript: dark jeans, a gray henley, boots that had seen some wear. Everything about him seemed designed to avoid attention.

"This is Cerval Colley," Aaron said. "He joined us two weeks ago. Came in through the London cell. Background in data analysis and pattern recognition. He's been helping me cross-reference the theft reports."

Cerval nodded to the room, his expression professionally neutral. When he spoke, his voice was smooth and unremarkable. The kind of voice you'd forget five minutes after hearing it.

"The pattern is elegant, actually." He moved to the holographic display, his fingers dancing across the controls with practiced ease. New data layers appeared, connections forming between the red markers like a web. "Whoever is doing this understands divine infrastructure better than most gods do. They're not just stealing artifacts. They're targeting specific nodes in the network. Communication channels first, then power conduits, then connection anchors."

"In English?" Lily asked.

"They're cutting the phone lines first, then the power grid, then the bridges." Cerval's lips quirked. The ghost of a smile that didn't reach his eyes. "By the time they're done, there won't be any way for divine energy to flow into the mortal realm at all. Gods and mortals will be completely separated."

The room absorbed that in silence. Alexis felt a chill run down her spine that had nothing to do with the temperature.

Complete separation. No more Scions. No more divine intervention. No more prayers answered or miracles performed. A world cut off from the cosmic powers that had shaped it since the beginning.

"How long?" someone asked. "How long until they finish?"

Cerval's expression didn't change. "At the current rate of theft? Two weeks. Maybe three. After that, the damage will be irreversible."

* * * *

The briefing dissolved into chaos after that. The productive kind, with people breaking into groups, assigning tasks, reaching out to other cells for coordination. Alexis found herself standing apart from it, watching the activity swirl around her like water around a stone.

She'd wanted to hide. To bury the boon, bury her guilt, pretend that everything was fine and she could go back to her ordinary life.

But there was no hiding from this.

People were suffering. Scions were losing their powers, their connections to their divine parents, everything that made them who they were. And somewhere out there, someone was orchestrating all of it with the cold precision of a surgeon removing organs one by one.

"Al."

Keats appeared at her elbow, his face drawn. She could see him fighting to keep his composure, but his hands were shaking. A tremor she'd never seen in him before.

"Sixty percent," he said quietly. "My abilities are already at sixty percent, and I just started *using* them. By the time I figure out how they're supposed to work, they might not work at all."

The vulnerability in his voice cracked something in her chest. She reached for his hand, lacing her fingers through his the way she had a hundred times before. His palm was cold, clammy with fear.

"We're going to fix this," she said. "We're going to find whoever's doing this and stop them."

"How?" He looked at her, searching her face for something to hold onto. "We don't even know who they are. We don't know how they're getting into these places, how they're bypassing divine security. We don't know anything."

"Then we find out." Alexis squeezed his hand, trying to project a confidence she didn't feel. "The artifacts were made by someone. Forged by divine smiths who understood how they worked. If anyone knows how to track them, how to stop them from being used this way—"

"The Artifact Smiths." Lily's voice cut in. She'd crossed the room to join them, her expression fierce despite the fear lurking behind her eyes. "Hephaestus. The Cyclopes. Wayland, Ptah, the others. They created these things. They might know how to uncreate them. Or at least how to find them."

"Do we know where any of them are?" Keats asked.

"Aaron's been tracking reports of Smiths going into hiding over the past few weeks. Some of them have been targeted too. Not killed, but scared. Driven underground." Lily's jaw tightened. "Whoever's doing this doesn't want anyone who could undo their work still standing."

Alexis thought about what Cerval had said. *Whoever is doing this understands divine infrastructure better than most gods do.*

That kind of knowledge didn't come from nowhere. It suggested someone ancient. Someone who had watched the divine-mortal bond being built, who understood its architecture intimately.

Someone, perhaps, who had existed since before the bond was forged at all.

Darkness has many faces, Chaos had said. *Not all of them are as fond of you as I am.*

Was this what he'd been warning her about?

"We need to find the Smiths," Alexis said, her voice steadier than she felt. "Before whoever's doing this finishes driving them underground. They're our best shot at understanding what we're dealing with."

"I'll start pulling together what we have on their last known locations," Lily said. "Aaron's got some contacts in the Greek pantheon who might know where Hephaestus is laying low. And there've been rumors about Wayland in Scandinavia."

"I can help with the data analysis."

They turned. Cerval had approached silently, his expression helpful and earnest. Up close, Alexis noticed his eyes were an unusual shade of gray. Pale and cool, like winter fog.

"I've already mapped the theft patterns," he continued. "If the Smiths are being targeted too, there should be overlap. Places where the thief has been, people they've contacted. I can cross-reference the data, see if anything useful shakes loose."

"That would be helpful," Lily said. "Thanks, Cerval."

He nodded, that ghost-smile flickering across his face again. "Just doing my part."

He moved away, already pulling up data on a tablet he'd produced from somewhere. Efficient. Competent. Invisible.

Alexis watched him go, something nagging at the back of her mind. She couldn't put her finger on it. A vague sense of wrongness, like a picture hanging crooked.

But there were too many other things to worry about. She filed the feeling away and turned back to Keats and Lily.

"Okay," she said. "Let's find the Smiths. And let's find whoever's trying to tear the world apart."

The boon still pressed against her soul. The secrets still sat heavy on her tongue. But for now, there was work to do, and people depending on her to do it.

Her personal crisis would have to wait.

The world was falling apart, and Alexis Rain was done hiding her head in the sand.

7

Keats looked like he was trying to push a boulder uphill with his mind.

He sat cross-legged on the meditation platform, his eyes closed, his hands resting on his knees with fingers curled into loose fists. Sweat beaded at his temples despite the cool mountain air. His jaw was clenched so tight Alexis could see the muscle jumping beneath his skin.

She stood at the edge of the platform, arms crossed, watching him strain against abilities that kept slipping through his grasp. Behind her, the White Mountains stretched toward a sky the color of old pewter, heavy clouds threatening rain that hadn't yet fallen. The air smelled of pine and approaching storm.

"Anything?" Lily asked. She was perched on the wooden railing, one leg dangling, her red hair whipping in the wind.

Keats's eyes opened. They were bloodshot, ringed with exhaustion. "Fragments. Nothing I can hold onto. It's like trying to catch smoke."

"Tell us what you saw," Alexis said. "Even fragments might be enough."

He rubbed his face with both hands, the gesture frustrated and weary. "Fire. Lots of fire. Industrial, not natural. A forge, maybe.

Mountains, but not these mountains. Volcanic. I saw a single eye, huge, watching. And heat. So much heat I could almost feel it burning."

"The Cyclopes," Lily said. "They work volcanic forges. Always have."

"That narrows it down to about a thousand volcanic regions worldwide." Keats's voice carried an edge of bitterness. "Helpful, right?"

"Hey." Alexis moved closer, crouching beside him so they were at eye level. His skin was clammy when she touched his arm, cold despite the effort he'd been expending. "You're doing more than anyone else could. Three weeks ago you didn't even know you had these abilities."

"Three weeks ago my abilities worked properly." He met her eyes, and she saw the fear underneath the frustration. "What if they keep degrading? What if by the time I figure out how to use them, there's nothing left to use?"

She didn't have an answer for that. None of them did.

"What else?" Lily pressed, her tone gentler than before. "Any other details? Sounds, smells, anything that might narrow the location?"

Keats closed his eyes again, reaching for the memory of the vision. "Salt. I smelled salt on the wind. And there was something… Greek. Old Greek, not modern. The way the forge was built, the symbols carved into the stone. It felt Mediterranean."

"Volcanic, Mediterranean, near salt water." Lily pulled out her phone, fingers dancing across the screen. "That could be Sicily. Or one of the smaller Greek islands. The Cyclopes were supposed to have forges under Mount Etna originally, but they moved around."

Alexis straightened, her mind already working through the problem. Keats's visions were fragmented, unreliable, but her gift had no such limitations. If the information existed somewhere, she could find it.

Where are the Cyclopes currently located? That didn't work. She tried rephrasing a few times and finally came to the most likely answer.

The answer came immediately: *Nisyros. Volcanic island, Dodecanese chain. Forge beneath the caldera. They have not moved in three hundred years.*

"Nisyros," she said. "Small volcanic island in the Aegean. Their forge is under the caldera."

Keats stared at her. "How do you—" He stopped himself, shaking his head. "Right. The gift. I keep forgetting you can just… know things."

"It helps to have a starting point." She offered him a hand up. "Your vision gave me that. Now let's go talk to some ancient blacksmiths."

* * * *

The entrance to the Cyclopes' forge was hidden in the throat of Nisyros's dormant caldera, accessible only through a path that wound between sulfur vents and pools of bubbling mud.

The trio stepped out of the ether at the caldera's edge, the transition from gray void to searing heat so abrupt it stole her breath. The air tasted of rotten eggs and hot metal. Steam rose from cracks in the yellow-white ground, and the earth itself seemed to pulse with barely contained energy. A giant's heartbeat thrumming beneath her feet.

They'd discussed letting Alexis transport them. Her ether access was the fastest way to travel, even if it made Keats nauseous and left Lily complaining about the cold. As long as they held Alexis's hands, they could move through the ether with her.

"Charming," Lily muttered, surveying the hellscape around them. "Lovely vacation spot."

"The forge is below us." Alexis pointed toward a crack in the caldera floor where the steam rose thickest. "There should be an entrance somewhere near that vent."

They picked their way across the unstable ground, the heat intensifying with every step. Alexis's boots stuck to patches of ground that were almost too hot to walk on. Sweat soaked through her shirt within minutes, plastering the fabric to her back.

The entrance, when they found it, was a vertical shaft that plunged into darkness. Carved steps spiraled down along its walls, the stone worn smooth by countless feet over millennia. The air rising from below carried the clang of hammers on metal and the deep bass rumble of bellows feeding an impossibly hot fire.

"Welcoming committee?" Keats asked, peering into the darkness.

"Probably not." Alexis started down the stairs, shadows gathering around her instinctively. "The Cyclopes don't like visitors."

The descent took longer than she expected. The stairs spiraled down and down, the temperature climbing with each turn until the air itself felt like a physical weight pressing against her skin. Orange light began to flicker from below. The glow of a forge fire so vast it lit the entire cavern.

They emerged onto a ledge overlooking a workshop the size of a cathedral.

The forge dominated the center of the space. A pit of molten rock fed by channels that seemed to tap directly into the volcano's heart. Massive bellows, each one larger than a house, pumped rhythmically on either side, sending blasts of air that made the flames roar white-hot. Anvils the size of cars were scattered throughout the cavern, their surfaces scarred by ages of use.

And working at those anvils, their single eyes reflecting the fire's glow, were the Cyclopes.

Alexis had expected them to be large. She hadn't expected them to be *this* large. Each one standing at least fifteen feet tall, their bodies thick with muscle built over millennia of smithwork. Their skin was the gray-brown of volcanic rock, rough and scarred from countless sparks and splashes of molten metal. And their eyes, single, enormous, centered in their foreheads, glowed with an intelligence that was ancient and alien and decidedly unfriendly.

The nearest one looked up from his work as they descended the final stairs. His hammer, a block of iron that must have weighed a ton, paused mid-swing.

"Scions." The word rumbled through the cavern like distant thunder, carrying contempt that had been fermenting for ages. "You are not welcome here."

The other Cyclopes had stopped working now. Five of them, Alexis counted, their massive forms turning toward the intruders with the slow deliberation of creatures who had never needed to hurry in their eternal lives.

"We're not here to cause trouble," she said, pitching her voice to carry over the roar of the forge. "We need information about the artifact thefts."

"The thefts." The lead Cyclops set down his hammer with a boom that shook the floor. "You mean the systematic destruction of everything we have built over ten thousand years. Yes, we are aware."

He moved toward them, each step covering ground that would have taken Alexis three strides. Up close, the heat radiating from his body was almost unbearable. Like standing too close to an open oven.

"We are also aware," he continued, his single eye narrowing, "that Scions bring nothing but trouble. Divine politics. Olympian squabbles. Every time the gods fight among themselves, we are caught in the middle. Our forges raided. Our work stolen. Our brothers killed."

"We're not here to raid anything," Keats said, stepping forward despite Lily's warning hand on his arm. "We're trying to stop whoever's taking the artifacts. Trying to save the divine-mortal connection before it's severed completely."

"And why should we care?" The Cyclops loomed over Keats, his shadow swallowing the young man entirely. "The divine-mortal connection has brought us nothing but servitude. Forge this weapon, build this tool, create this miracle. Always demands. Never respect."

"If the connection is severed, you'll be cut off too," Lily pointed out. "No more divine commissions means no more divine protection.

How long do you think this forge will stay hidden when the mortals start drilling deeper into the earth?"

"We have survived worse than mortal curiosity." But there was a flicker of uncertainty in the Cyclops's voice that suggested Lily's point had landed.

Alexis stepped forward, drawing the attention back to herself. Time for a gamble.

"My name is Alexis Rain," she said. "Daughter of Nyx."

The effect was immediate. All five Cyclopes went still, their massive bodies freezing in place. The lead one's eye widened, his gaze fixing on her with new intensity.

"Nyx," he breathed. The name carried weight. Reverence, maybe, or fear. "The primordial. The night itself."

"My mother was ancient when the Olympians were still learning to walk." Alexis held his gaze, drawing on shadows without conscious thought. They gathered around her feet, curled at the edges of her form, making her seem larger than she was. More *other*. "She remembers when your kind first learned to shape metal. She remembers the world before the gods claimed it."

"And yet you come to us as a supplicant." The Cyclops's voice had changed. Less hostile, more curious. "A daughter of night, begging for scraps of information."

"I don't beg." The words came out harder than she intended, but she didn't soften them. "I'm asking for help because someone is destroying everything your people built. Ten thousand years of work, being systematically unmade. You can refuse out of spite, or you can help us stop it. Your choice."

The cavern fell silent except for the roar of the forge. Alexis felt Keats and Lily flanking her, their tension palpable. The Cyclopes exchanged looks. Some communication passing between them that she couldn't read.

Finally, the lead Cyclops spoke.

"Brontes," he said. "I am called Brontes. And I will tell you what we know. Not for love of the Olympians, or their half-blood spawn. But because Nyx was old when we were young. And because you have fire in you, daughter of night. Fire enough to be interesting."

Interesting. The word echoed in her mind, carrying echoes of another voice, another conversation.

She was starting to wonder if being interesting was a blessing or a curse.

* * * *

Brontes led them to a side chamber, away from the worst of the heat. The walls here were lined with shelves holding artifacts in various stages of completion: weapons, tools, items Alexis couldn't identify. The air smelled of hot metal and something older, earthier. Ancient stone that had been here since before humans walked the earth.

"The artifacts being stolen," Brontes said, settling onto a stone bench that creaked under his weight, "are all connection points. Anchors that allow divine energy to flow into the mortal realm. Without them, the bond between worlds weakens. Eventually, it will shatter entirely."

"We know that much," Lily said. "What we need to know is how to stop it. How to find the artifacts, or failing that, how to create new ones."

Brontes's laugh was like boulders grinding together. "Create new ones? Child, it took us centuries to forge those artifacts. We built them at the dawn of the divine age, when the boundary between worlds was still soft and malleable. Now that boundary is hardened. Set. Even if we had centuries to spare, the conditions no longer exist."

"Then we need to recover the stolen ones," Alexis said. "Is there any way to track them?"

"Not directly. The artifacts are designed to be stable, self-contained. They don't leave traces that can be followed." Brontes's eye narrowed thoughtfully. "But we were not the only smiths. The Telchines worked with different methods. Binding magic instead of pure forging. Their artifacts carry signatures that can be read, if you know how."

"The Telchines." Keats leaned forward. "Where can we find them?"

"You cannot." Brontes's voice carried old grief. "The Telchines were hunted to extinction long ago. Zeus blamed them for a drought, wrongly, but divine justice rarely concerns itself with truth. He destroyed their island, scattered their forges, killed all but..." He paused. "All but one."

"One survived?" Alexis pressed.

"Perhaps. There were rumors, centuries ago, of a Telchine hiding in liminal space. The cracks between worlds where even gods cannot easily reach. If any of their kind still lives, that is where they would be."

"How do we get there?"

Brontes studied her for a long moment. "The liminal spaces are unstable. Treacherous. Even for a daughter of Nyx, the journey would be dangerous."

"Everything's dangerous lately," Lily muttered. "At least this danger might help."

The Cyclops rose, moving to a shelf lined with scrolls that looked older than writing itself. He selected one, handling it with surprising delicacy for hands that could crush stone.

"This contains what we know of the liminal paths," he said, offering it to Alexis. The parchment was warm against her fingers, almost alive. "It is incomplete, and much of it may be outdated. But it is a starting point."

"Thank you."

"Do not thank me." Brontes's voice was grave. "If you succeed, you may delay the severing. If you fail, the consequences will be severe. For all of us."

He turned away, returning to his forge and his work, the conversation clearly over. Alexis tucked the scroll into her jacket, feeling its weight against her chest. Another burden added to the collection she was already carrying.

"Well," Keats said quietly as they made their way back toward the stairs. "That was terrifying and only moderately helpful."

"Welcome to divine politics." Lily's voice carried exhaustion. "Where everyone hates everyone else, and the best you can hope for is grudging tolerance."

Alexis didn't respond. She was thinking about what Brontes had said. About fire, and being interesting, and the weight of her mother's name.

And about darkness, and its many faces.

* * * *

Back at the compound, Lily headed for the training room.

She needed to move. To hit something. To feel her body responding the way it was supposed to, even if that response was diminished. Sixty percent capacity, Aaron had said. Every day, a little less.

The training room was a converted barn, its wooden beams hung with punching bags and its floor covered in mats that smelled of old sweat and newer disinfectant. Lily grabbed a pair of gloves from the rack by the door and started wrapping her hands, the familiar ritual settling her nerves.

She wasn't alone. Another figure was already working the heavy bag at the far end. A young woman with honey-blonde hair and the compact build of someone who'd trained seriously. Her combinations were good, Lily noticed. Crisp, efficient, no wasted movement.

"Hey," Lily called out. "Mind if I join you?"

The woman paused, turning with a smile that brightened her whole face. She looked to be in her early twenties, with warm brown eyes and freckles scattered across her nose.

"Lily Abrams, right? I'm Ellie." She stripped off one glove to offer a handshake. Her palm was calloused, her grip firm. "I've heard a lot about you. The speed thing is pretty amazing."

"Less amazing lately." Lily shook her hand, noting the easy confidence in Ellie's posture. "You're new? I don't think I've seen you around."

"Arrived about three weeks ago, right before everything went crazy." Ellie's smile turned rueful. "Great timing, right? Join the super-secret divine organization just in time for the apocalypse."

Lily found herself smiling back. There was something likeable about Ellie. An openness that felt genuine in a world full of secrets and hidden agendas.

"Who's your divine parent?" Lily asked, moving to the bag next to Ellie's.

"Honestly? I'm not sure." Ellie resumed her stance, throwing a combination that made the bag shudder. "My abilities are kind of vague. Enhanced intuition, I guess? I can sometimes sense when things are about to go wrong. Not visions like Apollo's kids, just... a feeling."

"That sounds useful."

"It would be, if I could control it." Another combination, harder this time. "Mostly it just makes me anxious about everything."

Lily laughed. A real laugh, surprising herself. She'd been carrying so much tension lately that she'd forgotten what it felt like to talk to someone without secrets, without agenda.

"I know what you mean," she said. "My speed is supposed to make me feel powerful. Lately it just makes me feel slow."

"That's rough." Ellie's voice was sympathetic. "Is it the artifact thing? The divine connection weakening?"

"Yeah. Every day it's a little worse." Lily threw a punch that she'd have been faster at a month ago. It still connected solidly, but she could feel the difference. "We're working on it. Alexis has some leads."

"Alexis." Ellie's tone shifted to something like awe. "I haven't met her yet, but everyone talks about her like she's…"

"Like she's what?"

"I don't know. Special, I guess." Ellie shrugged, a little embarrassed. "Daughter of a primordial goddess, took down Phthonos… It's a lot to live up to."

"She's also my friend," Lily said, something protective stirring in her chest. "And she's dealing with stuff nobody should have to deal with alone. Don't put her on a pedestal. It makes it harder for her to be human."

Ellie nodded slowly. "That's actually good advice. Thanks."

They fell into a rhythm after that. Working side by side, occasionally trading tips or commentary. Ellie's technique was solid if unpolished. Lily found herself offering corrections without thinking about it, and Ellie received them with an eagerness that was almost endearing.

"Same time tomorrow?" Ellie asked as they wound down, both of them breathing hard and slick with sweat.

"If the world isn't ending." Lily grabbed a towel from the rack, wiping her face. "Which, given our luck, is about fifty-fifty."

Ellie's laugh echoed through the training room. Warm, genuine, the kind of sound that made you want to laugh along.

"I'll take those odds," she said. "See you tomorrow, Lily."

Lily watched her go, feeling something ease in her chest that she hadn't realized was tight. It was nice to have someone new to talk to. Someone who wasn't carrying the same weight of secrets and cosmic responsibilities.

Someone who seemed normal.

She headed for the showers, already planning tomorrow's session. The world might be falling apart, but at least she'd made a friend.

Small victories counted for something.

8

The scroll from Brontes was older than any language Alexis could read.

She'd spent the past two days studying it, the parchment spread across the intelligence center's main table like a patient awaiting surgery. The symbols weren't Greek, weren't any alphabet she recognized. Spiraling patterns that seemed to shift when she looked at them too long, lines that curved in directions that made her eyes ache.

But her gift didn't care about languages. It cared about information, and the scroll was full of it.

How do I reach the Telchine's cave?

The answer came in pieces, assembling itself from fragments of knowledge scattered across millennia: *Enter liminal space through the threshold at Cape Sounion. Follow the path that isn't there. Trust the direction that feels wrong. The cave exists in the crack between what is and what could be.*

Helpful. And completely insane.

"I found something."

Cerval's voice pulled her from her contemplation. He'd appeared at her elbow without a sound. She was starting to notice that about him, the way he moved like silence was his native element. His tablet glowed in the dim light of the intelligence center, casting shadows up across his angular features.

"The artifact theft patterns," he continued, sliding the tablet across the table toward her. "I cross-referenced them with the locations of known divine craftspeople. There's significant overlap."

Alexis studied the screen. A map of Europe and the Mediterranean, dotted with markers in two colors. Red for thefts, blue for smiths. The blue markers were clustered in patterns that seemed random until you looked closer. Then you noticed how the red markers circled them. Surrounded them. Cut off their escape routes.

"They're not just stealing artifacts," she said slowly. "They're isolating the people who could make new ones."

"Exactly." Cerval's gray eyes met hers, cool and assessing. "Whoever's doing this isn't improvising. They're executing a plan. One that accounts for every possible countermove."

"Any indication of who?"

"Not yet." He shook his head, and she caught a flicker in his expression. Frustration? Or something else? "The operational security is beyond anything I've seen. No signatures, no traces, nothing that points to a specific actor. Whoever they are, they understand divine systems at a fundamental level."

The words echoed what Brontes had said. What Aaron's briefing had suggested. Someone ancient, operating with knowledge that predated most gods.

Darkness has many faces.

"Keep digging," Alexis said. "Anything you find, bring it to me immediately."

"Of course." Cerval nodded, retrieving his tablet. That ghost-smile flickered across his face again. "Good luck with the Telchine. I hope you find what you're looking for." He drifted away, back into the shadows at the edge of the room. Alexis had questions.

But there was no time to dwell on it. They had a journey to make.

* * * *

Cape Sounion jutted into the Aegean like a finger pointing at infinity.

The ruins of Poseidon's temple crowned the clifftop, white marble columns catching the last light of sunset. Below, waves crashed against rocks worn smooth by millennia of assault, the spray carrying salt and the distinct smell of the sea. Tourists had left hours ago; the three of them stood alone among the ancient stones, the wind pulling at their clothes.

"So," Lily said, eyeing the temple with skepticism. "We're looking for a door that doesn't exist, to a place that might not be real, to find someone who's probably dead."

"That's the spirit," Keats muttered.

Alexis walked between the columns, letting her fingers trail across the weathered stone. It was cold despite the warm evening, carrying a chill that had nothing to do with temperature. Power hummed beneath the surface. Old power, the kind that remembered when gods walked openly among mortals.

Where is the threshold to liminal space?

Between the sixth and seventh columns. Where the shadow falls at the moment the sun touches the sea.

She counted columns, moving to the space her gift had indicated. The sun was a molten disc on the horizon, bleeding orange and red across the water. In minutes, it would dip below the edge of the world.

"Here," she said. "Keats, Lily, with me. When the sun touches the water, we go through."

"Go through what?" Lily asked, but she moved to Alexis's side anyway, trusting in spite of her skepticism.

"I'm not sure yet. Stay close."

Keats took her hand. His palm was warm, steadying. On her other side, Lily gripped her elbow, the contact grounding them together.

The sun kissed the sea.

The shadow between the columns stretched, impossibly, wrongly, and Alexis pulled them through.

* * * *

Liminal space was nothing like the ether.

Where the ether was gray and featureless, this was… everything. And nothing. The ground beneath her feet kept changing. Now stone, now sand, now solidified moonlight. The sky above cycled through colors that had no names, bleeding from violet to amber to a shade of green that made her teeth ache.

The air smelled of possibilities. Of doors opening and closing. Of choices made and unmade.

"This is insane," Lily breathed. She was still gripping Alexis's arm, her fingers digging in hard enough to leave bruises. "What *is* this place?"

"The space between," Alexis said. "Where reality hasn't decided what it wants to be yet."

"Great. Helpful." Lily's snark was undercut by the tremor in her voice. "Which way?"

That was the question. Paths branched in every direction, or no direction. Alexis could see three routes ahead that seemed to lead somewhere, but two of them felt wrong in ways she couldn't articulate. The third...

"Keats." She turned to him. His face was pale, his eyes unfocused in the way that meant he was reaching for a vision. "Can you see anything?"

"Trying." The word came through gritted teeth. Sweat beaded at his temples despite the ambient chill. "The static is worse here. Like trying to tune a radio during a thunderstorm." He closed his eyes, concentrating hard. "Left. I think. There's a shape in the static. A cave. Water dripping."

"Left it is." Alexis started forward, keeping hold of both of them. "Stay close. Don't let go. I don't know what happens if we get separated here."

They walked.

The path twisted through landscapes that changed with every step. A forest of crystal trees that chimed in an unfelt wind. A desert where the sand was made of crushed mirrors, reflecting versions of themselves that moved a half-second out of sync. A bridge over an abyss that seemed to contain stars. Not distant stars, but close ones, burning with light that warmed their faces as they crossed.

"This is wrong," Keats said suddenly. They'd been walking for what felt like hours, or minutes, or days. Time was as unstable as everything else here. "The path ahead. It doesn't feel right."

Alexis paused, reaching for her gift. *Which direction leads to the Telchine's cave?*

The answer was muddled, uncertain. *Forward. But also not forward. The way is blocked.*

"Something's in our way," she said. "My gift can't see past it."

"Let me try." Lily's voice had steadied. She released Alexis's arm and moved ahead, her body shifting into the ready stance of someone about to sprint. "Maybe I can scout ahead. See what we're dealing with."

"Your speed—"

"Is at sixty percent. I know." Lily's jaw tightened. "But sixty percent of superhuman is still faster than normal. And sitting here won't get us anywhere."

Before Alexis could argue, she was gone. A blur of motion that vanished around the bend in the path. The air displaced by her passage carried the smell of ozone and copper.

Seconds passed. Or longer. It was impossible to tell.

Then Lily was back, skidding to a stop with her chest heaving. Her face had gone white.

"We have a problem," she said.

"What kind of problem?"

"The kind with three heads and a bad attitude." Lily's voice cracked. "There's something blocking the path ahead. A guardian, I think. And Al?" She met Alexis's eyes, and the fear there was raw and real. "It's not some ancient relic that's been here forever. The ground around it is freshly disturbed. Whatever that thing is, someone put it there *recently*."

Alexis's blood went cold.

Someone else knew about the Telchine. Someone else had gotten here first and left a guard to stop anyone who came looking.

"What is it?" Keats asked. His hand found hers again, squeezing tight.

"A chimera," Lily said. "Lion, goat, serpent. The whole mythological package." She laughed, but there was no humor in it. "And it's big. *Really* big."

Alexis looked at the path ahead. The path they had to take if they wanted to find the Telchine, find answers, find any hope of stopping the artifact thefts.

Then she looked at her team. Keats, with his unreliable visions and his steady courage. Lily, diminished but unbowed, faster than anything human even at sixty percent.

And herself. Daughter of night. Granddaughter of Chaos. Carrying secrets that pressed against her soul like stones.

"Then we go through it," she said. "Together."

Keats nodded once, his jaw set.

Lily cracked her knuckles, a fierce grin spreading across her face despite the fear in her eyes. "I was hoping you'd say that."

They moved forward, into the unstable heart of liminal space, toward a monster that someone had placed specifically to stop them.

The trial wasn't over.

It was just beginning.

9

Liminal space was everything and nothing at once.

Alexis had thought she understood the concept. The spaces between spaces, the gaps where reality hadn't decided what it wanted to be. But walking through it was different from understanding it. The ground beneath her feet shifted between textures: solid stone one moment, packed sand the next, then a surface her boots sank into like clouds made solid.

The sky, if it could be called a sky, defied description. Colors she had no names for rippled overhead, bleeding into each other like watercolors on wet paper. Occasionally, she caught glimpses of other places through tears in the fabric of the space: a forest of trees made entirely of glass, their branches catching light that came from nowhere. A desert where the sand reflected images instead of light, showing fragments of moments that might have been memories or futures. An abyss filled with stars that burned in colors no earthly telescope had ever recorded.

"Don't look too long at any of it," Lily warned, her voice tight with concentration. "The liminal plays tricks. Shows you what you want to see, or what you fear to see, or sometimes what it thinks would be interesting. None of it's real. Or all of it's real somewhere. Either way, it's not useful."

Easy for her to say. Lily had been navigating these spaces for years, had learned their rhythms and their dangers. For Alexis, every step felt like a test. A constant negotiation with a reality that hadn't made up its mind about the rules.

Keats walked close beside her, his oracle sight flickering gold at the edges as he tried to make sense of a place where past, present, and future existed simultaneously. "I can't see anything clearly here," he muttered, frustration bleeding through his voice. "It's like trying to watch a movie where every frame is from a different film."

The path, such as it was, wound through landscapes that shifted as they watched. They passed through a forest where the trees grew upside down, roots reaching toward a sky that was also somehow a floor. They crossed a bridge over a river that flowed in both directions at once, its waters carrying fragments of conversations in languages that predated human speech.

At one point, they walked through what looked like a graveyard, except the headstones were blank and the graves were filled with light instead of earth. Alexis felt the pull of it. An almost irresistible urge to look closer, to see what names might appear on those empty stones, to discover what lay beneath that gentle glow.

Lily grabbed her arm and pulled her forward. "Don't. Those are the spaces where things that never existed are buried. You look too long, you start wondering if you're one of them."

They walked for what felt like hours but might have been minutes. Time moved differently here, stretching and compressing in ways that made Alexis's internal clock spin uselessly. The boon pressed against her consciousness with every step, a reminder of deals made in places even stranger than this.

And then the landscape crystallized around them, liminal uncertainty hardening into something almost like a cave, and Alexis saw what waited ahead.

* * * *

The Chimera was worse than Lily had described.

It crouched in the center of the path where liminal space had formed into something almost like a cavern. Walls of crystallized possibility rising on either side, a ceiling of frozen light overhead. The creature filled the space like a nightmare given flesh, easily fifteen feet tall at its lion's shoulder, its body a patchwork of impossibilities.

The lion head dominated the front. Maned in fire that crackled and spat without heat, eyes like molten gold that tracked their approach with predatory intelligence. From its back rose the goat head, smaller but no less alert, its horizontal pupils fixing on them with an intensity that felt like judgment. And the tail. The tail was a serpent unto itself, thick as a tree trunk and tipped with a head that hissed venom, its scales gleaming like oil on water.

The smell hit Alexis first. Sulfur and copper and something older, ranker. The musk of a creature that had been hunting since before humanity learned to fear the dark.

"Okay," Keats breathed beside her. "That's... that's a lot of monster."

"Three heads means three attack vectors," Lily said. Her voice was steady, professional. The soldier in her taking over. "Fire from the lion, probably some kind of charge attack. The goat might have defensive magic or sonic capabilities. The serpent is definitely venomous."

"How do you know all that?"

"I read." Lily's jaw tightened. "Also, the serpent is dripping something that's eating through the stone floor. So, you know. Context clues."

Alexis looked at the ground beneath the creature's tail. Sure enough, small craters pocked the crystalline surface where drops of venom had fallen, the edges still smoking faintly. The acid had eaten through material that reality itself had only recently decided should exist.

"The fresh disturbance Lily mentioned," she said, studying the area around the Chimera. Gouges in the walls where enormous claws had scraped. Deep furrows that would have required tremendous force. Scorch marks from the fire-mane that looked days old at most, the crystallized walls still bearing the heat-distortion of recent flame. "This thing was placed here recently. Within the last week, maybe less."

"Someone doesn't want us reaching the Telchine," Keats said.

"Then they should have picked a bigger monster." Alexis didn't feel the confidence she projected, but her team needed to see it anyway. "Here's the plan: Lily, you're our evasion. Keep it distracted, keep moving, don't let any of the heads lock onto you. Keats, I need your eyes. Even fragmented visions are better than nothing. Call out attacks before they land if you can."

"And you?" Lily asked.

"I'm going to hit it until it stops moving."

The Chimera's lion head swung toward them, nostrils flaring. It had caught their scent. The body tensed, muscles bunching beneath hide that looked thick as armor, and a low rumble built in its chest. The precursor to a roar that would announce the beginning of violence.

"Go," Alexis said.

Lily moved.

* * * *

Even at sixty percent, Lily was a blur.

She darted across the Chimera's field of vision, red hair streaming behind her like a banner of defiance. The lion head tracked her, jaws opening to release a gout of flame that scorched the air where she'd been a heartbeat before. The fire was real. Alexis felt the heat wash across her face from thirty feet away, saw the crystalline floor blacken and crack where the flames touched down.

The serpent-tail struck at Lily's shadow, missing by inches. The goat head bleated, a sound that carried harmonics wrong enough to make Alexis's teeth vibrate in her skull, and the air rippled with some kind of sonic attack that Lily simply outran, leaving the distortion to dissipate harmlessly behind her.

"Left flank!" Keats shouted. His eyes had gone distant, gold flickering at their edges as he reached for fragmentary visions through the static that clouded his sight. "The serpent's going to—"

Lily dodged right without waiting for him to finish. The serpent's strike slammed into empty ground with enough force to crack the crystal floor, venom spraying across the surface with a hiss of dissolving stone. Where the acid touched, reality itself seemed to flinch. The crystallized possibility losing coherence, becoming uncertain again before hardening into something new.

Alexis circled wide, shadows gathering around her fists like gauntlets made of darkness. The Chimera was focused on Lily. Exactly as planned. She came up on its blind side, where the goat head couldn't see and the lion's attention was elsewhere.

The creature's flank was a wall of muscle and hide that radiated heat from within. She could smell it now, the close-up musk of an ancient wrongness, a thing that had been stitched together from parts that should never have shared the same body.

She struck.

Darkness lashed out from her hands. Tendrils of primordial night that wrapped around the Chimera's hindquarters and *pulled*. The power felt different here in liminal space, more raw, less filtered through the layers of reality that usually stood between her and Nyx's domain. It responded to her will with an eagerness that was almost frightening.

The creature roared, all three heads voicing fury in discordant harmony. Lion's thunder, goat's scream, serpent's hiss combining into a sound that made the crystalline walls shudder. It stumbled, enormous bulk thrown off-balance, one rear leg buckling under her assault.

"Again!" Keats called. "Before it—"

The goat head turned toward her and screamed.

The sound hit her like a wall of broken glass. Alexis went to her knees, hands clamping over her ears as blood trickled from her nose.

The world spun, reality fracturing at the edges of her vision, and her connection to Nyx's power flickered under the sonic assault. The darkness around her fists dissipating like smoke in a hurricane.

She could feel the scream trying to shake apart something fundamental inside her. Not her eardrums, not her balance. Something deeper. Like it was trying to vibrate her soul out of alignment with her body.

The lion head swung toward her, jaws opening, fire building in its throat. A glow that started deep in its chest and rose like the sun climbing toward dawn…

Lily slammed into her from the side, carrying them both out of the flame's path. Heat scorched across Alexis's back, close enough to singe her jacket, hot enough that she felt the hair on the back of her neck curl and crisp. Then they were rolling across the crystal floor, Lily's arms wrapped around her, the world a tumbling confusion of light and shadow and the Chimera's continued roaring.

They came to rest against the cavern wall. Alexis's ears were still ringing, blood still trickling from her nose, but she was alive. Her back throbbed with what would become a serious burn if she didn't heal it soon.

"The goat," she gasped. "It's got some kind of—"

"Sonic weapon. Yeah, I noticed." Lily hauled her upright, her grip strong despite her own ragged breathing. A burn mark ran across her left forearm where she'd gotten too close to the flames. Red and angry, already blistering. "New plan?"

"Same plan. Need to take out the goat first."

The Chimera had recovered from their initial assault and was scanning the cavern, all three heads moving independently, searching for prey that had momentarily escaped. Keats had moved to a different position, trying to maintain sight lines while staying out of direct danger. He raised a hand, pointing.

"The goat is charging another scream! Twenty seconds!"

Twenty seconds. Alexis looked at Lily, saw the same calculation running behind her eyes. Not enough time to retreat, not enough space to evade. The sonic attack would fill this crystallized cavern like water filling a glass.

"How fast can you get me onto its back?"

Lily's eyes widened. "That's insane."

"That's not a no."

A fierce grin spread across Lily's face. The expression of someone who had been waiting for permission to do something crazy. "Hold on tight."

She grabbed Alexis around the waist and *ran*.

The world blurred. Alexis felt her stomach lurch as acceleration slammed her backward, wind tearing at her clothes and hair. The Chimera loomed ahead, growing larger, impossibly fast, and then Lily was leaping, using speed as thrust, carrying them both in an arc that cleared the lion's snapping jaws by feet.

For a moment, they were airborne. Alexis saw the Chimera below them. All three heads tracking their flight, the goat's mouth opening for the scream it had been building. The lion's mane blazing brighter, preparing another gout of flame. The serpent coiled to strike.

Then they landed on the Chimera's back.

Lily released her immediately, already moving to avoid the serpent-tail that whipped toward them. Alexis found her footing on the creature's spine. The hide rough as sandpaper beneath her boots, the heat from within making sweat break out across her entire body. The fire-mane crackled inches from her face, close enough that she could see individual flames dancing like living things, heat washing over her in waves that dried her eyes and parched her throat.

The goat head turned, mouth opening—

Alexis drove her shadow-wrapped fist into its throat.

The scream died in a strangled gurgle. Darkness poured into the wound, spreading like poison through veins, and the goat head's eyes rolled back. Its neck went slack, the sonic weapon silenced mid-charge, the building pressure dissipating into harmless vibration.

The Chimera screamed. Lion and serpent voicing rage that shook the crystalline walls. Cracks spread through the ceiling above them, fragments of frozen light raining down. The creature bucked wildly, trying to throw her off. Alexis grabbed a fistful of fire-mane, the flames licking at her fingers without burning. Nyx's power protecting her, barely. And held on.

Her shoulder wrenched. Her grip slipped. She caught herself, found new handholds, felt the creature's fury transmitted through every muscle and bone in its body.

"Keats!" she shouted over the chaos. "The serpent. Where's it going to strike?"

"Your right! Three seconds!"

She threw herself left as the serpent-tail stabbed at where she'd been. The strike was so fast she felt the wind of its passage ruffle her hair. Venom splattered across the Chimera's own back, and the creature howled as the acid ate into its hide. The sound of its own weapon turned against it.

"Lily! The tail!"

Lily was already moving. She blurred around the Chimera's hindquarters, a streak of red hair and determination, and Alexis saw a flash of silver. A knife, drawn from somewhere, slashing across the base of the serpent-tail in a strike too fast to follow.

The serpent head shrieked, ichor spraying from the wound in a black arc that painted the cavern wall. It wasn't severed. The thing's hide was too tough for that. But it was crippled, movements sluggish and uncoordinated, the venom it tried to spit dribbling uselessly down its own scales.

Two heads down. One to go.

The lion head twisted, trying to reach her. Flames roared from its jaws, but she was behind its neck, in the one spot the fire couldn't reach. It snapped at her, teeth closing on empty air as she ducked and wove, her body screaming with exhaustion, her grip weakening with every passing second.

"Alexis!" Keats's voice carried desperate warning. "It's going to roll! Get off!"

She felt the Chimera's weight shifting, the body preparing to throw itself onto its back and crush her beneath it. No time to climb down. No time to do anything but—

She gathered every scrap of shadow she could reach. Pulled from the darkness of the cavern, from the void between the stars visible through the liminal ceiling, from the primordial night that was her mother's domain. And drove it into the lion's skull.

The darkness punched through bone, through brain, through everything that made the Chimera a living thing. Alexis felt the creature's life force shatter under her assault. Ancient, furious, and finally ending. It was like feeling a star go out. Like standing in the moment between one heartbeat and the absence of the next.

The Chimera collapsed.

Alexis rode it down, rolling free at the last moment as the body crashed to the crystal floor. The impact shook the cavern, cracks spreading through the walls, dust and fragments raining from above. The crystallized possibility groaned under the weight of a dead impossibility.

Then silence.

* * * *

Alexis lay on her back, staring up at the frozen-light ceiling, every muscle in her body screaming.

The burn on her back throbbed with every heartbeat. Her shoulder ached where she'd nearly dislocated it holding on. Blood still crusted her upper lip from the sonic attack, and her ears rang with a high, persistent tone that made the silence feel incomplete.

But she was alive. They were all alive.

Footsteps approached. Two sets. Then Keats was there, kneeling beside her, his hands running over her arms and torso checking for wounds. His face was pale, green eyes wide with residual fear, but his touch was gentle, careful.

"That," he said, "was the most terrifying thing I've ever watched."

"Seconded." Lily dropped to sit beside them, breathing hard. Her knife was still in her hand, ichor dripping from its blade. The burn mark on her forearm had blistered badly. She'd need healing soon. "Also the most badass. Did you seriously punch through a Chimera's skull?"

"Seemed like the thing to do at the time." Alexis let Keats help her sit up, wincing as the motion pulled at her burned back. Her hands were shaking, she realized. The adrenaline was wearing off, leaving exhaustion and a bone-deep ache in its wake. "Nice work on the tail. That knife move was impressive."

"Impressed a girl can handle a blade?" Lily's grin was tired but genuine.

"Impressed anyone could hit a moving target that fast while running at superhuman speed. That's not normal combat training."

"I've had time to practice." Lily shrugged, but her expression softened. "And Keats. Those callouts. The timing on the serpent strike, the roll warning. Your visions might be fragmented, but what you're getting is *useful*."

Keats's cheeks colored. "I was mostly guessing. The static kept cutting in and out."

"Then you're a good guesser." Alexis reached for his hand, squeezing it. "We'd be dead three times over without those warnings."

He lifted her hand to his lips, pressing a kiss against her bruised knuckles. "Don't do that again. The riding-a-monster-while-it-tries-to-kill-you thing. My heart can't take it."

"No promises."

They sat together for a moment, the three of them, surrounded by the corpse of an impossible creature in a space between worlds. Bruised. Bleeding. Victorious.

The Chimera was already beginning to dissolve, reality reclaiming the matter that had been shaped into something impossible. Alexis watched the process with detached fascination. Flesh becoming light becoming possibility becoming nothing. In an hour, maybe less, there would be no sign the creature had ever existed except for the scorch marks and acid burns scarring the crystal floor.

A shift had occurred between them. Not relief at surviving, but something deeper. They'd fought as a unit. Each of them essential, each of them trusting the others with their lives. That kind of bond wasn't something you could manufacture. It had to be earned.

They'd earned it.

"So," Lily said eventually, breaking the contemplative silence. "Who wants to address the elephant in the room? Or I guess, the dead Chimera in the room?"

"Someone put it here," Keats said. "Recently. To stop anyone from reaching the Telchine."

Alexis looked at what remained of the creature's corpse. "This wasn't protection," she said slowly, the realization crystallizing. "The Telchine didn't put this here to guard themselves. This was a blockade. Someone *else* doesn't want us, or anyone, reaching the last Telchine."

"The same someone who's stealing artifacts?" Lily asked.

"Has to be." Alexis pushed herself to her feet, ignoring the protest from her aching muscles. "They're isolating the Smiths. Cutting off anyone who might be able to undo what they're doing. The Cyclopes said the Telchines had knowledge about tracking artifacts. Binding magic, signatures that could be read."

"So whoever's behind this is scared of what the Telchine knows," Keats concluded. "Scared enough to post a guard."

"Which means the Telchine definitely has something useful." Alexis offered her hands to help the others up. "Let's go find out what."

They moved past the dissolving Chimera, toward the path that continued beyond it. The cave entrance was visible now. A darker shadow against the already-strange landscape of liminal space, promising answers and almost certainly more danger.

Alexis walked forward, her team beside her. The boon still pressed against her soul. The secrets still sat heavy on her tongue. But here, now, in this moment, she wasn't carrying anything alone.

That counted for something.

Maybe it counted for everything.

10

The cave mouth gaped before them like a wound in reality.

Beyond the dissolving Chimera, the path had narrowed to a single point. A darkness so complete it seemed to swallow the strange light of liminal space entirely. The air that drifted from within carried the smell of salt and old metal, of things forged in ages when the world was young and malleable.

Alexis paused at the threshold, her body reminding her forcefully of what they'd survived. Her hands were still shaking. Fine tremors she couldn't control. The shadow-strike that had killed the Chimera had taken more out of her than she'd expected, leaving her feeling hollowed out, scraped raw.

"Hey." Keats's hand found hers, warm fingers threading through her trembling ones. "You okay?"

She wanted to lie. Wanted to say she was fine, that the fight hadn't affected her, that she was ready to push forward without pause. But standing here at the edge of the dark, with the adrenaline fading and the weight of everything pressing down, she couldn't manage it.

"I will be," she said instead. "That last strike... I've never channeled that much power before. It felt like—" She searched for words. "Like reaching into something bigger than myself and pulling out a piece of it."

Keats's thumb traced circles on the back of her hand, a small comfort that grounded her more than she wanted to admit. "Nyx's power?"

"Maybe. Or something older." She thought of Chaos, the vast presence that had called her interesting, that had extracted a boon she still hadn't told anyone about. The power she'd used against the Chimera had felt like night, yes, but also like void. Like the primordial nothing from which everything had emerged.

The boon pressed against her soul, a constant reminder of secrets she was keeping.

"Whatever it was," Keats said, "it saved our lives. All three of us." He lifted her hand to his lips, pressing a gentle kiss against her knuckles. The gesture was so tender, so unexpectedly sweet in the aftermath of violence, that Alexis felt something crack in her chest.

"Don't," she whispered. "If you're nice to me right now, I might fall apart."

"Would that be so bad?"

"We're in the middle of a mission."

"We're standing outside a cave in a dimension between dimensions after killing a mythological monster." His green eyes held hers, steady and warm despite everything. "I think the mission can wait thirty seconds while I tell you that you were incredible back there. Terrifying, but incredible."

"Terrifying?"

"You punched through a Chimera's skull with concentrated darkness. That's not a normal Tuesday activity, Al." But he was smiling as he said it. That crooked grin she'd loved since they were kids sparring at the dojo. "I'm saying… I'm glad you're on our side."

Lily's voice cut through the moment. "Not to interrupt the touching scene, but we should probably move. No telling how stable this space is after the fight."

Alexis squeezed Keats's hand once before releasing it. "She's right. Let's go."

"For the record," Lily added as they approached the cave mouth, "I also thought you were impressive. The nice romantic praise is Keats's department, but consider yourself professionally acknowledged."

Despite everything, Alexis almost smiled.

* * * *

The cave was older than anything Alexis had ever encountered.

She felt it the moment she crossed the threshold. A weight of years pressing against her consciousness, time accumulated in layers so thick she could almost taste them. The darkness here wasn't hostile; it was patient. Watching. Waiting to see what these intruders would do.

The passage widened as they moved deeper, the walls roughhewn but decorated with carvings that seemed to shift in the dim light. Alexis's eyes adjusted quickly, another gift from Nyx, the ability to see in darkness as clearly as day, and what she saw made her breath catch.

The carvings told stories. Figures that might have been gods, or might have been something else, working at forges that blazed with captured starlight. Creatures being shaped from raw possibility. Not born, but *made*. And threading through all of it, a repeating symbol: three circles interlocked, surrounded by waves.

The walls themselves seemed to breathe with history. Alexis let her fingers trail across the stone as they walked, feeling grooves worn smooth by countless hands across countless years. Some of the carvings had been damaged, deliberately, she realized, chunks of stone gouged out where faces had been, where names might have been written. Someone had tried to erase parts of this record.

The floor was worn in a path down the center, the stone polished by millennia of footsteps. Along the edges, she saw debris. Fragments of things that might have been tools or might have been weapons, too corroded by time to identify. This had once been a busy place. A place of work and creation. Now it felt like walking through the bones of something vast and dead.

"What is this place?" Lily whispered. Even her voice seemed muted here, absorbed by stone that had listened to secrets for millennia.

"The last refuge of the Telchines," a voice answered from the darkness ahead. "And you are either brave or foolish to have found it."

The speaker emerged from shadows that seemed to part around her like curtains.

She was small, barely five feet tall, with skin the gray-green of sea-weathered bronze and hair that fell in tangled ropes of silver and black. Her eyes were large, far too large for her face, and they held a depth that spoke of ages lived and losses beyond counting.

But it wasn't her appearance alone that spoke of age. It was the way she moved. Each step deliberate, weighted with the accumulated hesitation of someone who had learned that haste led to mistakes, and mistakes led to extinction. Her hands were gnarled, the fingers bent at wrong angles from injuries that had healed without proper setting, the knuckles swollen with work done across centuries. Scars marked her arms in patterns that might have been decorative or might have been damage. Marks of forge-work, of splattered metal and wayward flames.

She looked ancient. Not in the way of old humans, fragile, fading, but in the way of stone worn smooth by countless waves. Eternal. Enduring. And profoundly, bone-deep tired.

When she spoke, her voice carried the rasp of someone who had gone long periods without speaking. Years, perhaps, or decades. The voice of someone who had forgotten that words were meant to be used regularly.

"You killed my guard," she said. Her voice was like water over rocks. Soft, but with edges that could cut. "The Chimera was not mine to command, but it served to keep the curious at bay. Now you have destroyed it, and here you stand in the one place I thought safe."

"The Chimera wasn't protecting you," Alexis said. "It was blocking access to you. Placed there recently, within the last week. Whoever put it there didn't want anyone reaching this cave."

The woman's enormous eyes narrowed. In the dim light, Alexis could see that they had no whites. Just iris the color of deep ocean, stretching from lid to lid. Eyes made for seeing in darkness, in depths where no light had ever reached.

"And how would you know such a thing?"

"The ground was freshly disturbed. The scorch marks from its fire hadn't had time to weather. And—" Alexis hesitated, then decided honesty was the only currency that might work here. "The Cyclopes told us how to find you. They said if anyone knew how to track the stolen artifacts, it would be the last Telchine."

Pain flickered across the woman's face, or anger held too long to burn hot anymore. Her mouth twisted, revealing teeth that had been filed to points in some ancient practice Alexis didn't recognize.

"Brontes sent you." It wasn't a question. "That old fool. He always did talk too much to pretty faces." She studied them with those vast eyes, and Alexis felt herself being measured, weighed, judged against standards she couldn't comprehend. "I am Makelo. The last of my kind. And you will explain why I should not simply let this cave swallow you whole."

* * * *

Makelo led them deeper into the cave, through passages that wound and doubled back on themselves in ways that defied normal geometry. The air grew warmer as they descended, carrying hints of sulfur and heated metal. A forge, Alexis realized. Even in hiding, a Smith could not be separated from their craft.

The Telchine moved with surprising grace for someone who looked so ancient. Her bare feet made no sound on the stone floor, and she navigated the twisting passages without hesitation. A path walked so many times it had become instinct. But Alexis noticed the way her hands trailed along the walls as she moved, fingers finding handholds that might be needed if her legs failed. The caution of someone who had learned not to trust their own body.

"You said you're the last," Keats ventured. He was walking close behind Alexis, his hand occasionally brushing against her back. A quiet reassurance. "What happened to the others?"

Makelo didn't slow her pace. "What always happens to those who know too much. We were eliminated."

The word hung in the air, heavy with centuries of grief compressed into a single syllable.

The passage opened into a chamber that stole Alexis's breath.

It was vast. Cathedral-vast, with a ceiling lost in shadow far above. The walls were lined with alcoves, and in each alcove rested an artifact. Weapons, tools, jewelry, objects whose purpose Alexis couldn't guess. Hundreds of them, maybe thousands, arranged with the careful reverence of a museum or a tomb.

Light came from sources she couldn't identify. A soft glow that seemed to emanate from the artifacts themselves, each piece contributing its own particular illumination. Some glowed warm gold. Others burned cold blue. A few pulsed with colors that hurt to look at directly. Together, they created an illumination that was neither day nor night but something else. The light of things made rather than born.

The floor was inlaid with patterns in metal. Bronze and silver and something darker that might have been iron or might have been something else. The patterns spiraled inward toward the chamber's center, where the true heart of the space awaited.

At the chamber's center sat a forge. Not the industrial scale of the Cyclopes' operation, but something more intimate. A craftsman's forge, sized for delicate work. The coals glowed a deep, sullen red, banked but not dead. Waiting. Even after all these years, even after everything that had happened, the fire still burned.

Around the forge, Alexis could see the evidence of work in progress. Partially completed projects. Tools laid out in precise arrangements. A life interrupted but never truly abandoned.

"Holy shit," Lily breathed. "Is all of this…?"

"My people's work." Makelo moved to the forge, her small hands tracing its edge with affection. Her fingers knew every pit and scar in the metal, every repair made across the centuries. "What remains of it. Most was destroyed when they came for us. These pieces I saved. These pieces I guard."

She bent to adjust the coals. A motion so practiced it seemed unconscious. The fire brightened in response, as if recognizing her touch.

"When who came for you?" Alexis asked.

Makelo was silent for a long moment. When she spoke again, her voice carried the weight of grief so old it had calcified into stone.

"Zeus blamed us for a drought that withered his favored lands. A convenient excuse. We had nothing to do with it, could not have caused it even if we'd wished to. But we knew things the Olympians preferred kept secret. We understood how the bonds between realms worked, could see the architecture of divine power in ways even the gods themselves could not." Her vast eyes fixed on Alexis. "Knowledge is dangerous, child. Especially knowledge that could undo what the powerful have built."

"Zeus destroyed the Telchines over a lie?"

"Zeus destroyed our island. Sank it beneath the waves, drowned most of my siblings in a single night of divine rage." Makelo's voice was matter-of-fact, the emotion burned out of it long ago. But her hands had stilled on the forge, and Alexis could see the way her fingers trembled. Not with age, but with the memory of loss that never truly faded. "We numbered in the hundreds before that night. After… after, there were seven. Then four. Then two. Now one."

She turned to face them fully, and in her ancient eyes Alexis saw something sharp and fierce. A mind that had been working on this puzzle for millennia.

"But it wasn't truly Zeus's idea. He was… encouraged. Nudged. Someone whispered in his ear, fed his paranoia, convinced him we were a threat that needed eliminating."

"Who?"

"I never learned. But I've spent ages thinking about it." Makelo tilted her head, considering them. "Whoever it was understood divine politics intimately. Knew exactly how to manipulate Zeus's fears. And they didn't stop with us."

* * * *

"What do you mean?" Alexis asked.

Makelo gestured at the alcoves lining the walls. "These artifacts. Each one represents a connection point between divine and mortal realms. When we were destroyed, we thought that was the end of it.

Olympian jealousy, nothing more. But over the centuries, I've watched. I've listened. And I've noticed a pattern."

She moved to one of the alcoves, lifting out a small mirror framed in tarnished bronze. Her hands held it with the delicacy of someone handling a dying thing. Or perhaps a dead one.

"Hephaestus made this for a mortal queen who had earned Athena's favor. It allowed the queen to receive wisdom directly from the goddess. Disappeared three hundred years ago. The official story was theft by mortal bandits."

She set it down and moved to another alcove, her movements carrying the weight of ritual. Each artifact a station in some private devotion. "This amulet let a priest of Apollo predict natural disasters, saving countless lives. Vanished a century later. Blamed on a temple fire."

Another alcove. Her voice grew quieter with each revelation, as if speaking the losses aloud made them more real. "This ring granted its wearer the ability to speak with animals sacred to Artemis. The last person who wore it was found dead in the woods, the ring nowhere to be found. That was five hundred years ago."

Makelo turned back to them, her expression grim. "Every generation, a few more artifacts disappear. Every generation, the excuses are different. Theft, loss, destruction in various catastrophes. But the result is always the same. The connections weaken. The divine and mortal realms drift further apart."

"Someone's been doing this for centuries," Alexis said. The realization settled over her like a shroud. "Systematically. Patiently. Removing the things that bind the realms together."

"And eliminating anyone who might notice the pattern." Makelo's voice was bitter. "The Telchines. Certain oracles who saw too clearly. Smiths who asked too many questions. Everyone who knew what we knew is dead. That's not coincidence, children. That's extermination. Slow, careful, and nearly complete."

She returned to her forge, running her hands along its edge again. The firelight caught the scars on her arms, and Alexis realized they weren't random. They were records. Marks made deliberately, chronicling events or losses in a language only Makelo could read.

"There is one other thing," Makelo said, her voice dropping. "One creation that weighs on me above all others."

She moved to an alcove set apart from the rest, larger than the others, draped in cloth that had once been fine but had faded to gray with age. With trembling hands, she drew back the covering.

The alcove was empty.

"The Trident of the Seas," Makelo said. "Poseidon's symbol of authority. The artifact that anchors his connection to every ocean, every river, every drop of water that falls as rain." Her voice cracked on the words. The first genuine emotion she'd shown. "I made it. Three hundred years of work. Three hundred years of pouring everything I knew, everything I was, into a single creation. It was to be my masterwork. My legacy. The proof that Telchine craft could rival even divine creation."

Her hands clenched at her sides. "It was taken six months ago. And when it goes, when the last anchor breaks… the seas will forget their master. Storms will rage without guidance. The balance that has held for millennia will shatter."

Three hundred years. Alexis tried to imagine devoting three centuries to a single work. The patience, the dedication, the love that must have gone into every hammer strike, every careful shaping. And then watching it be stolen, used to unravel everything you'd worked to build.

"We'll get it back," she heard herself say. "We'll find whoever's behind this and we'll stop them."

Makelo looked at her with those enormous, depthless eyes. For a moment, Alexis thought she saw hope flicker there. Fragile, uncertain, afraid to believe.

"You are either brave or foolish," the Telchine said again. "But perhaps... perhaps that is what this moment requires."

* * * *

The weight of it was staggering.

Alexis found herself sitting on a stone bench near the forge, her legs suddenly unwilling to support her. Centuries. Not weeks or months or even years. *Centuries* of planning. Of manipulation. Of methodical, patient destruction of everything that connected gods and mortals.

"The current thefts," she said. "The ones happening now. They're not a new operation. They're an acceleration. Whoever's been doing this for centuries sped up."

"Something changed," Keats agreed. He'd taken a seat beside her, close enough that their shoulders touched. "Something made them abandon the slow approach and start moving fast."

Makelo studied them with those ancient, enormous eyes. "You said the Chimera was placed recently. That suggests whoever is behind this knows you're looking for answers. Knows you came to the Cyclopes. Knows you were headed here."

"How is that possible?" Lily demanded. She was pacing the length of the chamber, her restless energy finding no outlet. "We haven't told anyone outside the Network where we were going. And the Network is—"

She stopped. They all stopped.

"The Network," Alexis said slowly. "We discussed our plans in the compound. In briefings. With the whole team."

"You think there's a leak?" Keats's voice was sharp with disbelief. "Someone in the Network is feeding information to whoever's doing this?"

"I think someone placed a Chimera in our path before we even knew we were coming here." Alexis's mind was racing, fitting pieces together that she didn't like the shape of. "That requires advance knowledge. Inside knowledge."

Makelo made a sound that might have been approval. "You begin to see it. The scope of what you're facing. This isn't a thief you're hunting, children. This is a conspiracy that spans ages, with roots deep enough to have eyes everywhere. Even in places you think are safe."

"Then why tell us anything?" Lily asked. Her pacing had stopped, her body coiled with tension. "If you think we might be compromised, why not throw us out?"

"Because you killed the Chimera." Makelo's expression shifted. Not softening, but becoming something other than hostile. "That beast was ancient. Powerful. And you three young things, with your diminished abilities and your mortal fragility, brought it down. That speaks to something." Her gaze lingered on Alexis. "And because I know what you are, daughter of night."

Alexis felt her pulse quicken. "What do you mean?"

"I am old. Old enough to remember when the primordials walked openly, before they withdrew into their domains and let the younger gods play at ruling." Makelo moved closer, those vast eyes seeming to see through flesh to something deeper. "Nyx has not taken a mortal lover in ages beyond counting. Has not borne a half-human child since the world was young and such things were less remarkable. And yet here you stand."

"What does that have to do with anything?"

"Perhaps nothing. Perhaps everything." Makelo tilted her head, considering. "The acceleration you mentioned, the sudden rush to complete a plan that had been unfolding slowly for centuries. Something triggered it. Something changed the calculus." Her eyes never left Alexis's face. "When did you discover what you are, child? When did you first access your mother's power?"

Alexis thought back. The funeral. The attack. The night her powers had awakened and everything had changed. "A few months ago. Maybe… maybe six months now."

"And when did the accelerated thefts begin?"

The question hit like cold water. Alexis looked at Keats, at Lily, seeing the same realization dawning on their faces.

"Around the same time," Keats said quietly. "Aaron mentioned it at the briefing. The theft rate increased dramatically starting about six months ago."

"Coincidence?" Makelo's voice carried ancient skepticism. "Perhaps. Or perhaps whoever has been working toward this goal for centuries learned something that changed their timeline. Learned that a daughter of Nyx had been born. That the Night itself had produced an heir who might one day grow powerful enough to interfere with plans millennia in the making."

The weight on Alexis's chest doubled. The boon. The secrets. And now this, the suggestion that her existence had triggered an apocalyptic acceleration of a conspiracy older than most civilizations.

"That's insane," she heard herself say. "I'm eighteen. I've had powers for six months. How could I possibly be a threat to something that's been operating for centuries?"

"Because you are primordial." Makelo spoke the word like it meant something vast. "Not Olympian, not Titan. Primordial. Your mother is one of the first beings that ever existed. That blood carries weight. Carries *potential*. And whoever is behind this has learned to fear potential."

She turned away, moving back toward her forge with steps that suddenly seemed heavy with age.

"I will tell you what I know," she said. "I will teach you what I can about tracking the stolen artifacts, about reading the signatures they leave behind. But understand this: you are not fighting a thief. You are fighting something ancient and patient and thorough. Something that has been cutting away at the bonds between worlds for longer than your mortal civilizations have existed."

She looked back over her shoulder, those enormous eyes filled with what might have been hope or might have been despair.

"And it has noticed you. All of you. There will be no going back to ordinary lives. Not anymore."

Alexis thought of the boon pressing against her soul. Of Chaos, watching with ancient interest. Of Greer dissolving in the void. Of every choice she'd made that had led to this moment.

Makelo was right.

There was no going back.

There had never been any going back.

11

Keats watched Alexis pace the length of Makelo's chamber, and recognized the restless energy burning through her.

He'd seen it before. In the dojo when they were kids and she couldn't master a kata, in the weeks after her mother's death when grief had transformed into furious motion. Alexis Rain didn't know how to sit still when the world was falling apart. She processed through movement, through action, through demanding answers until the universe gave them up.

Right now, she was demanding answers from Makelo with an intensity that made even the ancient Telchine seem off-balance.

"Walk me through it," Alexis said, her boots clicking against the stone floor as she moved between the artifact alcoves. "From the beginning. What exactly are these things? Why do they matter so much that someone would spend *centuries* trying to destroy them?"

Makelo stood by her forge, small hands clasped before her, those enormous eyes tracking Alexis's movements with what might have been assessment or might have been memory.

"You remind me of someone," the Telchine said quietly. "An ally I had, long ago. She had the same fire. The same refusal to accept limitations."

"What happened to her?"

"She died." Makelo's voice was flat. "Trying to warn others about what was coming. No one listened. No one ever listens until it's too late."

Alexis stopped pacing. "I'm listening now."

A crack appeared in Makelo's armor of ancient wariness. She studied Alexis for a long moment, then nodded slowly.

"Very well." She moved toward one of the larger alcoves, gesturing for them to follow. "Let me show you what we built. And what someone has spent ages tearing down."

* * * *

The artifact Makelo led them to was a sphere of polished bronze, about the size of a grapefruit, covered in intricate engravings that seemed to shift and flow as Keats looked at them. It sat on a pedestal of black stone, and even from several feet away, he could feel warmth emanating from it, a hum like standing near a generator.

"This is a prayer anchor," Makelo said. "One of the first my people ever made. It was designed to capture the intent behind mortal prayers and channel that energy to the appropriate deity."

"Prayers need a physical object to work?" Lily asked. She'd taken a position near the chamber's entrance, her restless energy finding an outlet in constant vigilance. Always the soldier.

"Not always. Direct prayer can reach the divine, if the faith is strong enough and the god is listening." Makelo's fingers hovered over the sphere without touching it. "But the mortal world and the divine realm exist in different... frequencies. Different states of being. For energy to flow consistently between them, there must be bridges. Anchors. Points where the two realities touch."

"The artifacts," Keats said, understanding dawning. "They're not magical objects. They're infrastructure."

"Precisely." Makelo's vast eyes found his, and he saw approval there. "Think of the divine-mortal connection as a bridge between two mountains. The artifacts are the pylons that hold it up. Remove one, and the bridge sags. Remove enough…" She spread her small hands. "The bridge falls."

"And everyone on the bridge falls with it," Alexis finished. She'd stopped pacing, her attention fully focused on Makelo now. "The Scions. The demigods. Anyone caught between worlds."

"Not just them." Makelo moved to another alcove, this one containing what looked like a chalice made of silver and starlight. "The connection between divine and mortal realms isn't just about prayer and power. It's about balance. The mortal world generates certain energies, faith, hope, creativity, love, that the divine realm needs. And the divine realm provides structure, meaning, *stability* that keeps the mortal world from sliding into chaos."

Keats felt a chill run through him despite the warmth of the forge. "You're saying if the connection is severed, both realms suffer?"

"I'm saying if the connection is severed, both realms may eventually *collapse*." Makelo's voice carried the weight of someone who had thought about this for a long time. "Not immediately. Not obviously. But the mortal world would slowly lose its coherence. Magic would fade. Natural laws would become… inconsistent. And the divine realm, cut off from the faith that sustains it, would wither. Gods would weaken. Some might cease to exist entirely."

"That's insane," Lily said from her post by the entrance. "Why would anyone want that? Who benefits from both worlds dying?"

"That," Makelo said, "is the question I have been asking myself for longer than your civilizations have existed. And I have only theories."

* * * *

They gathered near the forge as Makelo explained, the ancient coals casting everything in shades of red and amber. Keats sat on a stone bench, Alexis beside him, their shoulders almost touching. Lily remained standing, but she'd moved closer, her vigilance temporarily set aside for the weight of what they were learning.

"The artifacts we created, my people, the Cyclopes, the other divine smiths, were designed in tiers," Makelo said. She'd produced a piece of parchment from somewhere and was sketching as she spoke, her small hands surprisingly steady. "The first tier are minor anchors. Prayer beads, blessed amulets, small tokens that connect individual mortals to their chosen deities. Important, but not critical. Losing them weakens the connection but doesn't break it."

She drew a larger circle. "The second tier are regional anchors. Artifacts that serve entire communities, cities, nations. The sacred standards that Roman legions carried. The totems of indigenous peoples. The holy relics housed in great temples. Losing these creates significant gaps in the bridge."

"And the third tier?" Alexis asked.

Makelo's stylus paused. When she drew the final circle, it was larger than the others combined.

"The third tier are the keystone anchors. There are only a handful in existence. Artifacts so powerful, so fundamental to the connection between realms, that losing even one would cause catastrophic damage." Her enormous eyes lifted to meet theirs. "Apollo's Lyre. Mjolnir. The Golden Fleece. And…" She hesitated. "And Poseidon's Trident."

The way she said the last artifact was different. Softer. More personal.

"You made it," Keats realized. "The Trident. That was you."

Makelo set down her stylus. Her hands, he noticed, had begun to tremble.

"I was young when I forged it. Young by Telchine standards, at least. Barely a thousand years old." A ghost of a smile crossed her weathered features. "Poseidon came to us because the Cyclopes were too busy with Zeus's thunderbolts, and my people specialized in binding magic. The Trident needed to command the seas, yes, but more importantly, it needed to anchor the divine presence throughout every ocean, every river, every drop of water on your world."

"How long did it take?" Lily asked, genuine curiosity breaking through her soldier's facade.

"Three hundred years." Makelo's voice softened with memory. "Three hundred years of gathering materials from the deepest trenches and the highest clouds. Three hundred years of binding spells so complex they gave me nightmares for centuries after. Three hundred years of pouring everything I knew, everything I *was*, into a single creation."

She fell silent, and in that silence, Keats understood something about the Telchine that he hadn't before. This wasn't just about artifacts or connections or cosmic infrastructure. This was about craft. About creating something so perfect, so essential, that it became part of the fabric of reality itself.

And someone was trying to destroy it.

"The current thefts," he said carefully. "Aaron briefed us before we left. Apollo's Lyre is already gone. Mjolnir's gauntlets, the Járngreipr, were taken last month. If the pattern holds…"

"They're working their way through the keystone anchors." Alexis's voice was grim. "Building up to the big ones."

"The Trident," Lily said. "It's a target."

Makelo's reaction was immediate and visceral. She stood abruptly, knocking over the parchment with her sketches, her vast eyes blazing with an intensity that made her seem, for a moment, not small at all.

"The Trident is not a target," she said. "It is *the* target. Do you understand what I'm telling you? Apollo's Lyre connects mortals to prophecy, to music, to the lighter aspects of divine truth. Mjolnir grounds the storms, maintains the balance between sky and earth. Both are critical, yes. But the Trident…"

She pressed her trembling hands flat against the forge's edge, steadying herself.

"The Trident anchors seventy percent of your world's surface. Every ocean. Every sea. Every river and lake and underground aquifer. If they take it, if they *destroy* it, the connection won't weaken. It will *shatter*. Completely. Permanently. There would be no rebuilding, no recovery. The divine and mortal realms would be severed forever."

The chamber fell silent except for the soft crackle of the forge's coals. Keats felt the weight of Makelo's words settling over him like a physical burden.

"Where is the Trident now?" Alexis asked. Her voice was steady, but Keats could see the tension in her shoulders, the tight line of her jaw.

"With Poseidon. In the deepest part of the Atlantic, in a palace that exists partly in the mortal ocean and partly in the divine realm." Makelo's hands had steadied, but her voice remained fierce. "It is protected by the god of the seas himself, by currents that would crush any vessel, by creatures older than your species. It should be unreachable."

"Should be," Lily repeated. "But whoever's doing this has already gotten past divine security a dozen times. They took Apollo's Lyre from *Olympus itself*."

Makelo's expression hardened. "Then we ensure they do not reach the Trident."

"How?" Keats asked. "You said yourself, you've been hiding in liminal space for ages because you couldn't stop them. What's different now?"

"You are different." Makelo's gaze moved between the three of them, lingering longest on Alexis. "A daughter of Nyx. An oracle of Apollo, however compromised. A child of Hermes with speed that even diminished could outrun most threats. And behind you, a network of Scions who are, for the first time in ages, *organized*."

She moved closer, and despite her small stature, her presence seemed to fill the chamber.

"I have spent millennia watching, waiting, gathering knowledge that no one wanted to hear. I know more about the artifacts than anyone living. I know how to track them, how to trace the signatures they leave behind, how to predict where the next theft will occur." Her enormous eyes burned with what looked almost like hope. "What I have lacked is anyone capable of *acting* on that knowledge."

"You want to help us," Alexis said. It wasn't a question.

"I want to protect my masterwork." Makelo's voice cracked on the word. "I want to ensure that three hundred years of my life's best effort does not vanish into whatever void these thieves are feeding. And if that means allying with a group of young half-bloods who were foolish enough to fight a Chimera and skilled enough to win…" The ghost of a smile crossed her ancient features. "Then so be it."

* * * *

Keats found Alexis standing alone near the chamber's entrance an hour later, staring at the passage that led back to liminal space.

Makelo had retreated to a side chamber to gather materials she said she'd need. Tracking tools, she called them, instruments designed to read the signatures that divine artifacts left behind. Lily had gone with her, curious about the Telchine's methods and likely also unwilling to leave their new ally unwatched.

Which left Keats and Alexis alone for the first time since… he wasn't sure when. Before the briefing, maybe. Before everything had started accelerating beyond their control.

"Hey," he said softly, coming to stand beside her. "You okay?"

She didn't turn, but she leaned into him when his shoulder touched hers. "I keep waiting for someone to tell me this is a drill. That we're being tested, and there isn't a centuries-old conspiracy trying to end the world."

"If it helps, I'm pretty sure even divine beings don't have drill budgets that cover Chimeras."

That earned him a small, tired laugh. "Fair point."

They stood in silence for a moment. Keats reached for his oracle abilities without thinking about it. A habit he'd developed in the weeks since discovering what he was. Usually he got nothing but static, fragments, the sensation of reaching for something out of grasp.

This time, something flickered.

He saw Alexis. Not as she was now, but as she might be. Standing in darkness so complete it seemed to have weight. Facing something vast and cold that he couldn't make out. And in her hand…

The vision shattered. Static flooded back in, and Keats gasped, his hand going to his temple.

"Keats?" Alexis turned to him, concern replacing the exhaustion in her eyes. "What is it? What did you see?"

He wanted to tell her. Wanted to describe the image that was already fading. Her, alone, facing something terrible. But the details were slipping away like water through his fingers, and all he was left with was a feeling. A sense of weight. Of importance.

Of inevitability.

"Nothing clear," he said, which was true. "Fragments. The usual."

She studied his face, and he saw her deciding whether to push. Deciding, in the end, to let it go.

"I hate this," she said quietly. "The not knowing. The pieces that don't fit. Makelo talks about a conspiracy spanning centuries, but she doesn't know who's behind it. We know someone in the Network might be compromised, but we don't know who. We know the Trident is the ultimate target, but we don't know when they'll make their move."

"We know more than we did this morning," Keats pointed out. "That's something."

"Is it enough?"

He didn't have an answer for that. So instead, he did what he'd done since they were kids facing problems too big to solve alone. He took her hand, laced his fingers through hers, and held on.

"We'll figure it out," he said. "We always do."

"Since when are you the optimist?"

"Since you started being the one who needed to hear it." He squeezed her hand. "We're in this together, Al. Whatever comes. You don't have to carry it alone."

Guilt flickered across her face, or fear. It was gone before he could identify it, replaced by a small, grateful smile.

"Together," she echoed.

But even as she said it, Keats couldn't shake the feeling that she was keeping something from him. Something important. Something that sat between them like a wall neither of them was willing to acknowledge.

He pushed the thought aside. They had enough problems without borrowing trouble.

"Come on," he said, tugging her gently back toward the main chamber. "Let's see what kind of tracking magic a three-thousand-year-old smith has up her sleeve."

Alexis let herself be led, but not before casting one last look at the dark passage behind them.

Keats pretended not to notice.

Some things, he was learning, were better left unasked.

At least for now.

12

The White Mountains compound had never felt so small.

Alexis stepped out of the ether with Makelo, Keats, and Lily in tow, emerging into the familiar grounds as the last light of evening painted the mountains in shades of amber and rose. The journey back from liminal space had been disorienting. Time moved strangely between worlds, and what had felt like hours in Makelo's cave had apparently been less than a day here. The compound's lights were flickering on, warm yellow squares against the deepening blue of twilight.

Home. She should feel relieved to be back. Instead, she felt the weight of everything they'd learned pressing down on her shoulders like physical stones.

Makelo stood beside her, the ancient Telchine looking even smaller and more weathered in the mundane light of the mortal world. She carried a worn leather satchel over one shoulder. Her tracking instruments, she'd called them. Tools that could read the signatures divine artifacts left behind. The only hope they had of staying one step ahead of whoever was systematically dismantling the connection between worlds.

"Interesting," Makelo murmured, her enormous eyes sweeping across the compound with an appraiser's gaze. "You've built something here. A sanctuary for half-bloods. My people tried something similar, once. Before…" She trailed off, the weight of history filling the silence.

"Before they were destroyed," Alexis finished quietly.

"Yes." Makelo's voice carried no self-pity, only fact. "I hope your sanctuary fares better than ours did."

The main building's door burst open before Alexis could respond. Aaron emerged at a near-run, his military bearing momentarily forgotten in what looked like genuine relief.

Behind him, more faces appeared. Operatives who had clearly been waiting, watching for their return. Alexis recognized some of them: Marcus from the London cell, Elena from the Scandinavian network, Javier who had been running communications while they were gone. Their expressions ranged from relief to curiosity to barely concealed fear.

Word traveled fast in the Network. They all knew the trio had gone looking for answers. Now everyone wanted to know what they'd found.

"You're back." Aaron stopped a few feet away, his sharp eyes cataloging each of them. Noting the exhaustion, the minor wounds they hadn't fully treated, the stranger in their midst. "We were starting to worry. Communications from liminal space are…"

"Non-existent," Lily supplied. "Yeah, we noticed."

Aaron's gaze fixed on Makelo. "And this is…?"

"Makelo. The last Telchine." Alexis gestured between them. "Makelo, this is Aaron Richardson. Son of Ares. He runs our intelligence operations."

"A child of the war god, running intelligence rather than fighting." Makelo's assessment was cool, clinical. "Interesting choice."

"War is ninety percent preparation and ten percent action," Aaron replied evenly. "My father taught me that the battles you prevent matter more than the ones you win."

Respect flickered in Makelo's expression, or the recognition of unexpected wisdom. "Then we may work well together. I have information your Network needs. And apparently, you have resources I lack."

Alexis watched the exchange with a strange sense of displacement. Here was a being thousands of years old, the last survivor of a decimated people, trading assessments with a son of Ares as if they were colleagues at a business meeting. The mundane framing of the extraordinary. She'd seen it so many times in the months since her awakening, but it still caught her off guard sometimes.

"You need medical attention," Aaron said, his gaze cataloguing their various injuries with practiced efficiency. "All of you. The briefing can wait an hour."

"The briefing cannot wait," Makelo countered. "Every hour we delay is an hour the enemy uses to advance their plans. Treat your wounds while I speak. You can multitask, I assume?"

Aaron's jaw tightened at the dismissal, but he nodded sharply. "Fine. We'll set up in the briefing room. Medical staff on standby." He turned to the gathered operatives still lingering by the door. "Fifteen minutes, main briefing room. This is priority alpha."

The operatives scattered, some heading inside to spread the word, others lingering to get a better look at Makelo. The ancient Telchine endured their stares with the patience of someone who had long ago stopped caring what others thought of her.

Keats appeared at Alexis's elbow, his warmth a comfort against the evening chill. "You okay?" he asked quietly. "You've got that look."

"What look?"

"The one where you're about to take the weight of the world on your shoulders and pretend it doesn't hurt."

She almost smiled at that. Almost. "We learned that everything we've been fighting for is part of a conspiracy older than recorded history. Excuse me if I need a moment to process."

"Take all the moments you need." He reached for her hand, squeezed once, then let go. "But don't forget. You're not processing alone. I'm right here."

The words should have helped. Instead, they reminded her of all the things she wasn't telling him.

"Briefing room," Aaron said. "I'll gather the key personnel. This sounds like something everyone needs to hear."

* * * *

The briefing room was crowded.

Word had spread quickly that the trio had returned with a guest. An actual Telchine, a being most had assumed was extinct. By the time Alexis took her place at the head of the table, nearly two dozen operatives had crammed themselves into the space. Some stood along the walls, others perched on windowsills. The air was thick with tension and the mingled scents of coffee, sweat, and anticipation.

Makelo stood beside the holographic display, looking profoundly out of place among the modern technology. Her weathered bronze skin and tangled silver-black hair marked her as something from another age entirely. Which, Alexis supposed, she was.

"Most of you know the basics," Alexis began, pitching her voice to carry. "Divine artifacts have been disappearing at an accelerating rate. Scion abilities are weakening. The connection between the divine and mortal realms is failing." She paused, letting the weight of the words settle. "What we learned today changes everything we thought we understood about what we're facing."

She nodded to Makelo, who stepped forward with a gravity that silenced the murmurs rippling through the room.

"I am Makelo," the Telchine said. Her voice, that water-over-rocks sound, somehow filled the space without effort. "Three thousand years ago, I helped forge the artifacts that bind your world to the divine realm. I am the last of my kind. Everyone else who possessed my knowledge has been systematically eliminated over the course of centuries."

She let that sink in. Alexis watched the faces around the room. Saw confusion give way to dawning horror as the implications registered.

"The thefts you've been tracking are not new," Makelo continued. "They are merely the acceleration of a pattern that has been unfolding for longer than most of your civilizations have existed. Someone, something, has been patiently, methodically dismantling the infrastructure that connects gods and mortals. Removing artifacts.

Eliminating those who might rebuild them. Cutting the bridges one strand at a time."

Aaron leaned forward, his tactical mind clearly working. "Why accelerate now? If they've been operating successfully for centuries, why change the approach?"

Makelo's gaze found Alexis. "We have theories. The timing coincides with certain... developments. But speculation matters less than fact. The fact is this: they are moving toward an endgame. And their ultimate target is Poseidon's Trident."

She gestured, and Aaron pulled up a holographic image of the Trident. A three-pronged weapon of gleaming bronze and captured sea-light.

"I created this artifact three thousand years ago," Makelo said. "It took three centuries to forge. It anchors the divine presence throughout every body of water on your world. Seventy percent of the planet's surface. If they take it, if they destroy it, the connection between realms won't weaken. It will shatter. Permanently. Irreversibly. There would be no rebuilding what is lost."

The silence that followed was absolute. Alexis could hear the hum of the building's ventilation system, the distant call of a night bird outside, the ragged breathing of the operative standing nearest to her. She watched the faces around the room. Saw the information landing like physical blows. Some people had gone pale. Others gripped the edges of tables or crossed their arms tight across their chests, as if trying to hold themselves together.

"How is that possible?" demanded a tall operative near the window. Marcus, Alexis thought, one of the newer recruits from the

London cell. His voice cracked. "The gods... they're supposed to be eternal. Invincible. How can someone dismantle everything they've built?"

"The gods are powerful, not omniscient," Makelo replied. "They created the system of connections over millennia, adding pieces as needed, never stepping back to see the whole architecture. They don't understand their own infrastructure the way my people did. The way I still do." Her voice carried no pride, only weariness. "And whoever is behind this understands it too. Perhaps better than anyone."

"Who?" The question came from multiple voices at once. "Who could have that kind of knowledge?"

"That is what we must discover." Makelo's enormous eyes swept the room. "But I can tell you this: whoever they are, they have been patient. Methodical. They have operated in shadows while empires rose and fell, while gods quarreled among themselves, while the mortal world changed beyond recognition. That kind of patience suggests something ancient. Something that thinks in centuries rather than years."

Aaron stepped forward, his tactical mind working through the implications. "You mentioned the thefts have accelerated recently. What changed? Why would a centuries-old operation suddenly speed up?"

Makelo's gaze found Alexis again. That same weighted look from the cave. "There are theories. New variables introduced into an ancient equation. But speculation is less important than action. The acceleration means they are approaching endgame. We have weeks, perhaps days, before they make their move on the Trident."

"What happens then?" someone asked from the back of the room. "If the connection shatters?"

"Both realms suffer," Makelo said flatly. "The mortal world loses its coherence. Natural laws becoming inconsistent, magic fading to nothing, the fabric of reality slowly fraying. The divine realm, cut off from the faith and belief that sustains it, withers. Gods weaken. Some cease to exist entirely." Her gaze swept the room. "And everyone caught between, every Scion, every demigod, every half-blood who carries divine essence in mortal flesh, faces a choice no one should have to make. Fade with one world, or be torn apart trying to exist in the gap."

Alexis felt the words land like blows. Around her, she saw her people, her Network, her responsibility, processing the scope of what they faced. Some looked terrified. Others looked determined. A few looked like they wanted to run and never stop.

She didn't blame them.

"What do we do?" The question came from Elena, the Scandinavian operative. A daughter of Freya who had lost her brother to divine politics before finding the Network. Her voice was steady, but Alexis could see her hands trembling at her sides. "If this conspiracy has been operating for centuries, if they've already eliminated everyone who tried to stop them... what chance do we have?"

It was the question everyone was thinking. Alexis could feel it in the air. The weight of hopelessness threatening to settle over the room like a shroud.

She stepped forward, drawing the room's attention back to herself. The boon pressed against her soul. The secrets pressed against her tongue. But this, this she could do. This she had to do.

"The Telchines didn't have us," she said. Her voice was steadier than she felt. "The oracles who saw too much, the smiths who asked questions, they were isolated. Picked off one by one because no one was watching each other's backs." She looked around the room, meeting eyes, acknowledging fear without surrendering to it. "That's what we built here. Not just a sanctuary. A network. We watch out for each other. We share information. We fight together."

"Pretty words," someone muttered. Alexis couldn't identify the voice. "But they had knowledge we don't. Resources we don't."

"They had knowledge," Makelo interjected, "but they lacked coordination. They lacked communication. They lacked—" She gestured at the room, at the technology, at the diverse collection of Scions from a dozen different divine bloodlines. "—this. In all my centuries, I have never seen half-bloods organize like this. Work together like this. Trust each other like this."

Her enormous eyes swept the room, and Alexis saw hope shift in the ancient Telchine's expression.

"You ask what chance you have," Makelo continued. "I tell you: you have the only chance anyone has ever had. Because you are not alone. Because when one of you falls, others will catch them. Because—" Her voice cracked, ancient grief bleeding through. "Because you will not abandon each other the way my people were abandoned."

The silence that followed was different from before. Less despairing. More contemplative. Alexis watched her people absorb Makelo's words, saw spines straightening, jaws setting, fear transforming into something harder. Something more useful.

"So what's the plan?" Aaron asked, ever practical. "You said they're moving toward the Trident. How do we stop them?"

"First, we identify them," Makelo said. "My tracking tools can read the signatures left by stolen artifacts. With your network's resources, we may be able to trace their movements, predict their next target, catch them in the act." She paused. "But understand. This will be dangerous. Whoever is behind this has killed to protect their secret. They will kill again."

"We've faced danger before," Lily said, her red hair catching the light as she stepped forward. "We'll face it again. That's what we signed up for."

Murmurs of agreement rippled through the room. Not everyone. Some faces remained pale, uncertain. But enough. Enough to matter.

"So what's the actual plan?" Javier asked, the communications specialist's practical mind cutting through the emotional weight. "Tracking signatures sounds good in theory, but we're talking about artifacts that could be anywhere in the world. How do we narrow it down?"

"The signatures don't travel far," Makelo explained. "When an artifact is moved through normal means, the trail fades within days. But when it's moved through divine channels, through spaces between worlds, through shadow-paths or ether gates, it leaves marks that last much longer. Whoever is doing this has been using such methods. I can read those marks."

"You said they're targeting the Trident next," Aaron said. "Can you use your tracking to predict when they'll make their move?"

"Not precisely. But I can identify the staging areas they've used before. The places where artifacts were gathered before being moved to wherever they're being stored or destroyed. If they follow the same pattern, we may be able to intercept them."

"And if they don't follow the pattern?" Marcus asked from near the window. "If they know we're onto them?"

"Then we adapt. We learn. We try again." Makelo's voice was hard as ancient stone. "That is how you fight something that has been winning for millennia. You make yourself unpredictable. You become the variable they cannot account for."

Her gaze found Alexis again, and there was something knowing in those vast eyes. Something that suggested she understood more than she was saying.

Alexis felt tension loosen in her chest. They weren't running. They weren't giving up. Despite everything, the impossible odds, the ancient enemy, the failing powers, they were still willing to fight.

Maybe that was enough. Maybe that was all you could ask of anyone.

* * * *

The briefing devolved into smaller conversations as people broke into groups, discussing implications, asking questions, trying to wrap their minds around the impossible scope of the threat. Alexis found herself drifting toward the edge of the room, letting others take the lead for once.

She watched her people work. Aaron had pulled Makelo aside, their heads bent together over tactical maps as they discussed deployment options. Lily was organizing the speedsters into reconnaissance teams, her natural leadership shining through despite the diminished powers that plagued them all. Others were checking supplies, reviewing equipment, preparing for a conflict that none of them fully understood.

This was what they'd built. Not just a sanctuary, but a functioning military organization capable of responding to cosmic threats. A year ago, she'd been a normal teenager grieving her mother's death. Now she was watching demigods from a dozen pantheons coordinate an operation to save the world.

The absurdity of it struck her sometimes. The sheer improbability of everything that had happened since her powers awakened. She'd fought a god. She'd met her primordial grandfather. She'd killed people. Or at least, she'd caused their deaths. She'd accumulated debts and secrets that would have crushed her a year ago.

And now she was standing at the center of humanity's last defense against an ancient conspiracy, trying not to fall apart while everyone looked to her for answers she didn't have.

She told herself it was strategic. Makelo and Aaron were deep in conversation about tracking methodologies, their heads bent together over a tablet displaying artifact signature patterns. Lily had gathered a group of the faster operatives, discussing reconnaissance possibilities with the kind of tactical focus that made her invaluable. Keats was—

Keats was laughing at something Lily had said.

Alexis watched from across the room as Lily touched Keats's arm, making a point about something, her red hair catching the light as she gestured animatedly. Keats responded with that crooked grin of his, the one Alexis thought of as hers, had always thought of as hers, and leaned in to hear better over the noise of the room.

It was nothing. She knew it was nothing. They were colleagues, friends, teammates who had fought together and trusted each other with their lives. Of course they had rapport. Of course they could make each other laugh. That was healthy. That was good.

So why did it feel like a knife sliding between her ribs?

The jealousy rose unbidden, toxic and familiar. She'd been fighting it for weeks. Longer, if she was honest. Ever since Lily had arrived and slotted so easily into their dynamic, bringing skills and speed and a quick wit that matched Keats's own. Ever since Alexis had started spending her nights in the intelligence center, researching threats alone, while Keats and Lily trained together, planned together, built the kind of easy partnership that came from shared hours and shared purpose.

She could see them from here. Keats leaning in to hear something Lily was saying, his body language open and engaged in a way that made Alexis's stomach clench. Lily gestured expansively, making some point about tactical positioning, and Keats nodded along, adding his own observations. They were good together. Complementary. A team.

When had Alexis stopped being part of that team?

The answer was obvious, and she hated it. She'd stopped being part of the team when she'd started keeping secrets. When she'd retreated into herself after Greer, after the boon, after every terrible choice she'd made in the name of protecting people from truths she thought they couldn't handle. She'd built walls, and now she was trapped behind them, watching through narrow windows as the people she loved connected without her.

She hated herself for feeling it. The world was ending, actually, literally ending, and she was standing here being jealous of her best friend for having a functional working relationship with her boyfriend. What kind of person did that make her?

She remembered a conversation with her adoptive mother, years ago, before Elizabeth Rain had been murdered and the world had revealed itself to be full of gods and monsters. They'd been talking about a friend of Alexis's. A girl who'd gotten jealous when Alexis spent time with other people. "Jealousy," Elizabeth had said, her voice gentle but firm, "isn't about the other person. It's about what we fear in ourselves. What we think we're lacking."

What did Alexis think she was lacking? Time, maybe. Presence. She'd been so focused on the threat, so determined to handle things herself, that she'd created distance without meaning to. And now that distance felt like a chasm, with Keats and Lily on one side and her on the other.

But what was the alternative? Tell everyone about the boon? Share the weight of Greer's death, the guilt that woke her in the small hours of the night? Admit that she was terrified, not of the enemy, but of herself. Of what she might become if this fight demanded everything she had?

The kind who's carrying too much alone, a treacherous voice whispered in her mind. *The kind who won't let anyone close enough to help.*

She pushed the thought away. Pushed the jealousy down. Buried it under the weight of duty and responsibility and the boon pressing against her soul like a constant reminder of all the secrets she was keeping.

"You look like you need some air."

Alexis startled. A young woman had appeared beside her. Honey-blonde hair, warm brown eyes, freckles across her nose. It took her a moment to place the face.

"Ellie, right?" she said. "You've been training with Lily."

"That's me." Ellie's smile was warm, genuine. The kind of openness that felt increasingly rare in Alexis's world of secrets and cosmic threats. "I've been wanting to introduce myself properly, but you're always so busy. Which, I mean, obviously. You're running a whole operation here while trying to save the world. That's a lot."

"It's something," Alexis agreed, a tired smile tugging at her lips despite herself. "Although, this is really Lily's show. Her brainchild, at least."

"Well, for what it's worth, I think you're doing an incredible job. Everyone here, they believe in what you've all built. In you." Ellie's eyes were earnest, almost uncomfortably so. "I know I'm new, and I don't know the history, but I can see the way people look at you. Like you're the reason they're still fighting."

The words should have been comforting. Instead, they added another weight to the pile Alexis was already carrying. *The reason they're still fighting. The one they're all depending on. The person who's supposed to have answers when the world falls apart.*

"Thanks," she said, and meant it, even if the gratitude was tinged with exhaustion. "I'm glad you're here, Ellie. We need all the help we can get."

"Can I ask you something?" Ellie's voice dropped, becoming more personal. "How do you do it? Stay so focused, I mean. Everything we heard, centuries-old conspiracies, the end of the divine-mortal connection, all of it, and you're standing here, holding it together. I'd be falling apart."

Alexis almost laughed. If Ellie only knew how close to falling apart she was. "You learn to compartmentalize," she said instead. "Focus on what you can control, set aside what you can't. Break the impossible into smaller pieces until they start looking manageable."

"That sounds like something someone taught you."

"My karate instructor, actually. Sensei used to say that every fight is won one move at a time. You can't think about the whole match. Just the next strike, the next block, the next breath." She paused, remembering the dojo, the smell of sweat and floor polish, the endless hours of practice that had built the foundation for everything she'd become. "Turns out that applies to saving the world too."

Ellie nodded slowly, absorbing it. "One move at a time. I can try that."

"You've got good instincts," Alexis said, surprising herself with the observation. "Lily mentioned you've been picking up combat training fast. And you seem to read people well. Knowing when someone needs space versus when they need company."

Ellie ducked her head, a pleased flush coloring her cheeks. "I try to pay attention. My mom always said that half of helping people is noticing when they need help in the first place."

"Smart woman."

"She was." The past tense hung in the air for a moment. "Cancer. Three years ago. That's why I started looking into the divine world. Desperate for answers, for miracles, for anything that might help. By the time I found out about Scions, it was too late for her. But at least I found people who understood what it was like to be different."

Alexis felt an unexpected kinship with the younger woman. Loss as a gateway into a larger world. They had that in common, at least.

"I'm sorry about your mother," she said. "And I'm glad you found us."

A shadow fell across them. Literally. Alexis looked up to find Cerval approaching, his gray eyes catching the light in a way that made them seem almost silver. He moved quietly, she noticed again. Like someone who'd learned to go unnoticed.

"Ellie," he said, nodding to the blonde. "I finished the analysis you asked about. The pattern recognition on the theft timelines."

"Oh! Great." Ellie's face lit up with a brightness that seemed disproportionate to the news. "Sorry, Alexis. I should go look at this. But if you ever need to talk, or… not talk and just sit in silence with someone, I'm around."

She hurried off with Cerval, and Alexis watched them go. Ellie chattering animatedly, Cerval responding with brief, measured words. There was something there, she thought. The way Ellie angled toward him, the careful attention in Cerval's responses. The beginning of something, maybe.

She caught fragments of their conversation as they moved away. Ellie asking about the analysis methodology, Cerval explaining something about temporal clustering in the theft patterns. His voice was smooth, professional, but there was something underneath it that Alexis couldn't identify. A carefulness that went beyond mere competence.

"He's good at that," Aaron said, appearing at her elbow. She hadn't heard him approach. Too lost in her own thoughts. "Making himself useful. Fitting in."

"You don't trust him?"

Aaron was quiet for a moment, his soldier's eyes tracking Cerval's retreat. "I trust the work he's produced. His analysis has been solid, his insights genuine. But..." He shook his head. "He feels too smooth. Too perfect. Like he's been trained to be exactly what we need."

"You think he's a plant?"

"I think we discussed the possibility of a mole already." Aaron's voice dropped lower. "And I think we should be careful about who has access to sensitive information until we know more. That's all."

It wasn't an accusation. It was the careful paranoia of someone who'd spent his life analyzing threats. Alexis filed it away, another weight added to the pile.

Good for them, she supposed. Someone should be finding connection in all this chaos.

The thought brought her attention back to Keats and Lily, still talking across the room. Still easy with each other in ways that made Alexis feel like an outsider in her own life.

Aaron appeared at her elbow again, a tablet in his hands. "Got a minute? There's something I want to show you. Privately."

She followed him to a quiet corner, grateful for the distraction from her own spiraling thoughts. Aaron pulled up a series of communications logs, timestamps highlighted in red.

"I've been running analysis on our internal communications since we discussed the possibility of a leak," he said, his voice low enough that only she could hear. "There are gaps. Small ones. A few minutes here and there where our secure channels showed activity that doesn't correspond to any logged conversations."

"Someone's using our systems to communicate externally?"

"Possibly. Or someone's been accessing files they shouldn't have access to and covering their tracks. Either way, it confirms what we suspected. Someone inside the Network is feeding information to the enemy." Aaron's jaw tightened. "I can't identify who yet. Whoever's doing this is good. They understand our security protocols well enough to work around them."

"Who has that level of access?"

"Core team members only. Me, Lily, a handful of senior operatives." He paused. "And anyone with technical skills who's been given temporary access for specific projects. Which, unfortunately, includes several of the newer recruits who've been helping with data analysis."

Cerval. He didn't say the name, but Alexis heard it anyway.

"What do you recommend?"

"Compartmentalize. Share our real plans only with people we're certain about. Feed different information to different groups and see what leaks." Aaron's soldier's eyes were cold with calculation. "It's not pretty, but it's how you catch a mole. Make them reveal themselves by acting on information only they had."

"Do it," Alexis said. "And keep me updated. Quietly."

Aaron nodded and moved away, already typing notes into his tablet. Another secret. Another weight. Another thing Alexis was carrying alone.

She needed to get out of here.

* * * *

The roof of the main building had become Alexis's refuge over the past weeks.

She climbed the access ladder now, emerging onto the flat expanse of weathered shingles and metal vents. The night had fully fallen while they'd been in the briefing, and the White Mountains rose around her like silent sentinels, their peaks silver-touched by starlight. The air was cold and clean, carrying the scent of pine and distant snow.

She sat with her back against an air conditioning unit, drawing her knees up to her chest, and let herself feel everything she'd been suppressing.

The cold seeped through her clothes, grounding her in her body. She could feel the rough texture of the shingles beneath her, the vibration of the AC unit humming against her spine, the distant sounds of the compound settling into its nighttime rhythms. Doors closing, voices murmuring, the occasional burst of laughter that seemed impossibly normal given what they'd learned.

How did people do it? How did they carry on with their lives when the foundations of reality were being systematically dismantled? Did they not think about it? Compartmentalize the horror into a box they could close when they needed to sleep, to eat, to laugh at a friend's joke?

Maybe that was the healthy response. Maybe Alexis was the broken one, sitting alone on a rooftop, cataloguing her fears like inventory.

The fear came first. Not fear for herself, that had burned away somewhere between Greer's dissolution and the Chimera's death, but fear for everyone depending on her. Fear that she would fail them. Fear that the conspiracy spanning centuries was simply too vast, too patient, too thorough to be stopped by a teenage half-blood and her ragtag network of outcasts.

The guilt came next. For the boon she hadn't told anyone about. For Greer, dissolved in the void because of choices she'd made. For every secret she was keeping from the people who trusted her most. The weight of it sat in her chest like a stone, cold and unmoving.

And beneath it all, the jealousy. Irrational, unwelcome, impossible to ignore. She loved Keats. She trusted Lily. She knew, *knew*, that there was nothing between them but friendship and shared purpose. But knowing didn't stop the feeling. Didn't stop the twist in her gut when she saw them laughing together, the whisper of inadequacy that said they were building something without her, that she was losing him by inches while she buried herself in research and secrets and the crushing weight of responsibility.

"Stop it," she said aloud, her voice small against the mountain silence. "Stop."

But feelings didn't follow orders. That was the problem. You could tell yourself something was irrational a thousand times and still feel it eating at you from the inside.

She thought about what Makelo had said. About the ally she'd lost. The one with the same fire, the same refusal to accept limitations. The one who'd died trying to warn people who wouldn't listen.

What had that ally's name been? Makelo hadn't said. After thousands of years, did names even matter anymore, or did they blur into faces, into feelings, into the general weight of loss accumulated over an immortal lifetime?

Alexis tried to imagine living that long. Watching everyone she loved grow old and die while she remained. Watching civilizations rise and fall, wars fought over causes that would be forgotten in a century. Watching the world change so completely that nothing familiar remained except her own endless, enduring self.

Would she become like Makelo? Weathered by time, hardened by loss, capable of speaking about genocide with the flat affect of someone describing weather patterns? Was that what awaited her if she survived this? Centuries of carrying knowledge no one else remembered, watching the patterns repeat while being powerless to stop them?

Or would she be like Makelo's lost ally? The one with fire, the one who refused to accept limitations? The one who died trying?

Was that her future? Fighting against something too big to stop until it finally crushed her? Pushing everyone away in the name of protecting them until she was truly alone?

The boon pressed against her soul, as it always did. Chaos, watching from the void. Interested. Waiting.

You are unexpected, he had said. *And in a universe this old, the unexpected is precious beyond measure.*

What did it mean to be unexpected? To be a variable that even primordial beings hadn't accounted for? Was that a gift or a curse? A weapon she could wield or a target painted on her back?

She didn't have answers. She was running out of questions that made sense.

The roof access hatch opened behind her.

Alexis didn't turn, but she knew the footsteps. She'd known them since they were children learning to walk, to run, to fight side by side.

Keats settled beside her without speaking, his shoulder warm against hers. For a long moment, they sat together, watching the stars wheel slowly overhead.

"You disappeared," he said finally.

"I needed air."

"You needed to be alone." It wasn't an accusation. An observation. "You've been needing that a lot lately."

The truth of it stung. "There's a lot going on."

"There's always a lot going on. That's not what this is." Keats's voice was gentle, but there was an edge beneath it. Frustration held carefully in check. "You've been pulling away for weeks, Al. And I've been trying to give you space, trying to trust that you'd come to me when you were ready. But watching you disappear into yourself… it's killing me."

The raw honesty in his voice cracked something in her chest. "Keats…"

"No, let me finish." He shifted to face her, his green eyes searching hers in the starlight. "I know you think you have to be strong for everyone. I know you think showing weakness means failing somehow. But Al, you're not failing anyone. You're drowning, and you won't let anyone throw you a rope."

"I'm not drowning."

"You're sitting alone on a roof in the dark after learning that everything we've been fighting for might be pointless. That seems pretty drowning-adjacent to me."

Despite herself, she almost smiled. Even now, he could make her almost smile. "Drowning-adjacent. Is that a clinical term?"

"It's a Keats term. I'm trademarking it." But his expression remained serious. "Talk to me, Al. Whatever's happening in your head, whatever you're carrying… you don't have to carry it alone."

The same words he'd said in Makelo's cave. The same offer she kept deflecting.

"I know," she said. And then, because she owed him something, even if she couldn't give him everything: "I'm scared, Keats. Not of the fighting or the danger. I can handle that. I'm scared that I'm not enough. That everyone's counting on me and I'm going to let them down."

"Why would you think that?"

"Because this thing we're fighting, it's beaten everyone who's ever tried to stop it. Makelo's entire people. Oracles, smiths, anyone who got too close to the truth. And they were ancient, powerful, knowledgeable in ways we can't even imagine. What makes me think we'll be different?"

Keats was silent for a moment, his thumb tracing circles on the back of her hand. When he spoke, his voice was thoughtful, measured.

"Maybe we won't be different. Maybe we'll fail too, and in a thousand years, some other group of half-bloods will be sitting in a cave hearing about how the Network tried and died." He paused. "But maybe that's not the point."

"What is the point?"

"We try anyway. Because it matters. Because the people we're protecting matter. Because giving up guarantees the outcome we're afraid of, and fighting at least gives us a chance." His green eyes found hers in the starlight. "My visions are failing. Lily's speed is fading. The whole divine-mortal connection is crumbling. And you know what? I'm still here. Still fighting. Still choosing to believe that what we do makes a difference."

"When did you become the philosopher?"

"Somewhere between 'your best friend has divine powers' and 'the world is ending.' Personal growth through apocalypse. I should write a self-help book."

This time, she did smile. Small and tired, but real. "I'd read that book."

"You'd be the first chapter. 'How to Save the World While Having a Complete Emotional Breakdown: A Case Study.'"

"Flattering."

"You know me. Always the charmer."

It was true. It just wasn't all of the truth.

Keats was quiet for a moment. Then he reached over and took her hand, lacing his fingers through hers the way he had a thousand times before.

"You're not alone in this," he said. "You have me. You have Lily. You have Aaron and Makelo and everyone in that building down there. We're not following you because we think you're infallible. We're following you because you fight even when you're scared. Because you care about people more than you care about being safe. Because when everything falls apart, you're the one still standing, trying to put it back together."

His hand tightened on hers.

"That's enough, Al. That's always been enough."

She wanted to believe him. She wanted to lean into his warmth, let go of the secrets, tell him everything. The boon, the guilt, the jealousy that was eating her alive. She wanted to be the person he saw when he looked at her, instead of the mess of fear and inadequacy she felt inside.

But the words wouldn't come. The walls she'd built were too high, too thick, too necessary.

"Thank you," she said instead. "I don't know what I'd do without you."

"You'd figure it out." He leaned his head against hers, his curls brushing her cheek. "You always do. But you don't have to. That's the point."

They sat together in the starlight, two small figures against the vast indifference of the mountains. Somewhere below, the Network continued its work. Planning, preparing, fighting against a conspiracy older than history. Somewhere in the void between worlds, Chaos watched with ancient interest. Somewhere in the dark, enemies moved pieces on a board that had been set up centuries ago.

And Alexis sat with the boy she loved, holding his hand, and felt more alone than she ever had in her life.

The truth was clear now. Makelo had laid it out in terms no one could deny. This wasn't a problem that would solve itself. This wasn't a threat that would fade if they waited long enough. Someone was trying to end the world as they knew it, and the only people standing in the way were a handful of half-bloods with diminishing powers and an ancient smith who had been hiding for millennia.

The ultimatum was implicit, unspoken but undeniable: commit fully to this fight, or watch everything burn.

Alexis looked up at the stars. The same stars that had watched over the Telchines before their destruction, over the rise and fall of civilizations, over every small tragedy and triumph in human history.

"I won't let them win," she said quietly. "Whatever it takes. Whoever I have to become. I won't let them sever the worlds."

Keats didn't ask who she meant by "them." Didn't ask what "whatever it takes" might cost.

He held her hand tighter and said, "Together."

She nodded, not trusting her voice.

They sat in silence for a while, watching the stars. Keats pointed out constellations. Something his mother had taught him, he said, before she'd disappeared from his life. Orion's Belt. The Big Dipper. Cassiopeia, the vain queen frozen in the heavens for her hubris.

"The Greeks saw stories everywhere," Alexis murmured. "Gods and monsters and heroes, written in the sky."

"They understood something we've forgotten," Keats said. "That the universe isn't just physics and chemistry. There's meaning woven into it. Purpose. Connection." He gestured at the stars. "Those aren't just burning balls of gas. They're markers. Reminders of what matters."

"And someone wants to cut us off from all of that."

"Yeah." Keats's voice hardened. "But they haven't won yet. And as long as we're still fighting, they haven't won."

Alexis thought about Makelo, three thousand years old, still fighting even when everyone else who remembered her world was gone. Thought about Aaron, methodically hunting for a mole even while the larger war raged around them. Thought about Lily and Ellie and all the others down in the compound, preparing for a battle they might not survive.

They were all carrying something. All fighting through their own fears and doubts. She wasn't special in that. She wasn't alone in that.

So why did she feel like she was?

Together.

The word echoed in her mind, a promise and a challenge. Together meant trusting people with the truth. Together meant letting go of the walls she'd built. Together meant admitting that she couldn't save the world by herself—that maybe she wasn't supposed to.

The boon pressed against her soul. The secrets pressed against her tongue. And somewhere in the cosmic dark, ancient forces moved their pieces around on that board that had been set up before humanity learned to write its own name.

Tomorrow, they would start hunting the thief. Tomorrow, they would begin the real work of protecting the Trident, of unraveling a conspiracy millennia in the making. Tomorrow, Alexis would have to be the leader everyone needed her to be—strong, confident, certain.

But tonight, she let herself lean against Keats's shoulder and watch the stars, two small figures holding onto each other against the vast indifference of the universe.

It wasn't enough. It couldn't be enough.

But it was all she had.

For now, it would *have* to be enough.

13

Alexis couldn't sleep.

She lay in the narrow bed of her quarters, staring at the ceiling, while the compound settled into its nighttime quiet around her. Keats breathed softly beside her, his body warm against hers, his arm draped across her waist in sleep. She should have felt comforted by his presence. Instead, she felt like a fraud.

The rooftop conversation played on loop in her mind. His words, *together, you're not alone, that's always been enough*, should have helped. Should have eased the weight pressing against her chest. Instead, they reminded her of everything she wasn't saying. The boon. Greer. The jealousy that coiled in her gut even now, even with him right here.

She slipped out of bed carefully, not wanting to wake him, and padded barefoot to the window. The White Mountains were silverblack under a half-moon, ancient and indifferent. The peaks rose jagged against a sky thick with stars. More stars than she'd ever seen in her old life, before the compound, before everything changed. At this elevation, the air was thin and cold, pressing against the window glass like something wanting in.

She could hear the wind moving through the mountain passes, a low constant whisper that never stopped. Somewhere far below, a night bird called. The sound echoing off stone faces that had watched civilizations rise and fall without caring. The compound itself was quiet, but it wasn't silent. Pipes creaked as water moved through the heating system. Footsteps sounded faintly from the corridor as someone, a guard, probably, made their rounds.

The cold seeped through the window glass, raising goosebumps on her bare arms. She should go back to bed. Should curl into Keats's warmth and let his presence anchor her. But she couldn't shake the feeling that she didn't deserve to be there. Didn't deserve to be held by someone who trusted her while she kept secrets that could poison everything.

Somewhere out there, an enemy older than history was moving pieces on a board she couldn't fully see.

And here she was, losing sleep over whether her boyfriend laughed too easily with another woman.

Pathetic, she thought. *The world is ending and you're jealous.*

But the jealousy wasn't the real problem. It was what the jealousy revealed. All the cracks in her foundation, all the places where her confidence had been built on sand instead of stone.

She thought of specific moments. The first time she'd seen Keats and Lily sparring, their movements synchronized like they'd been fighting together for years. The way Lily had touched his arm while making a point, casual and familiar. The inside jokes she didn't understand, references to missions she hadn't been part of, a history that existed before she arrived.

She thought of the briefing last week, when Lily had finished Keats's sentence and they'd both laughed at the same instant, and something in Alexis's chest had clenched so tight she couldn't breathe.

She thought of her parents, her real parents, the ones who'd raised her and loved her and died because of what she was. Charles would have told her she was being ridiculous. Elizabeth would have held her and reminded her that love wasn't a competition. But Charles and Elizabeth were dead, and she was standing at a window in the mountains, cataloguing all the ways she wasn't enough.

You're the daughter of Night, she told herself. *You've survived things that would break anyone else. Why can't you survive this?*

But the fear didn't answer to logic. It never had.

"You're doing it again."

She turned. Keats was sitting up in bed, watching her with eyes that caught the moonlight. He didn't look sleepy anymore. He looked like someone who'd been waiting for this moment.

"Doing what?"

"Standing at windows. Carrying things alone. Pretending you're fine when you're clearly not." He swung his legs over the side of the bed, but didn't stand. Giving her space, she realized. Even now, he was being careful with her. "Talk to me, Al. Really talk to me. Not the rooftop version where you give me enough to make me think you're opening up."

The words stung because they were true.

"I don't know what you want me to say."

"I want you to say what's going on. Not what you think I can handle. Not some edited version that protects me from the scary truth." He stood then, crossing the small room to stand in front of her. Close enough to touch, but not touching. "I'm not fragile, Alexis. And

I'm not going anywhere. Whatever it is, whatever you've been carrying, I can take it."

She wanted to deflect. To make a joke, change the subject, find some excuse to retreat. But Keats was standing there with his heart in his eyes, offering her something she'd been too afraid to accept.

Trust.

The word cracked something open inside her.

* * * *

"I've been jealous," she said.

The words came out small, almost childish, and she hated the sound of them. But once the first admission escaped, more followed, tumbling out like water through a cracked dam.

"Of Lily. Of you and Lily. The way you two work together. This easy rapport, the shared jokes, the way you *fit*. I watch you with her and I feel like I'm on the outside looking in. Like you're building something without me, and I'm too busy drowning in secrets to be part of it."

Keats's expression didn't change. He listened, steady and present.

"I know it's irrational," she continued, the words coming faster now. "I know you love me. I know Lily's not… she's not trying to take you away. But knowing doesn't make it stop. I see you laughing with her and something twists in my chest, and I hate myself for feeling it because it's *petty*. It's small. The world is literally ending and I'm jealous of my friend."

She turned back to the window, unable to meet his eyes. The mountains offered no judgment, only indifference.

"I've been pulling away because I don't know how to be around you without the jealousy showing. And I didn't want you to see this ugly, broken part of me. This part that can't even trust the person she loves."

Silence stretched between them. Alexis braced for disappointment, for judgment, for the moment he realized she wasn't the person he thought she was.

Instead, she felt his hands on her shoulders, turning her gently to face him.

"Look at me," he said.

She did. His green eyes were soft in the moonlight, but there was steel beneath the softness.

"Lily is family," he said. "She's the sister I never had. Someone who understands what it's like to have divine blood and human fears. I love her the way you love someone who's fought beside you, bled beside you, seen you at your worst and stayed anyway."

His hands moved from her shoulders to cup her face, tilting it up so she couldn't look away.

"But you, Alexis Rain, daughter of Night, most stubborn person I have ever met, *you* are my choice. You are who I want to wake up next to. You are who I want standing beside me when the world burns. You are my partner, my future, my *home*. And no amount of easy rapport with anyone else will ever change that."

Alexis felt tears pricking at her eyes. Tears she hadn't let herself cry in weeks. "How can you be so sure?"

"Because I've known you since we were kids learning to throw punches in a dojo that smelled like floor polish. Because I watched you bury both your parents and refuse to break. Because every day, you carry weights that would crush anyone else, and you still find room to care about people who can't protect themselves." His thumb brushed away a tear she hadn't felt fall. "I'm sure because I've seen who you are, Al. All of you. Even the parts you think are ugly."

He paused, and his voice dropped to something more intimate.

"Do you remember the first time we sparred after you got your powers? You were so afraid of hurting me. You pulled every punch, held back on everything, and I had to practically beg you to fight for real. And when you finally did, when you let go and showed me what you could do, you apologized. For being powerful. For being more than you used to be."

She remembered. The fear that she'd hurt him. The shame of being something other than the girl he'd grown up with.

"That's when I knew," Keats said. "That's when I knew you were still you. Still the person who'd rather hurt herself than risk hurting someone she loved. Lily's amazing. She's one of the best people I know. But she's not you. She's never been you."

He leaned closer, his forehead almost touching hers.

"You asked how I can be so sure? It's because I've watched you become something extraordinary, and you've never once let it make you cruel. You've never let power change who you are at your core. And that's why I love you. Not despite the darkness. Because of who you are inside it."

"And you still want this? Still want me?"

"I want you when you're strong. I want you when you're scared. I want you when you're jealous and irrational and standing at windows in the middle of the night." He leaned his forehead against hers. "I want you to let me in. That's all I've ever wanted."

* * * *

They stood like that for a long moment, foreheads touching, breathing the same air. The cold from the window pressed against Alexis's back, but she barely felt it. Everything she was aware of was Keats. His warmth, his steadiness, the certainty in his voice.

She'd been so focused on controlling everything, the mission, the secrets, her own emotions, that she'd forgotten what it felt like to trust. To let someone else carry part of the weight.

"I'm sorry," she whispered. "For pulling away. For not trusting you with this."

"Don't be sorry. Just... don't do it again." His lips curved into that crooked grin she loved. "Or at least, when you do it again, because you will, because you're you, let me call you on it sooner."

"Deal."

He kissed her then. Soft and slow, a promise rather than a demand. Alexis leaned into it, letting herself feel wanted, chosen, *enough*. The jealousy was still there, coiled somewhere in her chest, but it felt smaller now. Less like a monster and more like what it was: fear, wearing a different mask.

Fear that she'd lose him. Fear that she wasn't worthy of being loved. Fear that the person she was becoming, the one who made deals with primordials and killed without hesitation, wasn't someone anyone could love at all.

But Keats was still here. Still choosing her. And maybe that was what trust meant. Not the absence of fear, but the choice to believe anyway.

"There's more," she said when they finally broke apart. "Things I haven't told you. Things I've been carrying alone."

She felt him tense, then relax. "I figured. You've had that look. The one that says you're holding something heavy."

"I'm not ready to tell you everything. Not yet." The boon still pressed against her soul, a secret that felt too dangerous to share even now. "But I want to be. I'm *trying* to be."

"Then I'll wait." His voice was steady, certain. "When you're ready, I'll be here."

It wasn't perfect. It wasn't a complete unburdening, a full confession. But it was more than she'd given anyone in months.

It was a start.

* * * *

Morning came with pale light filtering through the window and the smell of coffee drifting from somewhere in the compound.

Alexis found Lily in the training room, working through forms with the kind of focused intensity that said she hadn't slept much either. Her red hair was pulled back in a messy ponytail, her movements sharp despite the hour. The training room was cold. The compound never got truly warm this high in the mountains. And Lily's breath fogged with each exhale.

"Hey," Alexis said from the doorway.

Lily paused mid-strike, turning with raised eyebrows. "Hey yourself. You look like someone who slept for once."

"I didn't. But I feel better anyway." Alexis stepped into the room, her bare feet quiet on the training mats. The mats were old and worn in the places where generations of fighters had practiced, the surface soft with accumulated use. "Can we talk?"

Wariness shifted in Lily's expression, or recognition. "Sure. What's up?"

Alexis took a breath. This was harder than she'd expected. Admitting jealousy to Keats had been one thing. He loved her, would forgive her almost anything. Lily was different. Lily was the person she'd been jealous *of*.

"I owe you an apology," she said. "I've been distant lately. Cold. And it wasn't about you. It was about me. About stuff I was dealing with. Badly."

Lily set down the practice knife she'd been holding. Her brown eyes were steady, unreadable. "Go on."

"I was jealous. Of you and Keats." The words felt like pulling teeth, but she forced them out anyway. "The way you two connect. It made me feel left out. Replaced. I know that's not fair to either of you. But I wanted you to know why I've been weird, and to tell you I'm working on it."

Lily was quiet for a long moment. Then, unexpectedly, she laughed. A short, sharp sound that held no mockery.

"God, Alexis. I thought you hated me."

"What?"

"You've been so closed off. Every time I tried to get closer, you pulled away. I figured I'd done something wrong. Overstepped somehow. Made you uncomfortable." Lily shook her head. "I've been walking on eggshells for weeks, trying to figure out how to fix whatever I broke."

Guilt twisted in Alexis's chest. She'd been so focused on her own feelings that she hadn't considered how her behavior might look from the outside.

"You didn't break anything," she said. "I did. I let my insecurities poison something that should have been simple."

"For what it's worth," Lily said, moving closer, "Keats talks about you constantly. Like, *constantly*. 'Al would know what to do.' 'Al handled something like this once.' 'Did you see how Al took down that Chimera?' It's honestly a little nauseating."

Alexis felt a surprised laugh escape her. "Really?"

"Yes. That boy is completely gone for you. Anyone with eyes can see it." Lily's expression softened. "And for what it's worth, I'm not interested. In him, I mean. He's great, but he's like a brother. The annoying kind who thinks he's funnier than he is."

"He does think that."

"Right?" Lily grinned. "So. Are we good? Because I don't want to keep tiptoeing around you. We've got a world to save, and that's hard enough without interpersonal drama."

"We're good." Alexis meant it. The jealousy wasn't gone. Feelings didn't vanish because you named them. But it felt manageable now. Smaller. "And Lily? Thanks. For being patient with me while I figured my stuff out."

"That's what teammates are for." Lily picked up the practice knife again, then held it out handle-first toward Alexis. "Now. You look like you could use some stress relief. Want to spar?"

Alexis took the knife. "You're going to regret asking that."

"Big talk from someone who punches through problems instead of around them."

"That Chimera had it coming."

They faced off across the mat, and for the first time in weeks, Alexis felt lightness in her chest.

* * * *

The sparring match lasted twenty minutes and left them both sweating and grinning.

Lily came in fast, testing Alexis's reflexes with a flurry of strikes that would have overwhelmed anyone slower. Her speed was diminished but still formidable. She moved like water, flowing around counters, finding angles that shouldn't have existed. Alexis gave ground at first, letting Lily set the pace, learning her patterns.

Then she stopped giving ground.

She caught Lily's wrist on an overcommitted strike, redirected the momentum, and spun her into a hold that should have ended the exchange. Lily dropped her weight, slipped free, and came up with a sweep that nearly took Alexis's legs out from under her.

"Not bad," Alexis admitted, recovering her balance.

"I've been practicing with diminished speed for months. You learn to compensate." Lily circled left, knife switching hands in a way that was meant to distract. "The question is, can you compensate for this?"

She feinted high and went low, a combination that Alexis barely caught in time. They grappled for position, neither willing to yield, until Alexis found an opening and pressed her advantage. Shadows flickering at the edges of her vision as her power responded to the challenge.

"No powers," Lily gasped, though she was grinning. "That's cheating."

"It's not cheating if I don't use them."

"The shadows literally moved."

"Shadows move. It's what they do."

They broke apart, both breathing hard. Lily was fast. Diminished powers or not, she moved like water, flowing around attacks that should have landed. Alexis was stronger, more grounded, her shadows giving her options that pure speed couldn't counter. They were evenly matched in ways that mattered.

The final exchange happened too fast to narrate. A blur of movement and counter-movement that ended with Alexis's practice knife at Lily's throat and Lily's elbow an inch from Alexis's temple.

"Draw," they said simultaneously.

Lily laughed, lowering her arm. "I could have had you."

"You could have tried."

They stood there for a moment, sweating and grinning at each other, and Alexis felt the last of the tension between them dissolve. This was what they were supposed to be. Partners, teammates, people who pushed each other to be better. The jealousy hadn't disappeared, but it had been replaced by something stronger: mutual respect.

"You're good," Lily said afterward, toweling off her face. "Like, *good*. The shadow thing is unfair, by the way."

"Says the woman who can literally outrun bullets."

"Used to. These days it's more like 'outrun slightly-slower-than-normal projectiles.'" Lily's expression flickered with frustration, then smoothed out. "But we work with what we have, right?"

"Right."

Keats appeared in the doorway, coffee cup in hand, watching them with an expression of amused satisfaction. "So. We're all friends now?"

"We were always friends," Lily said. "Some of us were just having feelings about it."

"I have it on good authority that feelings are terrible," Keats offered. "Inconvenient. Would not recommend."

Alexis threw her sweaty towel at his face.

He caught it without spilling his coffee. Oracle reflexes, even degraded ones, had their uses. And grinned at her. The easy, open grin of someone who knew exactly where he stood.

"War council in an hour," he said. "Aaron wants to finalize the plan. Makelo's been up since dawn working on tracking signatures."

The lightness in Alexis's chest shifted, making room for something else. Purpose. Determination.

She'd spent weeks being reactive. Responding to threats, dealing with crises as they arose, carrying secrets that weighed her down. Last night, she'd taken the first step toward changing that. This morning, she'd taken another.

Now it was time to stop being a victim of circumstances and start being the one who shaped them.

"An hour," she said. "I'll be ready."

She meant more than the meeting.

For the first time since the ether, since the boon, since Greer dissolved into nothing under her hands, Alexis felt ready to fight. Not defensively. Not reactively.

She was ready to *win*.

14

The war council assembled at dawn.

Aaron had commandeered the largest conference room in the compound, its walls now covered with maps, timelines, and artifact schematics. Holographic displays floated over the central table, showing real-time data feeds from Network cells around the world. The smell of strong coffee competed with the ozone scent of overworked electronics.

He stood at the head of the table, watching the key players file in. Alexis arrived with Keats and Lily, the three of them moving with an easy coordination that hadn't been there a few days ago. Something had shifted between them. Aaron didn't know the details and didn't need to. What mattered was that they were functioning as a unit again.

Makelo followed, her small form wrapped in layers of gray cloth that made her look like a bundle of old fabric come to life. Her enormous eyes swept the room's technology with a mixture of curiosity and disdain. Three thousand years old, and she still preferred her own methods.

The others trickled in: Elena from the Scandinavian network, her blonde hair pulled back in a severe braid. Marcus from London, still looking shell-shocked from the briefing two days ago. Javier, their communications specialist, tablet already in hand. And near the back, moving quietly to a corner seat, Cerval Colley. The analyst who'd proven surprisingly useful since his arrival.

Aaron's eyes lingered on Cerval for a moment. The man was competent, no question. His pattern analysis had been instrumental in understanding the theft timeline. But there was something about him that set Aaron's instincts humming. The same instincts that had kept him alive through three tours in divine-adjacent conflicts.

He filed the thought away. Paranoia was useful, but it couldn't be allowed to paralyze.

"Let's begin," he said, and the room fell silent.

* * * *

"We know three things with certainty," Aaron began, pulling up the first holographic display. A map of the world appeared, dotted with red markers. "First: twelve major artifacts have been stolen in the past six months. The pattern has accelerated dramatically. Four thefts in the last three weeks alone."

He gestured, and the display shifted to show a complex web of connections. "Second: thanks to Makelo's analysis, we understand that these aren't random targets. They're systematically removing the anchors that bind the divine and mortal realms together. Each theft weakens the connection further."

Another gesture. The hologram zoomed to focus on a single point. A glowing trident symbol in the Atlantic Ocean. "Third: their ultimate target is Poseidon's Trident. Take that, and the connection doesn't weaken. It shatters. Permanently."

"So we protect the Trident," Marcus said. "Station guards, set up defenses—"

"It's not that simple." Makelo's water-over-rocks voice cut through the room. "The Trident is held by Poseidon himself, in a palace that exists partially outside mortal space. We cannot walk up and offer to stand guard."

"Then what *can* we do?" Elena asked.

Aaron nodded to Alexis, who stepped forward. She looked different today, he noticed. More settled. More present.

"We can't guard the Trident directly," she said. "But we can identify the thief before they reach it. Makelo's tracking tools can read the signatures that stolen artifacts leave behind. If we can find where they've been staging their operations, we can intercept them."

"A trap," Lily said, understanding dawning. "We figure out where they're going to be and we hit them before they hit the Trident."

"Exactly." Aaron pulled up a new display. A timeline with projected theft windows. "Based on the acceleration pattern, we estimate they'll move on the Trident within the next two to three weeks. That gives us time to track, analyze, and position ourselves."

"What about warning Poseidon?" Keats asked. "He should know his artifact is being targeted."

Makelo made a sound that might have been a laugh or a sigh. "Poseidon has been warned. Through what channels remain functional. But the Sea God is not known for heeding the concerns of… lesser beings." The bitterness in her voice was ancient. "He believes the Trident is untouchable. That no one would dare move against him in his own domain."

"Pride," Alexis said quietly. "The same thing that got the Telchines killed."

"The same thing that has been killing divine-mortal relations since the beginning," Makelo agreed. "Gods do not change easily. They are creatures of pattern, of ancient habits. By the time Poseidon believes the threat is real, it may be too late."

"Then we make sure it's not too late," Aaron said. "We don't wait for divine permission. We act."

* * * *

The next hour was spent in detailed planning.

Makelo explained her tracking methodology. The way stolen artifacts left residual signatures that could be read at transition points, places where the veil between worlds was thin. With the Network's global reach, they could position observers at dozens of such locations, creating an early warning system.

"The thief must move through these transition points," she said, marking locations on the holographic map. "Cape Sounion, where you entered liminal space. The crossroads at Hecate's Grove. The threshold beneath Delphi. There are others. Dozens around the world. We cannot watch them all, but we can prioritize the ones nearest to recent thefts."

"I'll coordinate with the regional cells," Elena said, already making notes. "We have people near most of these locations. They can set up observation posts within forty-eight hours."

"Communication will be critical," Javier added. "If someone spots movement, the response team needs to mobilize immediately. I'm setting up dedicated secure channels. Encrypted, rotating frequencies. Anything we transmit stays inside the Network."

Aaron nodded approvingly. This was what the Network did best. Coordinated action across impossible distances, leveraging their scattered strength into something greater than the sum of its parts.

"What about the response team itself?" Marcus asked. "Who's going after the thief when we find them?"

"The trio," Aaron said, gesturing to Alexis, Keats, and Lily. "They've already faced this enemy's defenses. The Chimera in liminal space. They know what they're dealing with. And Alexis is our strongest combatant." He paused. "No offense to anyone else."

"None taken," Elena said dryly. "I've seen her fight. I'm comfortable being backup."

"We'll need more than backup," Alexis said. "If we're setting a trap, we need contingencies. What if they don't take the bait? What if they have forces we haven't accounted for?"

"Secondary teams positioned at each major transition point," Aaron said. "Ready to intercept or pursue depending on how things develop. We're not putting all our assets in one location."

"Good." Alexis's voice carried a new authority. Not demanding, but sure. "We should also consider that whoever's doing this has been operating for centuries without being caught. They're not stupid. They'll have countermeasures we can't predict."

"Then we stay flexible," Lily said. "Adapt when the plan goes sideways. That's what we're good at."

"Spoken like someone who's never met a plan she couldn't improvise around," Keats said, earning a small smile from Lily and a snort from Alexis.

The mood in the room had shifted. Still serious, still aware of the stakes, but with an undercurrent that felt almost like confidence. They had a plan. They had resources. For the first time since this crisis began, they weren't reacting.

They were taking the fight to the enemy.

* * * *

Aaron stayed behind after the others filed out, his attention caught by the data feeds.

The anomaly had been nagging at him for two days now. Ever since he'd started his quiet investigation into potential leaks. Small data packets, transmitted at irregular intervals, pulling information from their secure servers. The amounts were minuscule, barely noticeable against the normal flow of Network communications. But they were consistent. Persistent.

Wrong.

He pulled up the analysis he'd been running, frowning at the results. The packets were encrypted. Well encrypted, using protocols he didn't recognize. They originated from somewhere inside the compound's network, but the source point kept shifting, bouncing through different nodes in a pattern that seemed random but probably wasn't.

Someone with access to their systems was siphoning information. Someone good.

"Problem?"

Aaron turned. Cerval stood in the doorway, his gray eyes catching the light from the holographic displays. He'd moved so quietly Aaron hadn't heard him approach. Which was notable, given Aaron's training.

"Maybe," Aaron said carefully. "Something weird in our systems. I'm working on it."

Cerval moved closer, his attention shifting to the data on the screen. "Irregular packet transmission?" His voice was professionally curious. "I noticed some anomalous traffic when I was working on the theft timeline analysis. Assumed it was background noise, but…" He tilted his head, studying the patterns. "This doesn't look like noise."

"No," Aaron agreed. "It doesn't."

"Want help?" Cerval's offer seemed genuine. The eager assistance of someone who'd found their niche and wanted to prove their value. "Data analysis is kind of my thing. I might be able to trace the source more quickly than standard methods."

Aaron hesitated. Every instinct told him to keep this close, to trust no one until he understood what was happening. But Cerval's analysis had been invaluable so far, and Aaron couldn't investigate everything alone. Not with a war council to coordinate and a trap to set.

"Alright," he said finally. "But this stays between us for now. I don't want to cause panic over what might be nothing."

"Understood." Cerval pulled up a chair, his attention already focused on the data. "Let me take a look at the encryption protocols.

There might be a signature in the method they're using. Something that could help us identify the source."

Aaron watched him work, noting the quick, confident movements of someone genuinely skilled at this kind of analysis. Cerval was good. Maybe even as good as he claimed to be.

Which made the question even more pressing: was he exactly what he appeared to be, a talented recruit who'd arrived at the right time? Or was he something else entirely?

Aaron didn't have an answer yet. But he'd learned long ago that the most dangerous enemies were the ones who looked like friends.

He'd keep watching. Keep testing. And when the moment came to act, he'd be ready.

* * * *

By evening, the plan was in motion.

Elena had reached out to thirteen Network cells, establishing observation posts at priority transition points across three continents. Javier's secure communication channels were up and running, tested and retested for any sign of compromise. Makelo had calibrated her tracking instruments and was teaching a small team of volunteers how to read artifact signatures. Insurance in case something happened to her.

The compound hummed with purpose. For the first time since the crisis began, Aaron could see something other than fear in the faces around him. Focus. Determination. Hope.

He found Alexis in the strategy room, reviewing deployment maps with Keats and Lily. The three of them looked up when he entered, and he was struck again by the change in their dynamic. Whatever had been off between them was resolved now. They moved like a team again.

"Status report," Alexis said. Not a question. A request between equals.

"We're as ready as we're going to be," Aaron said. "Observation posts are going active over the next twenty-four hours. Response teams are on standby. If they move on any of our monitored transition points, we'll know."

"And the system anomaly?"

He'd briefed her privately about the data leak, keeping the circle small as they'd agreed. "Still working on it. Cerval's helping with the analysis. Nothing conclusive yet, but we're getting closer."

Alexis nodded slowly. "Keep me updated. If someone inside is feeding information to the enemy…"

"I know." Aaron met her eyes. "I know what it means. And I'm handling it."

"I trust you." The words were simple, but they carried weight. Alexis Rain didn't give trust easily. That she offered it now, to him, meant something.

"So," Lily said, breaking the moment with her characteristic directness. "We're ready. Now what?"

"Now we wait," Aaron said. "We watch. And when they make their move—"

"We'll be ready for them," Alexis finished. Her voice held the certainty of someone who'd stopped doubting and started deciding.

Aaron hoped she was right.

He hoped they all were.

Because somewhere out there, an enemy that had been winning for centuries was preparing their endgame. And no matter how solid the plan, no matter how ready they felt, Aaron knew one thing with absolute certainty:

Plans never survived contact with the enemy.

15

The temperature dropped fifteen degrees in the span of a single breath.

Alexis felt it before she saw anything. A wrongness that crawled across her skin like frozen static. She was in the command center reviewing Makelo's schematics of the Trident's protective wards when the sensation hit, cutting through her concentration with surgical precision.

"Something's here," she said, and the words came out flat, certain.

Keats looked up from his station, his oracle sight flickering gold behind his eyes. His face went pale. "Al—"

"I feel it." Lily was already on her feet, bow materialized in her hands, red hair catching the emergency lighting that had begun to strobe across the chamber. "That shouldn't be possible. We have wards. We have—"

The shadow coalesced in the center of the room.

It didn't step through a doorway or emerge from some hidden passage. It gathered. Darkness pulling toward a central point like water circling a drain, until something stood among them that had no business existing in this protected space.

A shade. A messenger of the dead.

The figure was humanoid but wrong in ways that defied easy description. Its edges blurred and reformed constantly, as if it couldn't remember what shape it was supposed to hold. Where its face should have been, there was only a suggestion of features. The echo of a person who had once existed, reduced now to purpose and function.

Around them, alarms began to wail. Makelo's voice crackled over the intercom, demanding status reports, but Alexis barely heard her. Her attention was fixed on the impossible thing that had breached three hundred feet of granite, divine protections, and six years of carefully constructed security.

"Stand down," she said, and the command carried enough authority that Lily's bowstring eased. "It's not here to fight."

"How can you possibly know that?"

"Because if it wanted us dead, we'd already be dead." Alexis stepped forward, putting herself between the shade and her friends. Her power stirred beneath her skin, primordial darkness recognizing something ancient in the messenger's form. "Shades serve Hades. They don't breach protected spaces for casual violence. They come for one reason only."

The shade's not-face turned toward her, and she had the unsettling sense of being seen. Truly seen, in a way that had nothing to do with eyes.

"Alexis Rain." The voice was like wind through dead leaves, carrying the weight of centuries. "Daughter of Nyx. Champion of the Scion Network."

"That's me." She kept her tone even, conversational, though her heart hammered against her ribs. "And you are?"

The Chaos Arena

"A messenger. Nothing more." The shade drifted closer, and the temperature dropped another five degrees. "I bring words from Kieran, Son of Hades. Lord of the Spaces Between. Architect of the Severance."

Behind her, she heard Keats suck in a breath. Lily's bowstring creaked as it drew tighter despite Alexis's command. Even the air seemed to hold itself still, waiting.

"Then speak," Alexis said. "What does the son of Hades want with us?"

The shade extended one blurred hand, and something materialized in its palm. A scroll of material that wasn't paper, wasn't skin, sealed with wax the color of dried blood.

"A formal challenge," the shade intoned. "Combat in the Chaos Arena. Binding terms. The outcome to be honored by all parties, enforced by cosmic law itself."

Alexis didn't take the scroll. Not yet. "The Chaos Arena. You're talking about neutral ground. Sacred ground."

"The only ground where such matters can be decided with permanence. Where victory cannot be disputed, where defeat cannot be escaped." The shade's voice remained eerily calm, almost gentle. "My master offers you this honor, Daughter of Night. Single combat. Champion against champion. Winner claims all."

"This is insane," Lily said. "Al, don't—"

"What are the terms?" Alexis kept her focus on the shade, though she could feel Keats's eyes burning into her back. His oracle sight would be showing him something. Futures branching and colliding, possibilities that might terrify him. She couldn't afford to look.

The shade's form rippled, as if pleased by the question. "Should Kieran emerge victorious, all Scions relinquish their opposition to his work. They cease interference with him and his associates. The severance continues without... heroic complications."

The words hit like physical blows. All Scions. Not just her. Everyone. The entire Network, bound by cosmic law to stand aside while divine connections were systematically destroyed. While Scions lost their powers, their identities, everything that made them more than ordinary mortals.

"And if I win?"

"Kieran ceases all artifact thefts. He returns what he has stolen. He submits himself to divine judgment for his actions."

It sounded almost fair. Almost balanced. But Alexis had learned enough about divine politics to know that nothing in this world came without hidden costs.

"Why now?" she asked. "Why challenge me directly when you've been operating in shadows for months?"

"Because shadows have limits." The shade's voice carried what might have been approval. "And because my master respects what you've built. The Scion Network stands where others fell. You have protected those who could not protect themselves. You have earned the right to face him as an equal."

"That's not an answer."

"It is the only answer you will receive." The shade extended the scroll further. "Accept or decline. Those are your choices, Daughter of Night. But know this: refusal will not stop my master's work. It will only prove that Scions lack the conviction to defend their own existence."

The words landed exactly where they were meant to land. Alexis felt them settle into her chest like stones, weighing her down with implications she couldn't ignore.

If she refused, Kieran's philosophy gained legitimacy. She would be admitting, in the eyes of cosmic law, that she didn't believe strongly enough in what Scions represented to stake her life on it. And he would continue his work anyway. Only now with the moral high ground.

If she accepted…

She thought of Makelo's words from days ago. The Trident. Poseidon's connection to the mortal realm, anchored in an artifact that had been forged before recorded history. Kieran's next target, almost certainly. The theft that would prove his operation had grown beyond anyone's ability to stop.

Unless.

Unless he needed the Scions out of the way first.

The realization hit her like ice water. "He can't take the Trident by stealth. Not with our defenses. Not with Makelo watching." She looked at the shade with new understanding. "This isn't about honor or conviction. This is about removing obstacles. A binding ruling that forces us to stand aside. That's the only way he gets to the Trident without a war."

"My master's motivations are his own," the shade replied, and there was something almost like respect in its wind-voice. "But you are not wrong to see strategy where others might see only challenge."

"Al." Keats's voice was strained. "We need to discuss this. We need—"

"I know what we need." She turned to face her friends, finally, and the weight of the moment pressed against her chest. Keats looked like he'd seen something terrible in his visions. His face was pale, his hands trembling where they gripped the edge of his workstation. Lily's expression was pure fury barely contained, her bow still half-drawn even though she knew it wouldn't help.

And beyond them, visible through the command center's glass walls, she could see other Scions gathering. Aaron, grim-faced and calculating. Ellie, hovering near the medical station with concern written across her features. Cerval, watching from the shadows near the server room with an expression she couldn't read.

All of them waiting. All of them depending on her to make the right choice.

"Give us a moment," she said to the shade. "If your master truly respects what we've built, he'll allow time for counsel."

The shade inclined its not-head. "You have until dawn. When the sun rises, I will require your answer."

It didn't vanish dramatically or fade into shadow. It simply stopped being there, as if reality had quietly edited it out of existence. The scroll remained, hovering in the air for a heartbeat before drifting down to land on the central console.

The temperature began to climb back toward normal.

"What the actual hell," Lily said, and the words seemed to break something loose in all of them.

Suddenly everyone was talking at once. Aaron demanding tactical assessments. Makelo's voice crackling through the intercom with questions about the breach. Ellie rushing in to check on Keats, whose oracle sight was still flickering erratically. Cerval offering to analyze the scroll for hidden mechanisms or traps.

Alexis let the noise wash over her for a moment, then raised her hand.

Silence fell.

"War council," she said. "Main briefing room. Everyone who needs to be there, ten minutes." She looked at Keats, at Lily, at the scroll that represented everything they'd been fighting against given form and weight. "We're not making this decision in panic. We're making it together."

* * * *

The briefing room felt too small for what they were discussing.

Alexis stood at the head of the table, the scroll unrolled before her. The text was written in something that shifted between languages. Greek, then Latin, then something older that hurt to look at directly. But the meaning was clear enough.

"Combat in the Chaos Arena," she read aloud. "Single champion for each side. Binding terms stated before witnesses. The outcome enforced by cosmic law, irrevocable and permanent."

"It's a trap," Lily said immediately. "It has to be."

"Of course it's a trap." Aaron's voice was flat, analytical. "The question is whether the trap is worth walking into."

"How can any trap be worth—"

"Because refusing also springs a trap." Makelo spoke for the first time, her ancient eyes heavy with knowledge that predated most civilizations. "I have seen this pattern before. The Arena challenge is not merely tactical. It is cosmic. Refusal carries weight that mortals, even Scions, rarely understand."

"Explain," Alexis said.

"The Chaos Arena exists outside normal space and time. It is neutral ground, yes, but it is also sacred ground. A place where disputes between powers can be resolved without destroying the world in the process." Makelo's form flickered, as it sometimes did when she spoke of things she'd witnessed in ages past. "To refuse a challenge there is to admit that your cause lacks legitimacy. That you do not believe in it strongly enough to defend it."

"That's insane," Lily protested. "We can believe in what we're doing without throwing Al into a death match with the son of Hades."

"Can you?" Makelo's gaze was uncomfortably direct. "Cosmic law cares nothing for intention or practicality. It sees only action. If Alexis refuses this challenge, every divine being watching, and many are watching, will take it as proof that Scions cannot defend their own existence. That they are, as Kieran claims, aberrations who lack the will to survive."

The silence that followed was heavy with implications.

"Then I accept," Alexis said quietly.

"No." Keats's voice cracked on the word. "Al, you don't understand what I'm seeing. The futures. They're branching in ways I've never experienced before. Some of them are dark. Very dark."

"Tell me."

He hesitated, his oracle sight flickering gold and then fading to something closer to amber. "I can't see clearly. Something is interfering. The same thing that's been blocking my visions for weeks. But what I can see..." He swallowed hard. "Kieran is powerful, Al. More powerful than we realized. His shadow manipulation might be as strong as your night powers. Maybe stronger. He's had years to master his abilities. You've had months."

"You think I'll lose."

"I think some versions of you lose. I think some versions of you—" He stopped, unable to finish.

"Die," Alexis completed for him. "Some versions of me die."

The word hung in the air like smoke.

"But not all versions," she continued. "Some versions of me win. Some versions of me end this."

"How can you be so calm about this?"

Alexis looked at him. Really looked, seeing past the fear and the flickering oracle sight to the boy who'd been her best friend since childhood. The man who'd stood beside her through impossible revelations and devastating losses. The partner who'd helped her understand that she wasn't alone, even when everything in her screamed that she had to carry this weight by herself.

"Because I'm not being calm," she said softly. "I'm terrified. But I'm also seeing something you might be missing."

"Which is?"

"He issued this challenge because he needs us out of the way. Not because he thinks he'll definitely win. Because he knows that without a binding ruling, we'll stop him. The Trident, Keats. That's what this is about. He can't take it while we're protecting it. So he's gambling everything on a single fight."

"And if you lose, we all lose," Lily said. "Every Scion, bound by cosmic law to stand aside. Do you understand what that means?"

"I understand exactly what it means." Alexis straightened, feeling something settle into place inside her chest. "It means this is important enough to risk everything. It means he's scared of us. Scared of what we can do if we're not bound by his terms. It means that for all his power and his philosophy and his access to spaces between, he still needs us neutralized before he can finish his work."

She looked around the room, meeting each gaze in turn. Aaron, who'd fought beside her since the beginning. Makelo, ancient and weary but willing to stand with them. Lily, fierce and loyal despite every reason to walk away. Keats, terrified for her but unable to stop her from being who she was.

And in the shadows, Cerval and Ellie, the newer members who'd joined their cause. Who believed in what the Network represented.

All of them watching her. All of them waiting.

"If I refuse," she said, "we lose anyway. Slowly, maybe. Piece by piece as he takes more artifacts and severs more connections. But we lose. At least this way, we have a chance."

"A chance isn't a guarantee," Keats said.

"No. It isn't." She reached across the table and took his hand, feeling the warmth of his skin against hers. "But it's more than we'll have if I say no. And there's something else."

"What?"

"He stated his terms. If he wins, we all stand aside." She smiled, and it was sharp enough to cut. "But I get to state my terms too. And I have some ideas about what to demand if I win."

* * * *

The shade returned at dawn, exactly as promised.

Alexis met it in the main chamber, alone. The others had argued about that. Keats especially had wanted to stand beside her, to show a united front. But this was her moment. Her choice. Her role in whatever was coming.

"Daughter of Night," the shade intoned. "You have considered my master's offer."

"I have."

"And your answer?"

Alexis looked at the creature. This echo of something that had once been human, reduced now to function and purpose. She wondered if it remembered what it had been. If it cared about the outcome of the challenge it carried, or if such concerns were beyond its diminished existence.

"I accept," she said. "But I have terms of my own."

The shade's form rippled with what might have been interest. "State them."

"If I win, Kieran ceases all artifact thefts immediately. He returns what he has stolen. Everything that he has taken, returned to its rightful place. And he submits himself to divine judgment for his actions against the Scion Network and the divine-mortal connection."

The shade was silent for a long moment. Then: "My master accepts your terms."

A flicker at the edge of Alexis's awareness. A wrongness in the response, too quick, too easy. But she couldn't grasp what it meant, and the shade was already continuing.

"The challenge will take place in three days' time. You may bring witnesses but no champions to fight in your stead. Only you and Kieran may enter the Arena itself. The outcome will be binding upon all parties, enforced by cosmic law, irrevocable and permanent."

"I understand."

"Then it is done." The shade extended one blurred hand, and the scroll that had been sitting on the console rose to meet it. The text shifted, new words appearing in that ancient, eye-hurting script. Her terms, recorded for eternity. "May your conviction prove stronger than my master's, Daughter of Night. May your love for those you protect carry you through the darkness."

It was an oddly gentle blessing from a messenger of the dead.

"Tell Kieran something for me," Alexis said as the shade began to fade.

"Speak."

"Tell him I'm not fighting for ideology. I'm not fighting for some abstract principle about what Scions represent or whether divine-mortal connections deserve to exist." She felt power stir beneath her skin, primordial darkness responding to the conviction in her heart. "I'm fighting for the people I love. For everyone who's counting on me to stand between them and whatever he's become. And that's a motivation he should be very worried about."

The shade paused in its dissolution, its not-face turning toward her one final time.

"I will deliver your message, Daughter of Night. I suspect my master will find it... illuminating."

Then it was gone, and Alexis was alone with the weight of what she'd agreed to.

Three days. Three days until she faced the son of Hades in combat that would determine the fate of everyone she'd sworn to protect. Three days to prepare for a fight that some versions of her didn't survive.

She turned to find Keats standing in the doorway, his face a mask of carefully controlled emotion.

"It's done," she said.

"I know." He crossed to her, took her hands in his. "I felt it. The visions shifted the moment you accepted. Some of the dark futures... they're still there. But others opened up too. Possibilities that didn't exist before."

"Good possibilities?"

"I can't tell yet. Something's still blocking me from seeing clearly. But Al..." He pulled her closer, resting his forehead against hers. "Whatever happens in that Arena, you need to remember something."

"What?"

"You're not alone. I know you can't take me in there with you. I know this is your fight. But you're carrying all of us with you. Everyone who believes in what we're building, everyone who's counting on you. That's not weight. That's strength."

She kissed him then, soft and desperate and full of everything she couldn't find words to say. When they finally broke apart, she managed a smile that felt almost real.

"Three days," she said. "Let's make them count."

Behind them, through the windows of the command center, dawn was breaking over the White Mountains. Light spilled across the peaks in shades of gold and rose, pushing back the darkness that had held dominion through the night.

But Alexis knew better than to see it as a metaphor. The real darkness was still out there, waiting. Watching. Preparing for a confrontation that would determine the shape of worlds to come.

She had accepted her role.

Now she had to become worthy of it.

16

"Nothing." Aaron's voice carried a frustration that Alexis had rarely heard from him. "Abso-fucking-lutely nothing."

The war room had transformed into something closer to an investigation center. Every screen displayed search results, database queries, network intercepts. The accumulated intelligence of six years of Scion tracking, and all of it had come up empty.

"That's not possible," Lily said. "We have files on every known Scion. Every suspected Scion. Every rumored Scion going back three generations. How can the son of Hades not exist?"

"He exists," Alexis replied quietly. "We felt him. The shade named him. Kieran, son of Hades, Lord of the Spaces Between." She let the words settle into the room. "He's real. Which means someone went to extraordinary lengths to keep him hidden."

Keats pulled up another database, his fingers moving across the keyboard with barely contained agitation. "I've cross-referenced every Underworld contact we have. Every oracle who's ever mentioned Hades. Every historical record of children born to the Big Three." He shook his head. "Zeus's offspring? Documented. Dozens of them across millennia. Poseidon's? At least a dozen confirmed. But Hades…"

"Hades doesn't father children," Makelo said. The ancient Telchine had been watching their search in silence, her form flickering at the edges like a candle in wind. "That has been the understanding for as long as gods have walked among mortals. He takes his marriage vows seriously. Persephone is… possessive."

"And yet." Alexis gestured at the shade's challenge, still sitting on the central console like an accusation. "Kieran exists. He's powerful enough to orchestrate a systematic theft of divine artifacts. He has access to abilities that let him breach spaces no Scion should be able to breach. And we have no idea who he is, where he came from, or how he's been operating right under our noses for what must have been years."

The silence that followed felt heavy with implications none of them wanted to voice.

"Someone's been protecting him," Aaron said finally. "Not just hiding him. Actively erasing his existence from every record we might access. That takes resources. Influence. The kind of power that goes beyond what any Scion should have."

"His father?" Lily suggested.

"Maybe. Or maybe…" Keats trailed off, his oracle sight flickering gold for a moment before fading to something dimmer. "I keep trying to see him. Every time I reach for a vision of who Kieran is, where he came from, what made him this way, I hit static. The same interference that's been blocking me for weeks." His jaw tightened. "Whatever's hiding him, it's the same thing that's been hiding everything else."

Alexis absorbed that information, filing it away with everything else they didn't understand. Another mystery layered on top of mysteries. Another shadow in a world that suddenly seemed full of them.

"Then we go in blind," she said. "We don't know his history. We don't know his training. We don't know what shaped his philosophy or what drives him beyond what he's chosen to tell us." She met each of their gazes in turn. "But we know he's powerful enough to challenge me directly. We know he believes strongly enough in his cause to stake everything on a single fight. And we know that he's scared enough of what we represent to want us neutralized before he makes his final move."

"That's not exactly comforting," Lily muttered.

"It's not meant to be comforting. It's meant to be honest." Alexis turned to Makelo. "You've seen Arena combat before. Tell us what I'm walking into."

* * * *

Makelo's briefing was the opposite of comforting.

"The Chaos Arena is not a battlefield," she began, her ancient voice carrying weight that made the air itself seem to thicken. "It is a crucible. A place where cosmic disputes are resolved through trial, where the outcome is determined not just by strength or skill, but by the truth of what each champion represents."

"That sounds almost philosophical," Keats said.

"Philosophy will not save her." Makelo's gaze fixed on Alexis with uncomfortable intensity. "The Arena exists outside normal space-time, carved from the raw fabric of Chaos itself. Physical laws function differently there. Powers that work predictably in the mortal realm may behave... unexpectedly. The Arena responds to conviction as much as capability."

"What does that mean practically?" Alexis asked.

"It means that doubt will kill you faster than any blade. It means that hesitation creates openings that cannot be closed. It means that whoever believes more strongly in their cause, whoever fights with more absolute conviction, has an advantage that transcends mere power." Makelo's form flickered again, and for a moment Alexis could see through her to the wall beyond. "I have witnessed Arena combat three times in my existence. Each time, the outcome surprised those who thought they could predict it based on relative strength alone."

"Has anyone ever died in the Arena?" Lily's voice was carefully controlled, but Alexis could hear the fear beneath it.

"Death is always possible. The Arena does not prevent lethal force. It ensures that whatever outcome occurs is binding upon all parties." Makelo paused. "But death is not the only way to lose. Surrender. Incapacitation. Loss of will to continue. All are valid conclusions. The Arena cares only that the dispute is resolved with finality."

"So I need to beat him without necessarily killing him."

"You need to defeat him in a way that leaves no room for dispute. Whatever victory looks like, death, surrender, or something else, it must be absolute." Makelo's expression grew troubled. "There is another thing you should understand about the Arena."

"Of course there is," Keats muttered.

"The Arena belongs to Chaos. It exists within his domain, shaped by his will, governed by his rules, such as they are." Makelo's voice dropped lower. "Chaos does not intervene in Arena combat. He observes. He witnesses. But his attention alone can be... destabilizing. Things happen in his presence that would not happen elsewhere. Possibilities that should be closed become open. Certainties become fluid."

Alexis felt a chill that had nothing to do with temperature. She'd met Chaos. She'd made a bargain with him that still hung over her like a blade waiting to fall. The thought of fighting for her life in his domain, under his gaze, with the weight of his attention pressing against reality itself...

"I can handle Chaos," she said, and hoped it was true.

"Can you?" Makelo's question wasn't accusatory. Curious. "You have met him, yes? You have walked in his realm and emerged intact. That alone speaks to something unusual in your nature. But meeting Chaos and performing under his scrutiny are different things. He finds certain outcomes... interesting. If he decides your combat is interesting, his attention may shape events in ways neither you nor Kieran anticipate."

The weight of the boon pressed against Alexis's consciousness. That undefined favor she'd promised in exchange for her escape from his realm. She hadn't told anyone about it. Not Keats. Not Lily. The secret sat in her chest like a stone, growing heavier with each day that passed.

"What else do I need to know?"

"Your witnesses can watch but not interfere. They will occupy adjacent space. Close enough to observe, too far to affect the outcome. If you fall, they cannot catch you. If you cry out, they cannot answer." Makelo's gaze softened. "This is by design. Arena combat tests the champion, not their allies. Whatever strength you carry into that space must come from within."

"But she'll know we're there," Keats said firmly. "She'll be able to see us. Hear us. That has to count for something."

"It counts for everything," Makelo agreed. "The Arena tests conviction. And conviction is often born from love."

* * * *

Later, when the briefings were done and the war room had emptied, Keats found a quiet corner and tried to see the future.

His oracle sight came reluctantly, flickering gold behind his eyes like a flame fighting against wind. He reached for the thread of tomorrow, the moment when Alexis would step into the Arena and face whatever Kieran had become, and felt reality shatter into fragments.

Not one future. Dozens. Hundreds. Branching and splitting and colliding in ways that made his head throb with pressure that bordered on pain.

He saw Alexis victorious, standing over Kieran's broken form while divine witnesses looked on in shock. He saw her falling, shadows consuming her light as Kieran's power proved too strong. He saw outcomes that made no sense. Both of them standing, both of them fallen, the Arena itself cracking under forces that shouldn't exist.

And threaded through all of it, that same interference. That ancient presence hiding at the edge of his sight, blocking the paths he needed to see, obscuring the truths he needed to understand.

"Keats?"

He opened his eyes to find Alexis watching him, her expression caught between concern and understanding. She'd seen him like this before. Lost in visions that refused to clarify, fighting against something that didn't want to be seen.

"The futures are shifting," he said. "More than they should be. Oracle visions are supposed to show probability. The most likely outcomes based on current trajectories. What I'm seeing is…" He struggled for the right word. "Chaos. Not the entity. The concept. Every time I try to fix on a single thread, it splits into dozens of others."

"What does that mean?"

"I don't know. Maybe the Arena itself disrupts normal prophecy. Maybe Chaos's presence makes the future more malleable than it should be." He hesitated. "Or maybe fate itself is being manipulated. By whatever's been blocking my visions. By whatever's been hiding Kieran from every record we have."

Alexis sat beside him, close enough that their shoulders touched. "Can you see any outcomes where I win?"

"Yes. Some of them are clear. Strong, even." He turned to look at her, and the gold in his eyes faded to something warmer. "But I can also see outcomes where you don't. Where the fight goes wrong in ways I can't predict or prevent."

"That's not exactly a pep talk."

"You don't need a pep talk. You need the truth." He took her hand, interlacing their fingers the way they'd done since they were children. "Something is interfering with fate itself. Not blocking my visions. Actively changing the probability of different outcomes. I don't know what it is or why it's happening. But you need to go into that Arena knowing that the rules might not work the way anyone expects them to."

"Including me."

"Including you. Including Kieran. Including Chaos himself." Keats squeezed her hand. "Whatever happens tomorrow, don't assume anything. Don't trust that your power will work the way it always has. Don't trust that his will either. Stay adaptive. Stay present. And remember..."

"Remember what?"

"That I'll be watching. That Lily will be watching. That everyone who believes in what you're fighting for will be with you in that space, even if we can't touch you." His voice roughened. "You're not alone, Al. You've never been alone. And tomorrow, when you step into that Arena, you're carrying all of us with you."

* * * *

The compound settled into a strange quietude as evening fell. Not peaceful. There was too much tension for peace. But closer to held breath. The calm before a storm that everyone could feel approaching.

Alexis found herself walking the corridors, observing the small moments that might be the last normal moments any of them experienced. Aaron hunched over his workstation, still searching for any scrap of information about Kieran, his dedication bordering on obsession. Cerval hovering near the server room, offering technical assistance that Aaron accepted with distracted gratitude. Makelo standing at a window, her ancient eyes fixed on darkness that held memories no one else could share.

And Ellie, moving between the wounded Scions who'd been brought in over the past weeks. Casualties of artifact thefts and divine power fluctuations that had left some of them damaged in ways conventional medicine couldn't address. The young woman's compassion was genuine, her care meticulous. She'd become a fixture in the medical wing, always ready with a kind word or a gentle touch when someone needed comfort.

"She's good at that," Lily said, appearing at Alexis's shoulder with her usual silent grace. "The caring thing. I think she means it."

"Most people do."

"Most people pretend to. Ellie…" Lily watched the other woman adjust a wounded Scion's blanket with unconscious tenderness. "I've been doing this long enough to recognize the real thing. Whatever else she is, she cares about people."

Alexis filed that observation away with everything else she was carrying. The intel gaps, the shifting futures, the weight of a fight she might not survive. "Are you ready for tomorrow?"

"I should be asking you that." Lily's voice carried fear, carefully masked behind her usual sharpness. "You're the one walking into a cosmic death match against the invisible son of the death god."

"I'm as ready as I'm going to be."

"That's not an answer."

"It's the only one I have." Alexis turned to face her friend. This woman who'd tested her with an arrow and become one of the most important people in her life. "Whatever happens tomorrow, I need you to promise me something."

"That depends on what it is."

"If I lose. If Kieran's terms become binding and all of you have to stand down. Don't give up. Find another way. The Arena's ruling might neutralize direct opposition, but there are always loopholes. Always angles that cosmic law doesn't anticipate." She gripped Lily's shoulder. "Promise me you'll keep fighting, even if it has to look different."

Lily's expression flickered through several emotions before settling on fierce determination. "I promise. But you're not going to lose."

"You can't know that."

"I know you." Lily's voice carried the absolute certainty that Alexis had come to rely on. "I know what you're capable of when you stop trying to carry everything alone. I know what you fight for and why. And I know that Kieran, whoever he is, whatever he's become, has never faced anyone like you." She smiled, and it was sharp enough to cut. "Give him hell, Al. Give him hell and come back to us."

* * * *

The final night came with the weight of everything unsaid.

Alexis and Keats found themselves in her quarters, the door closed against a world that would demand their attention again soon enough. For these few hours, nothing existed beyond the two of them. Their history, their present, and a future that remained stubbornly uncertain despite every attempt to see it clearly.

"I should be sleeping," Alexis said, though neither of them made any move toward rest. "Building strength for tomorrow. Instead I'm…"

"You're being human." Keats pulled her closer, his warmth a counterpoint to the cold dread that had been building in her chest all day. "Being scared. Being present. Being honest about what this means."

"What does it mean?"

"It means tomorrow might be different. Might be the last. Might be the beginning of something none of us can predict." His voice dropped to something barely above a whisper. "It means I might watch you walk into that Arena and never walk out again."

"Keats—"

"I'm not saying it to scare you. I'm saying it because we need to be honest about what's at stake." He pulled back enough to meet her eyes, and she saw the raw fear he'd been hiding all day. The terror of losing her that he'd buried beneath practical concerns and oracle attempts and strategic analysis. "I love you, Al. I've loved you since before either of us knew what love meant. And the thought of a world without you in it…"

She kissed him then, cutting off words that neither of them could bear to finish. The kiss was everything. Desperate and tender, fierce and gentle, carrying all the things they couldn't say aloud. All the futures they wanted to build together. All the memories they'd already made and the ones they might never have the chance to create.

"I'm coming back," she said when they finally broke apart. "I don't care what Makelo says about the Arena. I don't care what your visions show. I'm not leaving you. I'm not leaving any of this. I'm going to walk into that cosmic death match and I'm going to win because the alternative is unacceptable."

"Is that your strategy? Refusing to lose?"

"It's the only strategy that matters." She pressed her forehead to his, breathing in his presence like air. "Kieran fights for philosophy. For some abstract principle about what divine-mortal connections mean. I fight for you. For Lily. For Aaron and Makelo and everyone else who's counting on me. That's not equivalent. That's not even close."

"You believe that."

"I have to believe it. And tomorrow, in the Arena, I'm going to prove it." She smiled, and it felt almost natural. "Now shut up and hold me. We have a few hours before dawn, and I want to spend them remembering what I'm fighting for."

They didn't sleep. They held each other through the darkest hours of the night, speaking sometimes in whispers and sometimes in silence, finding comfort in presence when words ran out. Outside, the compound continued its quiet preparations. People moving, systems checking, everything building toward a dawn that would change things irrevocably.

But here, in this room, there was only Alexis and Keats. History and hope. Love that had survived revelations and betrayals and the discovery of divine heritage that should have changed everything.

It hadn't changed anything. Not the parts that mattered.

And tomorrow, Alexis would carry that truth into battle against a son of Hades who had never known anything like it.

* * * *

Dawn came too soon and too slowly at the same time.

Alexis stood at the compound's main entrance as gray light spilled across the White Mountains, painting the peaks in shades of rose and gold that felt like a promise she couldn't trust. Behind her, the entire Network had gathered. Not just the core team, but everyone who could stand, everyone who understood what was about to happen.

No one spoke. Words felt inadequate for a moment like this.

She'd dressed simply. Combat clothes that wouldn't restrict her movement, nothing ceremonial or symbolic. The Arena didn't care about appearances. It cared about truth. And the truth was that she was a daughter of night walking into judgment against the son of death, with everything she loved hanging in the balance.

Keats stood at her right shoulder. Lily at her left. The positions they'd held through every battle since this began. Her anchors, her constants, the people who would watch her fight and be unable to help no matter what happened.

"It's time," she said.

The ether welcomed her as it always did. That space between spaces that answered to her mother's blood and her grandfather's domain. But this time, instead of stepping through to a destination in the mortal world, she reached deeper. Toward something older. Toward a place that existed in the cracks between reality and unreality, where Chaos himself held court over the chaos of existence.

The transition felt different from any she'd experienced before. Not the familiar slide from one place to another, but more like falling. Or rising. Through layers of reality that thinned and shifted around her. Keats's hand found hers. Lily's presence pressed close on her other side. Together, they fell through the fabric of existence toward a place that had witnessed conflicts between powers since before the gods had names.

The Chaos Arena opened before them like a wound in the world.

And waiting in its center, shadows gathered around him like a cloak, stood Kieran.

The son of Hades who didn't exist in any record. The architect of severance. The champion of a philosophy that would remake the cosmos if given the chance.

He smiled when he saw her, and it was not the smile of a villain. It was the smile of a believer who knew, absolutely and completely, that he was about to change everything.

"Daughter of Night," he said, and his voice echoed across spaces that shouldn't exist. "Welcome to your judgment."

Alexis released Keats's hand. Stepped forward. Left everything she loved behind and walked toward a battle that would determine the fate of worlds.

"No," she said, and her voice carried the conviction of everyone she was fighting for. "Welcome to yours."

17

The Chaos Arena was nothing like Alexis had imagined.

She'd expected something like the Colosseum. Ancient stone, tiered seating, the weight of history pressed into every surface. What opened before her was closer to a wound in reality itself. The space stretched in directions that hurt to contemplate, vast and intimate simultaneously, its boundaries shifting at the edges of perception like a dream refusing to solidify.

The ground beneath her feet was solid. Dark stone shot through with veins of faint luminescence. But beyond the central platform, reality stopped. Not darkness. Not light. An absence that her eyes refused to process, sliding away from it the way water slides off glass.

The wrongness of it scraped against something fundamental in her brain. Some ancient survival instinct insisting that spaces should have walls, that up and down were concepts that *meant* something. Here, they were suggestions the Arena entertained only when it felt generous.

She breathed, and the air tasted of moments rather than molecules. Each inhale carried impressions that had no business being breathable: the memory of stars that had burned out before Earth existed, the echo of decisions that had shaped civilizations, the weight of every combat that had ever been decided in this impossible place.

Her lungs processed it all, converting cosmic significance into the simple chemistry her body required to function.

The stone beneath her feet hummed with attention. Not sentience, exactly. Nothing so pedestrian as awareness. But something older. Recognition. The Arena knew she was here. It had known she would come to this place, to this moment, since before she'd been born. Maybe since before her mother had descended from her realm to fall in love with a mortal man.

You're being watched, her instincts screamed. *By something that doesn't have eyes.*

Temperature existed here only as a concept. She felt neither cold nor hot, but somehow both. Her skin registering sensations that contradicted each other with cheerful disregard for physics. The air moved without wind, stirring her hair in patterns that followed no natural current. Light came from everywhere and nowhere, casting shadows that fell in directions that shouldn't exist.

"Holy shit," Lily breathed somewhere behind her.

The words felt inadequate, but Alexis understood the sentiment. This place existed outside the rules that governed normal existence. The air tasted of ozone and something older, something that predated the concept of air itself. Every breath felt borrowed from a universe that hadn't decided whether to allow her presence.

Alexis had thought she understood what it meant to touch the supernatural. She'd wielded primordial darkness, felt her mother's cosmic presence, even traded words with Chaos himself in the depths of his realm. None of it had prepared her for this. A place that existed specifically to witness the resolution of disputes between powers that shaped reality itself.

The Arena was judging her already. She could feel its assessment pressing against her consciousness like fingers testing the ripeness of fruit.

And they weren't alone.

The witnesses had already gathered.

* * * *

Alexis had seen gods before. She'd faced Phthonos in combat, met her mother in moments of cosmic intervention, even exchanged words with Zeus himself. But nothing had prepared her for this. The assembled might of Olympus, gathered in one impossible space to witness her fight for the right to exist.

They occupied positions around the Arena's perimeter, arranged on platforms that seemed to materialize from the void itself. Not sitting. Gods didn't sit for entertainment like mortals at a sporting event. They stood, or floated, or existed in ways that human language couldn't adequately describe.

Zeus dominated the central viewing position, his presence a storm barely contained in humanoid form. Lightning flickered in his eyes, and the air around him crackled with authority that made Alexis's divine blood sing in recognition. He watched her approach with an expression she couldn't read. Curiosity, perhaps, or evaluation.

Beside him, Hades was a study in controlled stillness. Where Zeus radiated power like a sun, Hades absorbed it like a void. His pale features revealed nothing, but his eyes tracked his son's form across the Arena with an intensity that spoke of things left unsaid between them.

Poseidon stood apart from his brothers, ocean-deep eyes carrying the weight of trenches that had never seen light. His presence made the air taste of salt and ancient things that lived where pressure crushed everything but will.

The Big Three, gathered in one place. The last time that had happened, according to the research she'd done, had been the dissolution of the Olympian Council three thousand years ago. The event that had shattered divine-mortal relations and sent gods retreating to their separate realms. Whatever was about to happen here, the cosmos was paying attention.

Alexis felt the cosmic significance of it pressing against her consciousness like a physical weight.

But they weren't the only witnesses.

Apollo blazed with contained radiance, his attention fixed on the Arena floor with the intensity of prophecy seeking fulfillment. Alexis caught the moment his gaze found Keats. Father and son, separated by divine law and cosmic circumstance, sharing a look that carried everything words couldn't express.

Hermes shifted restlessly, his form flickering between positions faster than mortal eyes could track. His daughter's speed was a pale echo of his nature, and watching him move made Alexis understand how much Lily held back in normal combat.

Athena observed with the cool assessment of strategy incarnate. Ares radiated barely contained violence, eager for bloodshed regardless of who provided it. Artemis stood with bow half-drawn, as if expecting the combat to spill beyond its designated boundaries.

Demeter stood apart from the war-touched gods, her presence a quiet rebuke to the violence about to unfold. Wheat-gold hair cascaded over shoulders draped in robes that shifted through every shade of growing things. She watched Alexis with eyes that held the patience of seasons. Neither approving nor condemning, waiting to see what would be harvested from the seeds being planted.

Near her, Dionysus lounged with deliberate irreverence, a goblet materializing in his hand only to dissolve and reform with each gesture. His smile carried the madness that lurked at the edges of ecstasy, and when his gaze met Alexis's, she glimpsed parties that had lasted centuries and revels that had driven mortals to beautiful, terrible things. He raised his shifting goblet in what might have been a toast or a warning.

Hephaestus had claimed a position that let him study the Arena's architecture rather than its occupants. The forge-god's attention traced the seams where reality met impossibility, his craftsman's eye cataloguing construction techniques that predated the Titans. Scars from eternal labor marked skin that glowed with banked heat, and Alexis remembered that her friend Makelo had learned his art from this god's example.

Aphrodite's presence was a wound in the air, beauty so concentrated it hurt to perceive directly. Alexis forced herself to look anyway, and found the goddess watching her with an expression that held neither the cruelty nor the frivolity mortals attributed to love's patron. Instead, there was something almost clinical. An assessment of the heart about to be tested.

She knows, Alexis realized with sudden certainty. *She knows this fight isn't about power or philosophy. She knows it's about love.*

Hera stood beside her husband like a storm waiting for permission to break. The Queen of Olympus radiated displeasure that had nothing to do with Alexis personally. This was the expression she wore when forced to witness contests that reminded everyone the gods had once been capable of producing half-mortal children. Her presence was a reminder that some wounds never fully healed, even across millennia.

And others. Gods Alexis recognized from research and some she didn't, minor deities and major powers all gathered to witness this moment when a half-mortal daughter of Nyx would face the hidden son of Hades for the right to determine the future of divine-mortal connection.

"I've never seen anything like this," Keats whispered. His oracle sight blazed gold, overwhelmed by the concentrated divine presence. "They're all here. Every major Olympian. This isn't protocol. This is history."

His voice cracked on the last word, and Alexis saw him press a hand to his temple in the gesture she'd learned meant his oracle sight was overwhelming him. Gold flickered in his eyes. Not the steady glow of controlled vision, but the strobing pulse of information he couldn't process fast enough.

"I can see—" He stopped, swallowed hard. "Futures. Hundreds of them. Branching from this moment like—" Another pause, his jaw tightening with the effort of containing what his gift was showing him. "Most of them end badly, Al. Most of them end with you—"

"Don't." She reached back without looking, found his hand, squeezed once. "Don't tell me how I die. Tell me how I win."

The gold in his eyes flared, then steadied. When he spoke again, his voice carried the resonance she'd learned meant prophecy rather than observation. "I can't see it clearly. Something's blocking the paths where you survive. Not darkness. Not like before. More like... conviction. Like the outcome depends on something that hasn't been decided yet."

"The Arena," Lily breathed, understanding dawning in her expression. "It's not a place for combat. It's a place for *choice*. The future can't be seen because it's being written in real-time."

"Theater," she added, but her voice carried awe despite herself. "They want everyone to know the outcome is legitimate. Witnessed by the powers that shaped the world."

Keats nodded slowly, some of the strain leaving his features as his gift settled into a less overwhelming rhythm. "Chaos Arena," he murmured. "I finally understand the name. It's not random. It's *undetermined*. The most powerful oracle in history couldn't predict what happens here, because what happens here creates the future instead of being created by it."

Alexis filed that information away with everything else she'd deal with later. Assuming later was something she got to experience.

Her attention had been captured by something else. Someone else. Standing apart from the Olympian gathering in a way that made the other gods' separation look like intimate closeness.

Chaos.

* * * *

He didn't occupy a platform. He didn't stand or float or exist in any way the other witnesses did. He was. A presence at the edge of everything, simultaneously there and not-there, watching with attention that preceded the concept of observation itself.

Alexis had met him before, in the depths of his realm when she'd been trapped and desperate. She remembered his voice like wind through places that had never known atmosphere. Remembered the deal she'd made. The boon she'd promised. That hung over her like a blade waiting for the moment he found it interesting to let it fall.

He noticed her looking. Of course he did. Chaos noticed everything that happened in spaces he'd shaped from his own nature.

And he smiled.

It wasn't a human expression. Couldn't be, from a being that had existed before humanity was a possibility in the cosmic order. But there was something in it that felt almost warm. Recognition. Anticipation.

Fondness.

Alexis saw Zeus notice the exchange. Saw the King of Gods stiffen almost imperceptibly, his lightning-touched gaze sharpening with sudden concern. He leaned toward Hades, murmured something too quiet for mortal ears to catch.

Whatever he'd said, Hades's response was a slight widening of his eyes. The only crack in his controlled facade.

They knew. Or suspected. Something about the way Chaos looked at her told them that the daughter of Nyx had become entangled with forces even gods approached with caution.

Alexis filed that concern away with everything else she'd deal with later, assuming there was a later, and turned to face her opponent.

* * * *

Kieran waited at the Arena's center, shadows pooling around his feet like loyal hounds awaiting command.

In the light of the divine assembly, such as light existed in this place, she could finally see him clearly. He was younger than she'd expected. Maybe mid-twenties, with features that spoke of Mediterranean heritage refined by something otherworldly. Dark hair fell across a face that might have been handsome if not for the cold certainty in his eyes.

He was taller than she'd expected from the glimpses she'd caught before. Nearly six feet, with the lean build of someone who'd trained his body as a weapon rather than an aesthetic choice. Shadows clung to him like a second skin, pooling in the hollows of his cheekbones and gathering in the folds of clothing that seemed woven from darkness itself.

But it was his stillness that unsettled her most. Alexis had faced plenty of dangerous opponents. Phthonos, the shade assassins, Greer in that final terrible confrontation. All of them had radiated threat through movement, through aggression, through the promise of violence about to be unleashed. Kieran radiated nothing. He existed, patient as a trap that had been set before she was born.

His eyes were his father's eyes, she realized. Hades's pale gaze, looking out from a face that bore no official record of its existence. Looking at her with the same flat assessment the Lord of the Dead had worn when they'd met. Cataloguing her strengths, her weaknesses, the precise moment when her existence would become irrelevant.

He's already decided I'm going to die here, she thought. *He's being polite about it.*

He looked at her with the patient confidence of someone who had already won and was waiting for reality to catch up.

"Daughter of Night," he said, and his voice carried across the impossible space without effort. "I'm glad you came."

"Did you think I wouldn't?"

"I thought you might let fear make your choice for you. Many would have." He spread his hands, shadows rippling outward from the gesture. "But you're here. Which means you believe strongly enough in your cause to stake everything on it. That deserves respect, even from an enemy."

"I'm not here because I believe in a cause." Alexis stepped forward, feeling the Arena respond to her presence. Stone warming beneath her feet, reality solidifying around her intent. "I'm here because you're threatening people I love. That's not philosophy. That's personal."

Surprise flickered in Kieran's expression. Or confusion. As if the concept of fighting for love rather than principle was foreign to his understanding. For one moment, she glimpsed the person behind the philosophy. Young, certain, and perhaps more fragile than his shadows suggested. Someone who needed to believe in his cause because the alternative was admitting he'd sacrificed everything for nothing.

"Personal." He tested the word like it was a new flavor. "Interesting. Most champions speak of duty and righteousness. Cosmic balance. The greater good." His smile carried an edge that made Alexis's instincts flare with warning. "You speak of love. We'll see if that's strong enough to save you."

"You think love is weakness." Alexis circled slowly, buying time while she assessed his stance, his positioning, the way shadows responded to his presence. "That caring about people makes you vulnerable."

"Doesn't it?" Kieran mirrored her movement, the two of them tracing an arc around the Arena's center like planets orbiting a point of mutual destruction. "Every person you love is a hostage fortune can take from you. Every connection is a crack in your armor. The Stoics understood this. The gods understood this, which is why they've spent millennia learning to care about nothing except their own power."

"The gods created Scions because they *did* care. They fell in love with mortals. They wanted children."

"They wanted amusements." His voice carried no heat. Only the flat certainty of someone stating mathematical fact. "Toys that would worship them. Weapons they could point at their enemies. Scions have never been about love, Daughter of Night. We've always been about utility. The difference between us is that I've accepted that truth, and you're still pretending otherwise."

Alexis felt the words land like blows, not because they were cruel, but because part of her had wondered the same things in her darkest moments. Had Nyx descended to the mortal realm out of love, or curiosity? Had the connection between divine and human ever been anything more than cosmic entertainment?

"You're wrong," she said, but the conviction she needed wasn't there. Not yet.

Kieran smiled, and it was almost kind. "Prove it."

He moved.

And Alexis learned what it meant to be outmatched.

* * * *

Kieran didn't attack like a Scion. He attacked like a force of nature.

Shadows erupted from the Arena floor in a wave of darkness that moved faster than her eyes could track. She barely had time to summon her own power, primordial night rising to meet primordial death, before the impact sent her skidding backward across stone that suddenly felt like ice.

Her night powers should have been equal to his shadows. Should have met his darkness with her own and found balance in the opposition. Instead, his attack cut through her defenses like they were suggestions rather than barriers.

Wrong, some part of her mind catalogued as she rolled away from a follow-up strike that would have taken her head. *His power feels wrong. Not stronger. Different. Like it's coming from somewhere else.*

She reached for that wrongness with her gift, forming the question before conscious thought could complete it: *What makes his shadows different from mine?*

The answer surfaced like something rising from deep water, and she didn't like what it told her.

His darkness wasn't drawn from Nyx's realm. From the primordial night that had existed before creation. His shadows tasted of endings. Of finality. Of the silence that followed the last heartbeat and the emptiness that filled the space where souls used to be.

Thanatos, she realized, rolling away from another strike that would have crushed her sternum. *He's not using Hades's power. He's channeling Death itself.*

That shouldn't have been possible. Thanatos was notoriously reluctant to share his dominion, even with full-blooded gods. For a half-mortal to access that kind of power—

The thought shattered as Kieran's next attack drove her backward, her defenses buckling under the weight of darkness that carried the cold of graves and the patience of inevitability. Every block cost her something. Every deflection left her fingers numb and her power trembling.

He's not fighting me, she understood with horrible clarity. *He's feeding on my power. Using it against me.*

She didn't have time to analyze the observation. Kieran was on her again, shadows forming into blades and tendrils and things with too many edges, pressing her back across the Arena floor in a retreat that felt increasingly desperate.

Every counter she attempted, he was already there. Every strategy she'd planned, he dismantled with casual efficiency. It was like fighting someone who knew her playbook. Who'd studied every move she might make and prepared perfect responses to each one.

"You're fast," Kieran observed, circling her with the patience of a predator who had cornered prey. "Faster than I expected. But speed isn't enough, Daughter of Night. Not against someone who's spent years preparing for exactly this kind of confrontation."

"Years." She circled opposite him, buying time to catch her breath while her mind raced through options that were rapidly dwindling. "How many years, exactly? How long have you been hiding from everyone who might have warned us about you?"

"Long enough to perfect my technique." He struck again. A casual gesture that sent a spike of shadow screaming toward her heart.

She twisted aside, felt the attack carve a line of fire across her ribs that told her she hadn't moved fast enough. Blood... her blood... spattered the Arena stones.

From the witness platforms, she heard Lily cry out. Keats's voice joined hers, calling her name with desperate urgency. But they couldn't help. They could only watch as she bled on sacred ground, outmatched by an opponent who'd been engineered to destroy her.

Engineered. The word surfaced in her mind with sudden clarity. Not trained. Engineered. By someone who knew exactly what she was capable of and had crafted the perfect counter.

The thought should have been terrifying. Instead, it sparked anger. Cold and hard and sharp as the blade that had cut her.

"Who made you?" she demanded, gathering her power for another assault. "Who spent years preparing you for a confrontation with me specifically?"

Kieran's smile flickered. "I made myself. I chose this path. I believe in what I'm doing."

"You believe in what someone taught you to believe." She attacked. Not with strategy this time, but with raw power, primordial night hammering against his shadows with force that made the Arena itself shudder. "Someone who knew exactly how to shape you into the weapon they needed."

For one instant, she saw doubt cross his features. Then his expression hardened, and his counterattack drove every thought from her mind except survival.

* * * *

The next several minutes were a blur of pain and desperation.

Alexis fought with everything she had. Every technique she'd learned, every power she'd awakened, every strategy she'd developed in her short time as a Scion. None of it was enough. Kieran met each effort with contemptuous ease, his shadows dancing around her attacks like they were playing a game only he understood the rules to.

Blood ran from a dozen wounds. Her left arm hung wrong where he'd twisted it in a clinch she'd barely escaped. Each breath brought fresh agony from ribs that might be cracked, might be broken, might be irrelevant if she didn't figure out how to turn this around.

She couldn't turn it around. The realization settled into her consciousness with the weight of cosmic certainty. She was losing. Not gradually, not dramatically. Losing, steadily and inevitably, to an opponent who'd been designed to destroy everything she was.

From her peripheral vision, she saw Keats pressing against the barrier that separated witnesses from combatants. His fists beat against nothing, his oracle sight blazing with desperate gold as he tried to find some future where this ended differently. Lily stood beside him, tears streaming down her face, shouting words that Alexis couldn't hear over the ringing in her ears.

They couldn't help her. They could only watch her die.

And the gods watched too. Impassive. Eternal. Witnessing judgment unfold as it had countless times before, in this place where disputes between powers were resolved with blood and conviction.

Only Chaos seemed different. His attention had sharpened somehow, his not-quite-presence leaning toward the combat with what might have been interest. As if the daughter he'd claimed as interesting had finally become interesting enough to warrant his full attention.

Kieran noticed her flagging. Noticed her defenses weakening, her attacks growing clumsy, her desperate gambles becoming predictable. He pressed his advantage with the methodical efficiency of someone completing a task rather than fighting a battle.

"This is mercy," he said, his voice carrying the same gentle sincerity she'd heard from the shade messenger. "What I'm doing, what you're trying to prevent, it's not cruelty. It's liberation. Divine-mortal connection corrupts both sides. Scions like us are proof of that corruption. Aberrations born from unions that should never have occurred."

He struck again, and she barely blocked. Her power faltering, her vision graying at the edges.

"When I've severed the last anchors, humanity will be free to evolve on its own terms. Gods will return to their proper realms. And beings like us…" His smile carried what might have been sadness.

"We'll fade. Gently. The last echoes of a mistake the cosmos is finally ready to correct."

His philosophy washed over her like cold water. He meant it. Every word. He genuinely believed he was doing the right thing. That destroying everything she was fighting to protect was an act of compassion rather than genocide.

And in that moment, wounded and bleeding and losing, Alexis found herself wondering if he was right.

Maybe Scions were aberrations. Maybe divine-mortal connection did corrupt everything it touched. Maybe the kindest thing would be to let it all fade away, to surrender to the severance he'd orchestrated, to accept that her existence was a mistake the universe was finally ready to undo.

The doubt crept through her like poison, weakening muscles that were already failing, dimming power that was already fading. She stumbled, went to one knee, felt the Arena stone cold against her palm as she tried to push herself back up.

Kieran loomed over her, shadows gathering for what would probably be the final blow.

"Surrender," he said, and the word carried genuine compassion. "End this with dignity. Accept that some battles aren't meant to be won."

Alexis looked up at him. At the son of Hades who'd been hidden and shaped and pointed at everything she loved like a weapon. At the true believer who couldn't imagine any truth beyond the one he'd been taught.

She thought of Keats, watching helplessly from the witness space. Of Lily, crying for a friend she couldn't save. Of everyone back at the compound who was counting on her to win this fight, to protect them from a future where they'd be forced to stand aside while everything they'd built was destroyed.

And she thought of the boon she'd promised to Chaos. The undefined favor that hung over her like a sword. The deal she'd made with a force that predated morality and probably didn't care about outcomes the way mortals understood caring.

He was still watching. Still interested. Still waiting to see what she would do when everything seemed lost.

"No," she said.

Kieran's shadows hesitated.

"I don't surrender." The words came from somewhere deeper than thought. From the part of her that had survived every loss, every revelation, every moment when the universe had tried to convince her that she didn't deserve to exist. "I don't accept that this battle isn't meant to be won. And I don't believe that love is weaker than philosophy."

She pushed herself to her feet. It hurt. God, it hurt. But pain was information, and she had more important things to focus on than the messages her body was screaming at her.

"You think you're offering mercy," she said, blood dripping from her wounds onto sacred stone. "But you've forgotten what mercy actually means. It's not deciding that other people don't deserve to exist. It's not choosing to erase everything that makes life complicated and messy and worth fighting for."

Kieran's expression shifted. The confident certainty flickered, replaced by something that looked almost like confusion.

"You're dying," he said. "Your power is failing. Your body is breaking. How can you possibly think you can still win?"

Alexis smiled, and it was sharp enough to cut.

"Because I'm not fighting alone."

18

Kieran didn't press his advantage.

That was the worst part. Alexis stood. Barely. Blood dripping from wounds she'd lost count of, power flickering like a candle in a storm, and he waited. Circling her with the patient confidence of someone who had already won and saw no need to rush the inevitable conclusion.

Her body catalogued the damage with merciless precision. Three ribs cracked, maybe four. Left shoulder dislocated from a throw she'd barely survived. A gash across her forearm that had exposed muscle. Burns where his death-touched shadows had kissed her skin, leaving marks that felt like frostbite and fire simultaneously. Each breath was an exercise in controlled agony, her lungs refusing to expand fully against the cage of broken bones surrounding them.

"You said something interesting," he observed, shadows pooling around his feet like obedient pets. "That you're not fighting alone. But look around you, Daughter of Night. Look at where you are."

She looked. She couldn't help it.

The Arena stretched around them in its impossible geometry. That wound in reality where cosmic disputes were resolved through blood and conviction. The divine witnesses watched from their platforms, impassive as statues, offering nothing but observation. Zeus with his lightning-touched eyes. Hades with his void-deep stillness. The assembled might of Olympus, gathered to witness judgment unfold.

And in the adjacent space, separated by barriers that couldn't be crossed, Keats and Lily. Helpless. Horrified. Watching her die by inches while the universe enforced the rules of sacred combat.

"They can't help you," Kieran said, following her gaze to her friends. "The Arena doesn't permit interference. Whatever strength you thought you'd draw from their presence, it's an illusion. In this place, you fight alone. You fail alone. You die alone."

"I'm not dead yet."

"No. Not yet." He tilted his head, studying her with an expression that carried something almost like respect. "You're stronger than I expected. More stubborn. Most opponents would have surrendered by now. Accepted the mercy of quick defeat rather than endure prolonged destruction."

"I don't surrender."

"So you've said. But stubbornness isn't the same as strength, and refusing to accept reality doesn't change it." He spread his hands, shadows rippling outward in a gesture that encompassed the Arena, the witnesses, the entire impossible situation. "You're losing, Alexis Rain. Not because I'm stronger, though I am, but because you're fighting for the wrong things."

The use of her full name caught her attention. Not "Daughter of Night." Not a title or a designation. Her name, spoken with something that sounded almost like familiarity.

"You don't know what I'm fighting for."

"Don't I?" His smile carried edges that cut. "You're fighting for connection. For the idea that divine and mortal can coexist, that beings like us represent something beautiful rather than something broken. You're fighting because you love people who would lose their powers if I succeed. Because you can't imagine a world where Scions don't exist."

He stepped closer, and she forced herself not to flinch despite every instinct screaming warnings.

"But have you ever asked yourself whether that world might be better?"

* * * *

The question landed like a blade between her ribs. Not physical this time, but somehow more painful for it.

"Better," she repeated. "You think destroying divine-mortal connection would make things better?"

"I think it would make things cleaner. Simpler. More honest." Kieran's voice carried the weight of absolute conviction. Not the desperate certainty of someone trying to convince themselves, but the calm assurance of someone who had thought through every angle and found their conclusion unassailable. "Consider what divine interference has given humanity. Wars fought in gods' names. Mortals manipulated as pawns in cosmic games. Children born between worlds, belonging fully to neither, carrying powers they never asked for and burdens they can't escape."

He began to pace, and even that simple movement carried the coiled potential of violence. His shadows moved with him, pooling and flowing like a tide responding to a moon only he could see.

"Do you know how many Scions have existed throughout history? Thousands. Tens of thousands. Heroes and monsters and everything in between. And do you know what they all have in common?" He paused, letting the question hang. "They all suffered. Every single one. Because that's what divine heritage gives you. Suffering dressed up as power, tragedy wearing the mask of destiny."

He gestured toward the divine witnesses. Toward Zeus and Poseidon and Hades and all the others who watched with ancient, unknowable eyes.

"Look at them, Alexis. Look. These beings who shaped your existence, who fathered and mothered and abandoned countless children across millennia. Do they look like they care about mortal suffering? Do they look like they've ever considered the cost of their interference in human affairs?"

She wanted to argue. Wanted to point out that her mother had protected her, that Apollo had risked everything to help Scions, that not all divine-mortal connections were corrupt. But her gaze found Hades, watching his son with that void-deep stillness, and she thought about Kieran. Hidden. Shaped. Pointed at everything she loved like a weapon.

What kind of father raised a child for this?

"Let me tell you about my childhood," Kieran said, as if reading her thoughts. "I was born knowing I was different. Knowing I was dangerous. My father visited me exactly seven times in twenty-three years. Once to confirm my existence, once to explain what I was, and five times to give me instructions. Not comfort. Not guidance. Instructions. Because that's what I was to him. Not a son. A tool. A solution to a problem he'd foreseen centuries before I was born."

His voice carried no self-pity, only the flat recitation of facts.

"I spent my childhood learning to hide. Learning to control powers that could kill with a touch. Learning to be invisible, because the alternative was being found. And being found meant being used. By my father. By his enemies. By anyone who understood what a child of Hades could do if properly motivated."

A crack appeared in his composed facade, quickly sealed.

"Do you know what it's like to grow up knowing your existence is a weapon? To understand, from the moment you're old enough to understand anything, that you weren't born from love? That you were created to serve a purpose. And that purpose involves destroying everything that makes life worth living?"

Alexis found she couldn't answer. Because she did know. Not the specifics of his experience, but the weight of carrying powers she'd never asked for. The burden of a heritage that came with expectations she'd never chosen.

"Gods don't love mortals," Kieran continued, his voice dropping to something almost gentle. "They use them. Collect them. Discard them when they become inconvenient. Even the ones who seem benevolent. They're operating on timescales we can't comprehend, with motivations we'll never fully understand. We're not their children. We're their experiments. Their entertainment. Their mistakes."

"That's not—"

"Not true?" He laughed, and the sound carried genuine amusement rather than mockery. "Tell me about your father, Alexis. Your mortal father. The one who raised you, loved you, died for you. Now tell me about Nyx. When did she hold you? When did she comfort you? When did she do anything except watch from cosmic distance while you stumbled through revelations that should have been explained to you from birth?"

The words hit targets she'd thought she'd armored. Charles Rain. Adoptive father, murdered by forces connected to divine politics. Elizabeth. Adoptive mother, killed in the crossfire of cosmic disputes. And Nyx, her biological mother, who had protected her in abstract ways but never once appeared to explain, to comfort, to be present.

She remembered the moment she'd learned what she was. The confusion. The terror. The desperate wish that someone, anyone, would appear to help her understand. And Nyx had been… absent. Watching from whatever realm primordial goddesses inhabited, offering nothing but silence.

"I'm not attacking you," Kieran said, watching her face with something that looked almost like sympathy. "I'm telling you the truth that no one else will speak. Divine-mortal connection isn't sacred. It's parasitic. Gods take from mortals. Attention, worship, genetic material. And give back nothing but complications and suffering."

"We have powers," Alexis managed, but the words came out weaker than she intended. "Abilities that—"

"That mark us as targets. That make us weapons in disputes we didn't choose. That ensure we'll never have normal lives, normal relationships, normal deaths." His shadows stirred around him, and she could feel the sincerity radiating from him like heat from a forge. "You think your powers are gifts? They're chains, Alexis. Beautiful chains, perhaps. Useful chains. But chains nonetheless, binding us to cosmic conflicts that have been raging since before humanity learned to walk upright."

* * * *

He attacked without warning.

The shadows came faster this time. A wave of darkness that moved like living hatred, seeking out every crack in her defenses with surgical precision. Alexis summoned her night powers to meet them, but her darkness felt weak against his. Diluted. Like comparing candlelight to a consuming void.

Their powers clashed in the center of the Arena, and the contact felt wrong in ways she couldn't articulate. Her shadows were cold. The cold of starless nights and empty spaces between worlds. His shadows were colder still. The cold of endings, of finality, of the absolute zero that waited at the end of all things.

She tried to hold the line, but his darkness devoured hers. Consumed it. Absorbed it into itself like a black hole swallowing light.

He's not fighting me, she realized as the impact drove her backward. *He's feeding on my power. Using it against me.*

The blow that followed caught her in the chest, lifting her off her feet and sending her crashing into the Arena floor. Stone cracked beneath her. Something else cracked inside her. Another rib, maybe, or something more fundamental.

She tried to rise, but his shadows wrapped around her legs, cold as graves, patient as death. They didn't squeeze. Didn't crush. They held, reminding her that she was beaten. That continuing to fight was prolonging the inevitable.

"The battle has paused," Kieran said, standing over her with shadows swirling around him like a cloak of triumph. "Not by agreement, but because I've stopped attacking and you can barely stand. This would be a good time to listen."

She wanted to attack. Wanted to summon everything she had and throw it at him in one desperate gamble. But her power flickered and guttered, and the shadows holding her legs tightened enough to remind her that struggling was pointless.

So she listened.

"You want to know what I'm fighting for?" Kieran asked. "Not cruelty. Not destruction. Not even victory, though I'll take it. I'm fighting for liberation. For a future where humans evolve on their own terms, without divine interference shaping their destiny. For a world where no child is ever born into the impossible position of being half one thing and half another, belonging fully to nothing."

"You're describing extinction," Alexis said, forcing the words past the pain in her chest. "Scions would cease to exist."

"Yes. Eventually. Gently." His voice carried no triumph, only quiet certainty. "The ones who exist now would live out their lives as their powers gradually faded. No new Scions would be born. Within a few generations, divine-mortal hybrids would be a memory. A strange chapter in human history, finally closed."

"And that doesn't bother you? Being one of the last? Knowing that everything you are would... end?"

"It comforts me." The admission carried weight that made her reassess everything she thought she'd understood about him. "I didn't ask for this existence, Alexis. I didn't choose to be born between worlds, to carry powers that make me a target for forces I barely understand. I was shaped into what I am by circumstances beyond my control. Like you. Like every Scion who ever lived."

He released the shadows holding her legs and stepped back, giving her room to rise if she could. It wasn't mercy. It was confidence. He knew she wasn't a threat anymore.

"The difference between us is that I've accepted the truth. Scions are aberrations. Beautiful, powerful, tragic aberrations. We exist because gods couldn't keep their hands off mortal affairs, couldn't resist meddling in human evolution, couldn't stop treating the world as their personal playground. And the kindest thing anyone can do is ensure that no more children are born into this impossible inheritance."

"By destroying the artifacts that anchor divine-mortal connection."

"By severing the link cleanly, permanently, compassionately. Yes." His shadows stirred, ready to resume the attack whenever he chose. "I'm not a monster, Alexis. I'm a surgeon. The connection between realms is diseased, and I'm cutting it out before the infection spreads further. The fact that it hurts doesn't make it wrong."

* * * *

She managed to push herself to her knees, but rising further was beyond her. The conversation continued from this position. Supplicant and conqueror, even if Kieran didn't seem to see it that way.

She wanted to argue. She needed to argue. Everything he was saying struck at the foundation of everything she'd been fighting for. The belief that Scions mattered, that divine-mortal connection was worth preserving, that her existence meant something beyond cosmic accident.

But the words wouldn't come.

Because some part of her, the part that had watched her parents die, that had been hunted and manipulated and forced into battles she'd never chosen, that part wondered if Kieran was right.

What had divine connection given her, really?

She thought of Charles. Her adoptive father, teaching her to ride a bike, helping with homework, making terrible dad jokes that she'd pretended to hate but secretly loved. He'd died in a car accident that wasn't an accident. Divine politics reaching into her mortal life and taking the person who'd actually been there for her childhood.

She thought of Elizabeth. Her adoptive mother, planning birthday parties and attending parent-teacher conferences and staying up late to talk about nothing and everything. She'd died at the compound, caught in the crossfire of cosmic disputes she'd never even known existed.

Two people who had loved her without reservation. Two people whose only crime was caring for a child who turned out to be more than human. Two graves that existed because gods couldn't stop playing games with mortal lives.

And what had she gotten in return? Powers she'd had to discover alone. A heritage that came with enemies built in. A destiny that had been shaped by forces who'd never asked her permission, who'd used her and those she loved as pieces in games she barely understood.

Maybe it would be better. Maybe a world without Scions, without divine interference, without the constant weight of cosmic significance pressing down on mortal shoulders... maybe that world would be simpler. Cleaner. More honest, as Kieran said.

Maybe she'd been fighting for something that didn't deserve to survive.

The doubt crept through her like poison, finding all the cracks in her conviction and widening them into chasms. She thought of Keats. His oracle abilities, the visions that came unbidden, the future he could see but never fully control. Would he be happier as simply human? Without the weight of prophecy? Without the father who appeared only in moments of crisis and vanished when the immediate danger passed?

She remembered his face after the visions. The exhaustion. The fear. The way he sometimes looked at her like he'd seen something terrible and couldn't unsee it. Was that a gift? Or was it exactly what Kieran said. A chain, beautiful and useful, but a chain nonetheless?

She thought of Lily. Her speed fading as Hermes's artifacts were stolen, her connection to her divine heritage growing weaker with each passing day. The grief when she'd realized what was happening. The fear of becoming ordinary.

But also, the relief? The complicated, guilt-laden relief of maybe not having to be special anymore? Lily had never said it out loud, but Alexis had seen it in her eyes. The weight of being Hermes's daughter, of carrying speed that set her apart from everyone around her, of never being able to be normal.

She thought of herself. Daughter of primordial night, carrying powers she'd never asked for, fighting battles she'd never chosen, watching people die because gods couldn't stop playing their eternal games with mortal pieces.

What would it be like to be simply human? To wake up without shadows answering her call? To look at a situation and not have answers surfacing from depths she didn't understand? To be ordinary?

Maybe Kieran isn't the villain, whispered the part of her that was tired of fighting. *Maybe she was.*

"I can see you thinking," Kieran said quietly. "I can see the doubt. That's not weakness, Alexis. It's wisdom. The ability to question your own certainties is what separates true conviction from blind faith."

"If I'm so wise, why am I losing?"

"Because wisdom isn't the same as strength. Because questioning your beliefs makes you human, but it also makes you vulnerable." He raised one hand, shadows gathering around it like storm clouds forming. "You could still surrender. Accept that I'm right. Walk away from this Arena with your life, if not your pride, intact."

"And watch you destroy everything I love?"

"Watch me free everyone you love from chains they didn't choose to wear." His voice carried genuine compassion that made her want to scream. "The people waiting for you back at your compound, they'll lose their powers, yes. But they'll gain something more valuable. Normal lives. Human lives. The chance to be something other than pawns in cosmic games."

Normal lives. Human lives. The words echoed in her mind like bells tolling for something she'd never realized she was mourning.

What would it be like to be simply human? To wake up without the weight of divine heritage pressing against her consciousness? To love Keats without worrying that their relationship was another thread in some cosmic tapestry being woven by forces beyond their comprehension?

What would it be like to be free?

* * * *

The Arena felt different now. The cosmic significance that had pressed against her when she'd first arrived had faded into something hollow, and the divine witnesses who'd seemed so important now looked like what Kieran had described them as. Ancient beings playing games with mortal lives, watching with detached interest as their experiments tore each other apart.

Even Chaos, standing apart in his terrible neutrality, seemed less like a grandfather and more like a collector admiring specimens in a jar.

She'd given him a boon. An undefined favor, callable at any time. She'd made a deal with a force that predated morality, that probably didn't understand love or loyalty or any of the things she'd told herself she was fighting for.

Had she been fooling herself this whole time? Pretending that her cause was righteous when she was just another piece being moved across a board she couldn't see?

The boon pressed against her consciousness like a weight she'd been carrying so long she'd forgotten it was there. That undefined promise she'd made in desperation, in the depths of Chaos's realm when escape seemed impossible. She'd told no one. Not Keats. Not Lily. Not anyone who might have helped her understand what she'd agreed to.

Because carrying burdens alone was what she did. Because asking for help felt like weakness. Because she'd convinced herself that she had to be strong enough to handle everything by herself.

And look where that got you, whispered the doubt. *Alone. Broken. About to lose everything because you were too proud to let anyone carry the weight with you.*

"You're not answering," Kieran observed. "That tells me everything I need to know."

"It tells you I'm thinking. That's all."

"It tells me you know I'm right." He didn't say it with triumph. He said it with something that sounded almost like sorrow. "You've spent months fighting for a cause you believed in, and now you're realizing that the cause itself might be the problem. That's not defeat, Alexis. That's enlightenment."

"Enlightenment." The word tasted bitter on her tongue. "Is that what you call it when someone convinces you that everything you love is a lie?"

"I call it truth. The hardest kind. The kind that makes you question everything you thought you knew." His shadows shifted, and she knew the pause was ending. The mercy he'd shown by explaining rather than attacking was running out. "Last chance, Daughter of Night. Surrender. Accept that I'm not your enemy. That I'm trying to save everyone, including you, from a future of endless cosmic manipulation. Or fight on, and lose everything."

She looked at him. At this son of Hades who believed so completely in his cause that he was willing to destroy everything she loved to achieve it. At the true believer who couldn't imagine any truth beyond the one he'd been taught.

And she realized, with something that felt like despair settling into her bones, that she didn't have a counter-argument.

His philosophy was rational. Internally consistent. Even compassionate, in its own terrible way. He wasn't lying about believing that Scions were aberrations, that divine-mortal connection was disease, that the kindest thing would be to let it all fade away.

He was wrong. She believed that with everything she had left. But she couldn't articulate why. Couldn't find the words that would counter centuries of careful reasoning with something more than desperate hope.

"I won't surrender," she said, and the words came out hollow. Empty. A refusal without conviction behind it.

Kieran nodded, as if he'd expected nothing else.

"Then I'll end this quickly. You've earned that much, at least."

His shadows moved.

And Alexis, wounded and doubting and unable to find the strength she needed, raised her failing defenses for what she knew would be the final exchange.

She was going to lose.

Not just the fight. The faith. The belief that had carried her through everything. The conviction that her existence meant something, that the people she loved were worth protecting, that divine-mortal connection was a gift rather than a curse.

She was going to lose all of it.

And she didn't know how to stop it.

19

The shadows hit her like a wall of frozen darkness.

Alexis felt something break inside her, not bone, though that too, but something deeper. Something that had been holding her together through months of impossible revelations and desperate battles and losses that had carved pieces out of her soul.

She hit the Arena floor hard enough to crack the ancient stone. The impact drove the air from her lungs, and for a moment she couldn't breathe, couldn't think, couldn't do anything but lie there as her body catalogued the damage with the clinical precision of shock.

Broken ribs, at least three, maybe more. She could feel them grinding against each other with every shallow breath, bone scraping bone in a symphony of wrongness. Her left arm hung at an angle that made her stomach lurch when she caught sight of it, dislocated at the shoulder, possibly fractured at the elbow, the fingers twitching with nerve damage she didn't want to think about.

Blood ran from a gash across her forehead, blinding her right eye with crimson warmth. She blinked, tried to clear it, and more blood flowed to replace what she'd wiped away. The wound was deep. She could feel the exposed edge of her skull when she probed it with her functioning hand, a discovery that sent her mind skittering away from the implications.

Every breath was agony. Every heartbeat felt like it might be her last. And somewhere beneath all of it, beneath the physical wreckage of her body, something worse was happening. Her power, the primordial darkness that had answered her call since she'd first awakened, flickered and guttered like a candle in a hurricane. She reached for it and found only embers where an inferno had been.

And above her, shadows gathering around him like a cloak of triumph, stood Kieran.

"It's over," he said. Not gloating. Not cruel. Stating fact. "You fought well, Daughter of Night. Better than anyone expected. But conviction isn't enough. Not against someone who's spent years preparing for exactly this moment."

She tried to rise. Her arms wouldn't cooperate, the left one screaming protest through shattered joints, the right one trembling with exhaustion that went deeper than muscle. Her power flickered and died like a candle flame drowned in water.

The taste of blood filled her mouth. She'd bitten through her lip at some point, she couldn't remember when, and the copper tang mixed with something else. Something that tasted like defeat.

"Stay down," Kieran advised, almost gently. "There's no shame in losing to a superior opponent. Accept the terms. Let this end with what dignity you have left."

Dignity. The word echoed in her mind like mockery. What dignity did she have? She was lying broken on the floor of a cosmic arena, about to lose everything she'd sworn to protect, and she couldn't even muster the strength to stand.

She turned her head, a small motion that sent spikes of pain through her neck, made her vision swim with gray at the edges, and found the barrier where Keats and Lily waited. They were pressed against the invisible wall, faces twisted with horror and desperation. Keats was shouting something, his oracle sight blazing gold, but she couldn't hear the words. The Arena's rules held. Witnesses could watch. They couldn't interfere.

She was alone.

Completely, utterly alone.

* * * *

The weight of her failures settled over her like a burial shroud.

Everyone depending on her. Aaron back at the compound, hunting for a mole he might never find, she should have helped more, should have used her gift to narrow the search instead of trusting that he could handle it alone. Makelo, who'd joined their cause because she believed Alexis could protect the Trident, three thousand years of solitude ended by hope, and now that hope was bleeding out on sacred stone.

Ellie, compassionate and eager, who'd looked at Alexis like she was something worth following. Cerval, quiet and competent, who'd trusted the Network with his loyalty despite whatever secrets he carried. Jamie, still learning what it meant to be a Scion, still believing that the compound was a safe place to figure it out.

All of them counting on her to win this fight. To prove that Scions weren't aberrations. To earn their right to exist through blood and conviction.

And she was failing them. All of them. Every single person who'd ever believed in her.

She thought of Greer, the Scion she'd killed in the ether. He wasn't her first real kill, she'd had to defend herself in the mountains when she and Keats were searching for Aaron. But, he was a man who'd been manipulated like Kieran but hadn't gotten the chance to see beyond his manipulation. His face haunted her. The surprise in his eyes when her shadow blade had found its mark. The way he'd crumpled, all that conviction draining away with his life.

She'd told herself it was necessary. Told herself she'd had no choice. But lying here, broken and defeated, she wondered if that was true. Maybe there had been another way. Maybe she'd chosen violence because it was easier than finding an alternative.

Maybe she was exactly the kind of weapon Kieran accused all Scions of being.

The boon pressed against her consciousness like a stone. That undefined favor she'd promised Chaos, her grandfather, if such a word meant anything to a primordial force, in exchange for her escape from his realm. She'd told no one. Had carried the secret alone, adding its weight to all the other weights she'd insisted on bearing by herself.

What had she been thinking? Making deals with entities that predated morality. Keeping secrets from the people who loved her. Pretending she could carry everything alone when she'd never been strong enough for that kind of burden.

She thought of the jealousy she'd felt, that poisonous doubt about Keats and Lily, the whispered fear that she wasn't enough, that he'd eventually realize she was a broken girl pretending to be a hero. The weeks she'd spent watching them together, cataloguing every touch and smile and shared joke, building a case for her own inadequacy.

Even after they'd resolved it, even after that night on the rooftop when he'd chosen her and she'd chosen trust, the memory of those feelings shamed her. How could she claim to fight for love when she'd spent weeks doubting the love that was right in front of her?

How could she claim to be worthy of protection when she couldn't even protect herself?

* * * *

Kieran's words echoed in the hollow space where her conviction had been.

Maybe he was right. Maybe Scions were aberrations, beautiful, powerful, tragic, but ultimately mistakes that the cosmos was ready to correct. Maybe divine-mortal connection was parasitic, gods taking from mortals and giving nothing back but complications and suffering.

Look at what it had cost her. Parents dead. Friends endangered. A life that had never been normal, could never be normal, would always be caught between worlds that didn't want her.

She remembered the day she'd learned about her birth mother. The world tilting sideways as she realized the person she'd called Mom had never conceived her. Yet, the woman had loved Alexis, of that she was certain.

She'd thought that was the biggest revelation until she'd understood she wasn't even fully human.

And look at what she'd done with that

inheritance. Made deals with primordial forces. Kept secrets from people who trusted her. Carried burdens alone when she should have shared them, pushed people away when she should have let them in.

She thought of Keats, in those first weeks after they'd gotten together. The way she'd held back, kept parts of herself hidden, refused to be fully vulnerable even with someone who'd already seen her at her worst. He'd been so patient. So willing to wait for her to trust him.

And she'd repaid that patience with jealousy and silence and the constant, grinding fear that she wasn't enough.

Maybe she deserved to lose.

Maybe everyone would be better off if she stopped fighting.

The thought slithered through her mind like poison, and she didn't have the strength to fight it off. Her body was broken. Her power was failing. Her conviction had crumbled under the weight of Kieran's philosophy and her own accumulated doubts.

What was left?

Nothing. Nothing but a broken girl lying on ancient stone, bleeding out in front of gods who watched with detached interest and friends who couldn't help her no matter how desperately they wanted to.

* * * *

The divine witnesses observed in silence.

Zeus with his lightning-touched eyes, watching another mortal fail another test. Hades with his void-deep stillness, expression unreadable as his son stood triumphant. Apollo, radiant with contained light, unable to help his own son's partner despite everything he'd risked for Scions.

She wondered what Apollo was thinking. Whether he was angry at her for failing. Whether he was already calculating how to protect Keats from the fallout of her defeat. Whether he even cared about the girl his son loved, or whether she was another piece on the board to him.

And Chaos, standing apart in his terrible neutrality, watching with interest that felt less like concern and more like entertainment.

She'd thought she was special to him. Thought that being his granddaughter, walking freely in his realm, earning his attention meant something beyond cosmic curiosity. But maybe Kieran was right about that too. Maybe gods, even primordial forces, didn't love. Maybe they collected. Used. Discarded.

The boon she'd given him felt less like a promise between family and more like a chain around her throat. One day he'd call it in. One day he'd ask something of her, and she wouldn't be able to refuse, and whatever happened then would be one more consequence of her own foolish choices.

She should have told someone. Should have told Keats, at least. But she'd kept the secret because keeping secrets was what she did. Because carrying burdens alone was easier than trusting people not to break under the weight.

Because she'd always believed, deep down, that she wasn't worth the trouble of sharing.

* * * *

"Surrender," Kieran said, and his voice carried something that sounded almost like compassion. "You've proven your courage. No one watching can doubt your conviction. But conviction without strength is stubbornness, and stubbornness isn't a virtue, it's a death sentence."

He crouched beside her, close enough that she could see the genuine belief in his eyes. He wasn't enjoying this. Wasn't savoring her defeat. He was a true believer offering mercy to someone he'd defeated fairly.

Up close, she could see details she'd missed before. A small scar above his left eyebrow, training accident, maybe, or something worse. The faint tremor in his hands that suggested this fight had cost him something too, even if he'd never admit it. The exhaustion lurking behind his conviction, the weariness of someone who'd been carrying his own impossible burdens for far too long.

They weren't so different, she realized. Both shaped by forces beyond their control. Both trying to do what they believed was right. Both convinced they were fighting for something worth the cost.

The only difference was that his philosophy led to ending everything, and hers... hers led here. To this moment. To broken bones and failing power and the bitter taste of defeat.

"You don't have to die here, Alexis. The terms don't require your death, just your acceptance of the outcome. Surrender, and you walk away. Your friends walk away. Everyone at your compound continues their lives, just... different. Simpler. Free from the weight of divine inheritance."

Free.

The word cut through the fog of pain and despair. Free from powers she'd never asked for. Free from a heritage that came with enemies built in. Free from the constant pressure of cosmic significance pressing down on mortal shoulders.

What would that be like?

She tried to imagine Keats without his oracle sight. Without the visions that plagued him, without the knowledge of futures he couldn't change, without the father who appeared only in crisis and vanished when the danger passed. Would he be happier? More... human?

She remembered him after a particularly bad vision, shaking, pale, unable to speak for nearly an hour. She'd held him through it, felt the tremors gradually subside, wished she could take the burden from him. Maybe Kieran was offering exactly that. Maybe losing the oracle sight would be a mercy rather than a loss.

She tried to imagine Lily without her speed. Without the desperate running that had defined her life since her mother's death, without the divine heritage that made her a target, without the connection to a father who'd never been there for the moments that mattered.

She remembered Lily talking about her mother, the grief that still surfaced sometimes, the anger at Hermes for not being there. Maybe being fully human would let her finally grieve properly. Finally move on. Finally be something other than her father's daughter.

She tried to imagine herself without night. Without the shadows that answered her call, without the gift that retrieved information she'd never consciously learned, without the weight of being the daughter of a primordial goddess who'd never once appeared to comfort her.

Maybe it would be better. Maybe they'd all be happier as simply human, unburdened by the complications of divine blood.

Maybe she should surrender.

* * * *

The thought settled into her consciousness with the weight of defeat.

She couldn't win this fight. Couldn't counter Kieran's philosophy with anything more than desperate hope. Couldn't find the strength to rise when her body was broken and her conviction had crumbled.

All she had left was stubbornness, and Kieran was right, stubbornness wasn't a virtue. It was another form of pride, another way of pretending she was stronger than she was.

I can't do this.

The admission felt like dying. Like something essential inside her was finally giving up, finally accepting what she should have known from the beginning.

I'm not enough. I never was.

She thought of her parents, Charles and Elizabeth, who'd loved her despite not understanding what she was. They'd died because of divine politics. Because gods played games with mortal lives and didn't care about the pieces they broke.

She thought of Nyx, her biological mother, who'd protected her from afar but never once appeared to explain, to comfort, to be present when presence was what Alexis needed most.

She thought of all the Scions who'd come to the Network seeking safety, seeking family, seeking proof that their existence meant something. She'd promised to protect them. To fight for them. To prove that divine-mortal connection was worth preserving.

And she'd failed. Was failing. Would fail.

"I'm sorry," she whispered, and she wasn't sure if she was talking to Keats, to Lily, to everyone she'd let down, or to herself. "I'm sorry I wasn't enough."

Her eyes started to close. Not unconsciousness, something worse. Surrender. The slow release of everything she'd been holding onto, the final acceptance that some battles couldn't be won.

The Arena waited. The gods watched. And Alexis Rain, daughter of Nyx, champion of the Scion Network, prepared to give up.

Then she heard his voice.

* * * *

It shouldn't have been possible.

The Arena didn't permit interference. Witnesses could watch, but they couldn't affect the outcome. Those were the rules. Those had always been the rules, since before the gods had names and cosmic law was first written into the fabric of existence.

But Keats had never been good at following rules that stood between him and the people he loved.

Alexis.

Not a shout. Not a desperate cry. Her name, spoken with a clarity that cut through the fog of pain and despair like a blade of golden light.

She opened her eyes.

He was still behind the barrier, she could see him pressed against that invisible wall, his face wet with tears, his oracle sight blazing so bright it hurt to look at. But somehow, impossibly, his voice was reaching her. Not through the air. Not through any physical medium.

Through their bond. Through years of friendship and months of love and a connection that had nothing to do with divine heritage and everything to do with choosing each other, over and over, no matter what the universe threw at them.

She saw the strain on his face, the cost of what he was doing. His oracle abilities weren't meant for this. They were meant for seeing, not reaching. But he was bending them anyway, pushing past every limit, refusing to accept that cosmic law could keep him from the person he loved.

Alexis, listen to me.

She listened.

You're not fighting for ideology. You're not fighting because you're right and he's wrong. You're not fighting to prove that Scions deserve to exist or that divine-mortal connection is sacred or that your mother's choices were justified.

His voice cracked, but he kept going.

You're fighting for people, Al. For Jamie at the compound who found his mother after years of thinking she'd abandoned him. For Lily, who finally has family again after losing everything. For Aaron, who's spent his whole life protecting Scions because someone has to. For everyone at that compound who doesn't fit anywhere else but found a place anyway.

She heard him. Heard him.

That's not aberration, Alexis. That's not a mistake the cosmos needs to correct. That's love. That's family. That's the whole point of everything we've been building.

Something stirred in the hollow space where her conviction had been.

Kieran thinks he's offering mercy by taking that away. He thinks he's liberating people from chains they didn't choose. But he's forgotten what it feels like to belong somewhere. To have people who'd fight for you, die for you, love you even when you're broken and bleeding and convinced you're not enough.

Keats's voice dropped to something barely above a whisper, but she heard every word as if he were speaking directly into her heart.

You are enough, Al. You've always been enough. Not because you're powerful or because you're a daughter of Nyx or because you can win this fight. You're enough because you love people. Because you fight for them. Because even when everything seems hopeless, you don't stop trying to protect the ones you care about.

A pause. She could see him gathering himself, pushing through whatever barrier was trying to reassert itself, refusing to let cosmic law have the last word.

Do you remember the first time you told me about your gift? We were sitting in your bedroom, and you were so scared I'd think you were a freak. You said you'd understand if I wanted to keep my distance.

She remembered. The fear in her chest. The certainty that he'd pull away once he knew what she was.

I told you that knowing things didn't make you a freak. It made you the most interesting person I'd ever met. And you looked at me like no one had ever said anything like that to you before.

His voice broke, but he kept going.

That's when I knew, Al. That's when I knew I was going to love you for the rest of my life. Because you were so convinced you were broken, and all I could see was someone worth fighting for.

Tears she hadn't known she was capable of producing anymore tracked down her cheeks, mixing with the blood.

Don't give up. Please. Not because the universe needs you to win, but because I need you. Because Lily needs you. Because everyone back home is waiting for you, believing in you, knowing that you'd never abandon them no matter how hard things get.

She felt something shift inside her chest. Not her broken ribs, something deeper. Something that had been crumbling under the weight of Kieran's philosophy and her own accumulated doubts.

It started to rebuild.

Come back to me, Alexis. Fight for us. Fight for love. And when you win, because you will win, come home.

The connection faded, his voice slipping away as the Arena's rules reasserted themselves. But the words remained, burning in her consciousness like flames that couldn't be extinguished.

You're fighting for people.

That's not aberration. That's love.

Alexis opened her eyes, opened them, and looked at Kieran with something that felt like clarity for the first time since the battle began.

He was still crouching beside her, waiting for the surrender he was certain would come. But something in her expression made him pause, made uncertainty flicker across features that had been so confident moments before.

"I'm not done," she said.

And despite everything, the broken bones, the bleeding wounds, the exhaustion that went deeper than physical, she began to rise.

20

Rising hurt more than falling had.

Every broken rib screamed protest as she shifted her weight, bone grinding against bone in ways that sent white-hot spikes of agony through her entire torso. Her dislocated arm hung wrong, a dead weight that pulled at her shoulder socket with every movement, sending fresh waves of nausea rolling through her stomach. The gash across her forehead had clotted enough to stop actively bleeding, but dried blood crusted her right eye half-shut, and her vision swam with exhaustion that went deeper than physical.

She got one knee under her. The motion made her cry out, a sound she barely recognized as her own voice, as fractured ribs shifted against damaged tissue. Her good arm trembled, muscles screaming from the abuse they'd already endured, threatening to give out entirely.

Get up, she told herself. *They're watching. Keats is watching. Get up.*

She pushed through the pain. Through the exhaustion. Through the part of her mind that was cataloguing all the reasons why this was impossible, why her body couldn't support this demand, why she should stay down and accept defeat.

Her leg straightened. Her spine protested every degree of vertical movement. Her vision grayed at the edges, and for a moment she thought she was going to pass out, thought her body was going to betray her at the last possible moment.

But she rose anyway.

One foot under her. Then the other. Standing, barely, swaying, held upright more by will than by any physical capability, but standing.

The Arena seemed to hold its breath.

Kieran stepped back, shadows coiling around him in defensive patterns that spoke of sudden uncertainty. He'd been so confident moments ago, so certain that victory was inevitable, that she'd accept the mercy of surrender rather than continue a fight she couldn't win.

He hadn't expected her to stand back up.

"This is pointless," he said, but some of the assurance had leached from his voice. "You're barely conscious. Your power is failing. One more exchange and you'll—"

"You're wrong."

The words came out stronger than she'd expected. Not a whisper. Not a desperate gasp. A statement, clear and certain, that cut through his objections like a blade through shadow.

"I've been wrong about a lot of things," she continued, feeling something shift inside her chest as she spoke. "I thought I had to carry everything alone. Thought I had to be perfect, be strong, be worthy of the people counting on me. I kept secrets because I didn't trust anyone else to help carry the weight. I doubted the people who loved me because I couldn't believe I deserved to be loved."

She took a step toward him. Her broken ribs ground together. Her vision flickered. She took another step anyway.

"But you're wrong too, Kieran. About everything that matters."

* * * *

He raised his hands, shadows gathering for another attack, but something in her expression made him hesitate. Made him wait to hear what she would say before he ended this.

"Your philosophy is rational," Alexis acknowledged. "Internally consistent. Even compassionate, in its own way. You're not lying when you say you believe in what you're doing. You genuinely think that severing divine-mortal connection is an act of mercy."

"It is."

"No. It isn't." She shook her head, and clarity settled into her consciousness, not the desperate certainty she'd been clinging to before, but something deeper. Something that didn't need to be defended because it was. "You're not wrong because your logic is flawed. You're wrong because you've forgotten what it feels like to belong to someone."

The words landed. She saw them hit, saw something flicker in his eyes that wasn't arrogance or conviction or any of the things she'd seen there before.

It was recognition. And fear.

"I know what it's like to carry burdens alone," she continued. "To believe that no one else can understand, that sharing the weight would break the people you care about. I know what it's like to feel like an aberration, like you don't fit anywhere, don't belong to anything, exist in the spaces between worlds that don't want you."

She was close to him now. Close enough to see the way his shadows trembled at their edges, uncertain for the first time since the battle began.

"But I also know what it's like to find a place anyway. To build something with people who are as broken as you are, as lost, as convinced they don't deserve to exist. That's not aberration, Kieran. That's family."

* * * *

Power stirred inside her, not the desperate flare she'd been fighting with before, but something steadier. Something that didn't come from fear or determination or the need to prove herself worthy.

It came from love.

The difference was like night and day. Like cold and warmth. Like drowning and breathing.

Before, her power had been a weapon, something she'd wielded through will and desperation, forcing it to obey through sheer stubbornness. It had felt like fighting a current, like swimming upstream, like demanding that darkness serve her because she had no other choice.

Now it felt like coming home.

The shadows didn't answer her call, they welcomed it. The primordial darkness that was her birthright stopped being something she controlled and became something she *was*. Not a tool. Not a weapon. An extension of herself, as natural as breathing, as effortless as love.

She thought of Keats, watching helplessly from the adjacent space, loving her enough to break the rules of cosmic combat to reach her. The power swelled in response, not because she was thinking about him, but because loving him was part of who she was now, and her power had finally learned to draw from that truth.

She thought of Lily, fierce and loyal, who'd become a sister in everything but blood. The darkness warmed, softened, became something protective rather than destructive.

She thought of Aaron, methodical and protective, who'd dedicated his life to keeping Scions safe. Of Makelo, ancient and grieving, who'd found hope again in their compound. Of Ellie and Cerval and Jamie and everyone else who'd come to the Network seeking family.

She thought of everyone at the compound, the wounded and the whole, the frightened and the brave, all of them building something together in a world that had never made room for them.

That was what she was fighting for. Not ideology. Not principles. Not the abstract concept of divine-mortal connection.

People. Her people. The family she'd chosen and the family that had chosen her.

The power responded to that truth, swelling inside her with a warmth that had nothing to do with cosmic heritage and everything to do with the simple, profound reality of loving and being loved in return. It didn't feel like power anymore. It felt like purpose. Like belonging. Like the certainty that she would never, ever be alone again.

"You want to know the difference between us?" she asked, and her voice carried across the Arena with authority that made the watching gods shift in their eternal stillness. "You fight because you believe. I fight because I love. And belief can be challenged, argued, undermined by better logic and more consistent philosophy."

She raised her good hand, and the darkness answered, not the cold, desperate power she'd been throwing at him before, but something else. Something that burned with the heat of connection, of belonging, of everything he'd tried to convince her was corruption.

"But love doesn't need to be defended. It just needs to be true."

* * * *

Kieran attacked.

His shadows surged toward her in a wave of darkness that should have been overwhelming, the same attack that had shattered her defenses before, that had driven her to the Arena floor and left her bleeding and broken.

This time, she didn't try to block it.

She walked through it.

The first tendrils of his shadow reached her and... stopped. Not deflected. Not destroyed. *Stopped*, unable to find purchase against whatever she'd become. They curled around her like smoke around a flame, seeking weakness and finding none, dissipating into wisps of confused darkness.

Another step. His shadows reformed, tried again, blades this time, sharp edges of concentrated death aimed at her heart, her throat, her eyes. They slid off her like water off glass, leaving no mark, causing no pain.

Kieran's eyes widened. He threw more power at her, everything he had, she realized, watching the desperation creep into his movements. Shadows became a storm around her, a hurricane of darkness that blocked out the Arena's strange light, that should have torn her apart, that would have destroyed anything based on power or conviction or the need to be right.

She walked through it like it wasn't there.

Step by step. Heartbeat by heartbeat. The son of Hades threw death at her, and the daughter of Nyx moved through it like a woman walking through rain, aware of it, touched by it, but fundamentally unchanged.

"That's not possible," he said, and for the first time since she'd met him, he sounded afraid. His voice cracked on the words. "Your power was failing. You were broken. How are you…?"

"I was fighting for the wrong reasons." She was still walking toward him, inexorable, inevitable. Each step brought her closer. Each step drove him back. "I was trying to prove something. Trying to win an argument. Trying to defend a position I wasn't sure I believed in."

Another step. Another wave of shadows that couldn't touch her. He was retreating now, backing away from something he couldn't understand, couldn't counter, couldn't defeat with all the power and philosophy he'd accumulated over years of preparation.

"Now I'm fighting for the people I love. And that's enough. That's always been enough."

She reached him.

He threw one last desperate attack, everything he had, shadows gathering into a single point of absolute darkness aimed directly at her heart. It should have killed her. It should have ended her. It carried the weight of Thanatos himself, the cold finality of death made manifest.

She caught it in her hand.

The darkness writhed against her palm, tried to consume her, tried to spread up her arm and into her chest and stop her heart. But her own shadows rose to meet it, not fighting, not destroying, *holding*. Containing. Accepting the darkness without being consumed by it.

She closed her fist, and his attack dissolved into nothing.

* * * *

The Arena responded to the shift in the battle.

Alexis felt it, the ancient space recognizing something in her transformation, in the power she'd found by letting go of everything except what mattered most. The stone beneath her feet hummed with approval. The void at the edges of reality leaned closer, interested in ways it hadn't been before.

And Chaos, still standing apart in his terrible neutrality, smiled.

Not the curious smile he'd worn before. Warmer. Pride.

Kieran threw everything he had left at her. His shadows became a storm, a hurricane of darkness that should have torn her apart, that would have destroyed anything based on power or conviction or the need to be right.

It couldn't touch what she'd become.

She reached through his defenses like they weren't there. Her hand, the one that wasn't broken, found his chest, and she pushed.

Not with power. Not with divine authority or primordial darkness or any of the cosmic forces that had been colliding since the battle began.

With truth.

Kieran flew backward, his shadows scattering like startled birds, and hit the Arena floor with the same bone-jarring impact she'd felt minutes ago. His carefully maintained composure shattered. His philosophy crumbled around him like a house built on sand.

And Alexis stood over him, wounded and bleeding but unbroken, and spoke the words that would end this.

"You've forgotten what it feels like to have someone worth fighting for. Or," she hesitated. "Or, you simply never had that. That's why you lost, Kieran. Not because I'm more powerful, because I'm more connected. I have people who love me. People I'd die for. People who'd die for me."

She looked down at him with something that wasn't hatred or triumph. It was closer to pity.

"When was the last time you had that? When was the last time anyone loved you because you were you, not because of what you could do, not because of the cause you served, but you?"

He didn't answer. He didn't have to. The hollow devastation in his eyes spoke for him.

Never. The answer was never.

* * * *

Shadows gathered around Alexis's hand, not his this time, but hers. The primordial darkness that was her birthright, the power of Nyx that had been waiting for her to understand what it was for.

She could end him. One strike, one surge of power, and the son of Hades would be nothing but a memory. The Arena would accept his death as a valid conclusion. The gods would witness. The outcome would be binding.

Kieran saw it in her eyes. Saw the power building. And he didn't try to defend himself.

"Do it," he said, and his voice carried exhaustion that went beyond physical defeat. "Finish this. I've lost. My philosophy failed. Everything I believed in..."

He laughed, and the sound was broken.

"I thought I was offering mercy. Liberation. A gift to a world that didn't understand it needed saving." His eyes found hers, and she saw something there that made her chest ache. "I was wrong. I see that now. End it. Please."

The shadows around her hand pulsed with lethal potential. One strike. One moment. One choice that would prove, once and for all, what kind of champion she truly was.

She thought about killing him.

Thought about it. Not in the abstract way she'd considered it during combat, when survival demanded decisive action. But now, with him broken beneath her, with victory secured and nothing standing between her and vengeance.

He'd tried to destroy everything she loved. Had orchestrated the theft of artifacts that anchored divine-mortal connection. Had nearly succeeded in his plan to erase Scions from existence. Had nearly killed her, would have killed her, if Keats hadn't found a way to reach through cosmic law itself.

She had every right to end him. Every justification. No god watching would condemn her for it, and many would probably approve.

But she thought about Charles. About Elizabeth. About the people who had raised her, loved her, taught her what it meant to be human even before she knew she was something more. They wouldn't have wanted this. Wouldn't have wanted their daughter to become someone who killed a beaten enemy because she could.

She thought about Keats. About what he'd said through the barrier. *You're enough because you love people. Because you fight for them.*

Killing Kieran wouldn't be fighting for anyone. It would be fighting *against* him, and he was already defeated. Already broken. Already lost.

She thought about the compound. About all those Scions building something together, trying to prove that divine-mortal connection could be beautiful instead of tragic. What would it mean if their champion won by becoming exactly what their enemies accused them of being? Another weapon. Another killer. Another proof that Scions were dangerous and needed to be contained.

And she thought about Kieran himself. About the childhood he'd described, the father who visited seven times in twenty-three years. The loneliness. The certainty that he was nothing more than a tool, a weapon, a solution to someone else's problem.

He'd never known what it felt like to be loved. Never understood that belonging was possible. He'd built his entire philosophy on the absence of connection because connection was something that had been denied him from birth.

Killing him would prove his philosophy right. Would demonstrate that love and mercy were illusions, that power was all that mattered in the end, that the strong destroyed the weak and called it justice.

Alexis let the power fade.

"No."

* * * *

Kieran stared at her like she'd spoken in a language he didn't understand.

"What?"

"I said, no." She stepped back, her shadows dissipating into the Arena's impossible air. "I'm not going to kill you."

"The terms…"

"The terms require victory. They don't require execution." She looked down at him, this broken true believer who'd been so certain of his righteousness, and made a choice that felt more important than anything else she'd done in the Arena. "I won, Kieran. The fight is over. But I don't get to decide who deserves to exist. That's another difference between us."

He pushed himself up on one elbow, confusion warring with something else in his expression. "I tried to destroy everything you love. I would have severed divine-mortal connection permanently if you'd lost. And you're showing me mercy?"

"I'm showing you what you forgot existed." She turned to face the divine witnesses, the gods who'd watched this battle unfold, who'd seen her fall and rise and choose compassion over vengeance. "I claim victory. The terms are satisfied. Kieran, son of Hades, ceases all artifact thefts and submits to divine judgment."

The Arena responded. She felt it in her bones, a cosmic acknowledgment that resonated through every layer of reality. The ancient space recognized her victory. The binding terms locked into place.

It was done.

Today, she'd won. She'd survived. She'd proven that love was stronger than philosophy, that belonging mattered more than power, that the daughter of Night could stand against the son of Death and choose mercy over destruction.

The barrier between the combat space and the witness space dissolved. And Keats was there, holding her before she could fall, his arms the only thing keeping her upright as exhaustion finally claimed its due.

"You did it," he whispered into her hair. "Al, you did it. You won."

"We won," she corrected, leaning into his warmth. "I heard you. Through the barrier. You reached me when nothing else could."

His arms tightened around her.

"Always," he said. "I'll always reach you. No matter what or who says I can't."

Lily appeared beside them, her face wet with tears she wasn't bothering to hide. "Don't you ever do that to me again," she said, and her voice cracked on the words. "I thought, when you went down, I thought—"

"I know." Alexis reached for her with her good arm, pulling her into the embrace. "I know. I'm sorry. I'm so sorry I scared you."

The three of them stood together in the center of the Chaos Arena, wounded and weeping and holding onto each other like they'd never let go.

Around them, gods prepared to pass judgment. Behind them, Kieran lay broken on the stone, his philosophy shattered, his future uncertain. Above them, the void that was Chaos's domain hummed with satisfaction at a conflict well resolved.

But for this moment, this single, precious moment, none of that mattered.

Alexis was alive. She was loved. She was home.

Everything else could wait.

21

The Arena held its breath.

Alexis stood in the center of that impossible space, held upright by Keats and Lily, as the weight of what she'd done settled into reality. The binding terms had locked into place. The combat was concluded. She had won.

But victory, she was beginning to understand, came with complications that weren't covered in the terms.

The divine witnesses began to move.

It wasn't dramatic, gods didn't need to be dramatic when their very presence reshaped the fabric of existence. They shifted, descended, gathered closer to the combat floor as if drawn by forces even they didn't control. The Arena's impossible geometry accommodated them, space folding and unfolding to create a configuration that felt less like an amphitheater and more like a courtroom.

A divine courtroom, with Alexis at its center.

She could feel their attention pressing against her like physical weight. Each god carried a different quality of regard, some curious, some calculating, some carrying emotions she couldn't name. For a half-mortal Scion to defeat a direct divine offspring in binding combat... the implications rippled through the assembly like stones dropped into still water.

Zeus reached the floor first, or perhaps he'd always been there and had chosen this moment to make his presence felt. His form radiated authority that made the air itself feel heavier, lightning flickering behind his eyes as he surveyed the aftermath of the battle.

His gaze found Kieran, broken and defeated on the Arena stone. Then it moved to Alexis, and something in his expression shifted in ways she couldn't interpret.

"The combat is concluded," he announced, and his voice carried the weight of cosmic law being spoken into existence. "The terms are satisfied. Alexis Rain, daughter of Nyx, stands victorious. Kieran, son of Hades, is bound by the conditions of his defeat."

Formal words. Ritual words. The kind of declaration that had been made in this space since before human civilization had learned to record its own history.

But Zeus's attention wasn't on the formalities. His attention was on Chaos.

* * * *

The primordial force hadn't moved from his position of terrible neutrality, but something about his presence had changed. He was more present now. More focused. Watching Alexis with an attention that made even the King of Gods uncomfortable.

"You fought well, granddaughter."

The words rippled through the Arena like stones dropped into still water. Every divine witness stiffened. Poseidon's ocean-deep eyes widened. Apollo's radiance flickered with sudden concern. Even Hades, void-still and inscrutable, turned to stare at the interaction unfolding before them.

Chaos had spoken. Chaos, who observed but never participated. Chaos, who predated the gods and would outlast them. Chaos, who found the affairs of divine and mortal alike too small to warrant his attention.

He had spoken to Alexis. Called her granddaughter. And his voice carried something that sounded almost like warmth.

Around the Arena, the divine reactions told a story of their own.

Aphrodite watched with an expression that mixed satisfaction with something more complex, as if the outcome had confirmed a theory she'd been developing. Love's patron understood, perhaps better than any other witness, what had happened. What had defeated the son of Hades.

Athena's grey eyes narrowed with strategic calculation. Alexis could almost see the goddess processing implications, updating her understanding of the board and its pieces. A half-mortal who could defeat divine offspring through conviction alone... that changed equations that had been stable for millennia.

Ares looked almost disappointed, not that Alexis had won, but that she hadn't killed Kieran. The god of war had little use for mercy, less for the philosophical implications of choosing compassion. His attention had already begun to drift, seeking violence elsewhere.

But it was Apollo's reaction that caught Alexis's attention. The sun god's radiance had dimmed, his focus entirely on Keats. Father and son, separated by divine law and circumstance, sharing a look that carried pride and fear and something that might have been hope. Keats had broken the rules of the Arena to reach her. Had bent his oracle abilities in ways they weren't meant to be bent.

Apollo had noticed. And he wasn't sure whether to be proud or terrified of what his son was becoming.

"You'll visit again," Chaos continued. Not a question. Not a command. A statement of fact, delivered with the certainty of a being who could see possibilities that gods and mortals would never comprehend.

Alexis felt Keats tense beside her. Felt Lily's grip tighten on her arm. They didn't understand what they were witnessing, how could they?, but they could sense its significance.

"I'd like that," she replied.

And meant it. Despite everything, the boon she'd promised, the undefined favor hanging over her like a blade, she meant it. Chaos was her grandfather. The ether was her inheritance. Whatever complications that relationship might bring, she couldn't bring herself to fear him.

Maybe that made her foolish. Maybe it made her brave. Maybe, as Zeus tended to believe, it made her both.

The King of Gods was staring at her now with an intensity that made her divine blood sing with warning. His lightning-touched eyes saw more than physical reality, they saw patterns, implications, the threads of fate being woven into configurations he'd never anticipated.

And he was deeply, profoundly concerned.

* * * *

"Brother." Zeus's voice was pitched low, meant only for Hades, but Alexis's enhanced senses caught every word. "Did you see that? Did you see how he looked at her?"

Hades had descended to the Arena floor, his attention fixed on his fallen son. But he paused at Zeus's words, something flickering across his pale features.

"I saw."

"Chaos doesn't speak to anyone. He observes. He witnesses. He does not engage." Zeus's voice carried controlled urgency. "And, he certainly doesn't call anyone 'granddaughter' with that tone. That... familiarity."

"She's Nyx's daughter. Chaos is Nyx's progenitor. The connection exists."

"The connection doesn't explain what I witnessed. That girl has given him something, Hades. A boon, if I'm not mistaken." Zeus's lightning flickered with agitation. "She's either the bravest mortal-born I've ever encountered, or the most foolish." He glanced offhandedly at Kieran lying on the floor of the arena. "Possibly both."

Alexis kept her expression neutral, but inside, her heart hammered. He knew. Zeus had recognized what she'd done, understood the implications of the deal she'd made in Chaos's realm.

He knew, and he was afraid.

"Whatever she's set in motion," Zeus continued, his voice dropping even lower, "it's beyond our sight. Beyond the Fates' weaving, perhaps. If Chaos has a favorite, if he decides to act on her behalf—"

"The implications would be catastrophic," Hades finished. "Chaos acting is never subtle. The last time he took direct interest in mortal affairs, civilizations fell."

"Then we need to watch her. Carefully. Whatever game she's playing..."

"She's not playing a game." Hades's voice carried certainty that made Zeus pause. "Look at her, brother. Look. Does that appear to be someone engaged in cosmic manipulation? Or does it appear to be a girl who made a desperate bargain to survive and hasn't understood its consequences?"

Zeus looked. Alexis felt his gaze like physical pressure, divine scrutiny searching for deception or hidden agenda.

She met his eyes without flinching. Let him see what was there, exhaustion, pain, the fierce protectiveness of someone who'd fought for the people she loved and won. Nothing hidden. Nothing false.

After a long moment, Zeus looked away.

"Perhaps," he conceded. "But foolishness and innocence don't make the danger less real. Whatever she's promised Chaos, whatever he intends to ask of her, it will shape events in ways none of us can predict." He turned to Hades and, in his authoritarian voice, said for all to hear, "Your son. What do you intend to do with him?"

* * * *

Hades moved toward Kieran with the measured steps of someone approaching something fragile.

That was wrong, Alexis thought. Everything about Hades's demeanor was wrong. He should have been angry, coldly furious at a son who'd embarrassed his bloodline, who'd lost a binding combat to a half-mortal Scion, who'd been defeated not by superior power but by something as simple as love.

Instead, the God of the Underworld looked... grieved. Concerned. Like a father approaching a wounded child, not a lord coming to discipline an errant servant.

The other gods noticed too. She saw Poseidon's confusion, Athena's calculating interest, even Hermes pausing his restless movement to watch this unprecedented display of divine paternal feeling.

"Kieran." Hades's voice was gentle in ways that made the watching gods shift with confusion. "Can you stand?"

Kieran looked up at his father with eyes that held nothing but devastation. His philosophy had crumbled. His certainty had shattered. Everything he'd believed, everything he'd fought for, had been undone by a girl who didn't fight for ideology but for love.

"I failed," he said. "Everything I tried to accomplish—"

"Was based on beliefs that were given to you." Hades crouched beside his son, and the motion was so unexpectedly human that Alexis felt something shift in her understanding of the god. "Beliefs that I should have questioned long ago. That I should have protected you from."

"Father?"

The word came out broken, confused, not the cold formality Kieran had used when speaking of Hades before, but something younger. Vulnerable. The voice of a son who had never understood why his father had been so distant, so absent, so willing to let him be shaped into a weapon.

"I visited you seven times," Hades said quietly, and the confession carried weight that made the Arena itself seem to listen. "Seven times in twenty-three years. I told myself it was for your protection, that too much attention would make you a target, that distance was a form of love." His pale eyes glistened with something that couldn't possibly be tears, because gods didn't weep. "I was wrong. I let you believe you were nothing more than a tool because I was too frightened to show you what you were to me."

"What was I?" Kieran's voice cracked. "What am I?"

"My son." Hades helped Kieran to his feet with the careful support of someone who'd wanted to do this for years and never allowed himself. "My son, who deserved better than the life I gave him. My son, who was taught to believe in severance because I never taught him to believe in connection.

"Not here." Hades adjusted his grip on Kieran, supporting his son with the tenderness that had been absent for twenty-three years. "We have much to discuss, you and I. Truths that should have been spoken before any of this began."

Zeus watched the interaction with an expression that mixed confusion with dawning realization. "Hades. What are you...?"

"The girl's terms specify divine judgment." Hades's voice carried authority that brooked no argument. "As Kieran's father, that judgment falls to me. I will deal with my son as I see fit."

"And, how do you see fit? After what he's done, the artifacts stolen, the connections severed, the chaos he's caused across every pantheon—"

"What he's done was in service of beliefs someone else planted in him." Hades's pale eyes met Zeus's, and something passed between them that Alexis couldn't read. "I'm beginning to suspect, brother, that we've been playing the wrong game entirely."

The words hung in the Arena like a revelation waiting to be understood.

* * * *

"The wrong game?" Zeus's lightning flickered. "Explain."

"Kieran didn't conceive this plan. He doesn't have the resources to orchestrate thefts across multiple divine realms, to hide from oracle sight, to engineer a confrontation specifically designed to neutralize the Scion Network." Hades's voice carried the weight of a truth he'd only begun to comprehend. "Someone taught him his philosophy. Someone provided him with access, with information, with the means to become exactly what he became."

"Who?"

"That's what I intend to discover." Hades adjusted his grip on Kieran, supporting his son with a tenderness that seemed out of place for the God of Death. "But I have my suspicions. And if I'm right..."

He didn't finish the sentence. Didn't need to. The implications were clear enough in the sudden tension that gripped the divine assembly.

Someone had manipulated Kieran. Someone had used the son of Hades as a weapon, pointed him at the divine-mortal connection, and let him believe he was acting on his own conviction.

Someone was still out there. Still watching. Still moving pieces on a board that none of them had seen.

"The artifacts," Alexis said, and every divine eye turned to her. "My terms specified that Kieran returns what he stole. But he accepted too quickly. I felt it at the time, something wrong about how easily he agreed."

Hades nodded slowly. "Because he hasn't personally stolen anything. His... associates handled the actual thefts. The terms bind him, not them. The artifacts will remain missing."

The loophole. She'd known something was wrong when Kieran accepted her conditions without negotiation. Now she understood why.

Beside her, Keats went rigid. "Then nothing's changed. Lily's still losing her speed. Scions everywhere are still being weakened. We won the battle but..."

"But we lost the war," Lily finished, her voice hollow. "All of this. Everything Alexis went through. And the artifacts are still gone."

The bitter truth settled over them like a shroud. Victory in the Arena had felt so complete, so absolute. But Kieran had been a symptom, not the disease. The real threat, the hidden architect who'd shaped him, who'd orchestrated the thefts, who'd been working toward goals none of them understood, was still out there.

"Then the operation continues," Alexis said, forcing strength into her voice despite the exhaustion dragging at her bones. "Even with

Kieran defeated. Even with the binding terms in place. Whoever's behind this…"

"Will continue their work." Hades's expression grew troubled. "Which is why I need to speak with my son. Privately. Away from ears that might carry what they hear to interested parties."

He was looking at the assembled gods as he said it, and Alexis realized with a chill that he suspected the manipulation went deeper than Kieran. That someone among the divine witnesses might be connected to whatever force had orchestrated all of this.

Zeus seemed to reach the same conclusion. His lightning-touched eyes swept across the gathered Olympians, searching for… something. Deception, perhaps. Or the presence of something that didn't belong.

"Go," he said finally. "Deal with your son as you see fit. But Hades, if your suspicions prove correct, if there's something larger moving in the shadows…"

"You'll be the first to know." Hades began to fade, taking Kieran with him into whatever realm gods went when they didn't want to be followed. "Watch the girl, brother. Not because she's dangerous, but because whatever game is being played, she may be the only piece on the board who isn't being moved by someone else."

They vanished. Father and son, disappearing into the spaces between existence, leaving behind questions that wouldn't be answered today.

* * * *

The divine assembly began to disperse.

One by one, the gods withdrew to their own realms, Poseidon to his depths, Apollo to his radiance, the others to whatever domains they called home. But their departure felt less like the conclusion of a proceeding and more like a retreat. Like beings who'd witnessed something that disturbed their understanding of how the cosmos worked.

Zeus lingered longest. His gaze moved between Alexis and the space where Chaos still maintained his terrible neutrality, and the concern in his expression hadn't faded.

"Daughter of Nyx," he said finally, and his voice carried weight that pressed against her consciousness. "You've won a victory today. Earned it, through conviction and courage that exceeded what anyone expected."

"But?" She heard the unspoken word hanging in the air.

"But, victory in the Arena is only the beginning. The terms you've secured, they're binding, but they're not complete. Whoever orchestrated this crisis, whoever shaped Kieran into the weapon he became, they're still out there. Still working toward goals none of us understand."

He stepped closer, and the proximity of the King of Gods made her divine blood burn with awareness of power that could unmake worlds.

"And you," he continued, "have entangled yourself with forces that even I approach with caution. Whatever bargain you've struck with Chaos, whatever he's asked of you or will ask, be careful. He is not malevolent, but he is not safe. The primordial forces that existed before the gods... they operate by rules we don't comprehend."

"I understand."

"Do you?" His lightning-touched eyes searched hers. "I wonder. But perhaps that's for the best. Perhaps someone who understood what they'd agreed to would never have had the courage to agree at all."

He turned away, began to fade like his brother had.

"One more thing, daughter of Nyx."

"Yes?"

"The mercy you showed Kieran, the choice not to kill when killing was within your right, that was well done. Whatever the future holds, remember that moment. Remember that you chose compassion when vengeance was easier." His form was nearly transparent now, barely more than lightning and suggestion. "It may be the most important choice you've made today."

He vanished, leaving Alexis alone with Keats and Lily in an Arena that suddenly felt too vast, too empty, too full of questions that wouldn't be answered for a long time.

Chaos remained. Watching. Silent now, but present in ways that made the void itself seem alive.

She didn't look at him. Didn't acknowledge the boon that hung between them, the undefined favor that would be called in someday, the entanglement that Zeus and Hades had recognized and feared.

That was a problem for another day.

Today, she'd won. She'd survived. She'd proven that love was stronger than philosophy, that belonging mattered more than power.

"Let's go home," she said.

Keats and Lily helped her toward the ether, toward the path that would take them back to the compound and the celebration that waited. Behind them, the Chaos Arena faded into the impossible spaces from which it had been carved.

But the questions it had raised, about manipulation and hidden architects and games being played on cosmic scales, those would follow them home.

22

The compound erupted when they stepped through the ether.

Word had traveled somehow, through oracle visions, divine communication, or the mysterious way that news of cosmic significance always seemed to spread faster than physics should allow. By the time Alexis, Keats, and Lily materialized in the White Mountains, every Scion who could stand was waiting for them.

The cheering hit her like a physical force. Voices raised in triumph, in relief, in the desperate joy of people who'd been waiting to learn whether they'd be allowed to exist for another day. Hands reached for her, touching her shoulders, her arms, her blood-stained combat clothes, as if confirming she was real, she was here, she'd won.

"She did it!"

"Alexis won!"

"The Arena, she won!"

Jamie was the first to reach her, the young Scion who'd only recently discovered his heritage, pushing through the crowd with tears streaming down his face. He threw his arms around her despite her wounds, and she felt him shaking against her chest.

"You saved us," he whispered. "You saved all of us."

Behind him, his mother, the woman he'd spent years believing had abandoned him, watched with an expression that mixed pride and grief and overwhelming relief. When Alexis caught her eye, she mouthed two words: *Thank you.*

Makelo stood at the edge of the crowd, too tall to blend in, watching with ancient eyes that had seen civilizations rise and fall. The Cyclops had been alive for three thousand years. He'd watched the gods withdraw from mortal affairs, watched divine-mortal connection fade to a thread, watched everything she'd loved disappear into the mists of history. And now she was watching a nineteen-year-old girl be celebrated for proving that Scions still mattered.

She didn't cheer. She didn't cry. She nodded, once, slow, carrying the weight of millennia, and something in her expression told Alexis that she'd given her something she'd stopped hoping for centuries ago.

Ellie pushed through the crowd next, her concern focused Alexis's wounds. "You're hurt, let me…"

"Later." Alexis caught her hands, squeezed gently. "Let them have this moment first."

And there were so many of them. So many faces she'd come to know over the past months, the frightened and the brave, the newly awakened and the long-hidden, all of them here because they'd believed in something worth fighting for. They surrounded her now, their joy washing over her like warm water, and for a moment, one moment, she let herself believe the victory was complete.

Rose coordinated the celebration with quiet efficiency, producing food and drinks from somewhere, organizing the chaos into something resembling a party. Alexis caught her eye across the crowded common room, and the girl smiled, a rare expression that softened her usually somewhat concerned features.

Cerval moved through the edges of the crowd, refilling cups and adjusting speakers, doing the invisible work that kept things running smoothly. He'd always been like that, competent and present but somehow easy to overlook. When he passed near Alexis, he paused long enough to murmur, "Well done," before disappearing back into his quiet efficiency.

The words washed over her in waves she couldn't process. She was still exhausted, still wounded despite the basic healing she'd had managed during their journey home. Her ribs ached with every breath. Her arm hung in a makeshift sling. And somewhere beneath the surface celebration, a hollow feeling had taken root that wouldn't let her join in the joy. Soon, she'd have the time to really suit and focus on her healing. It would not be pleasant.

She'd won. But she'd also lost something she couldn't name.

"Easy," Keats murmured, his arm around her waist the only thing keeping her upright.

"They need the truth."

"They'll get it. But not yet. Not tonight." His voice was gentle but firm. "Tonight, let them believe we won completely. Tomorrow is soon enough for complications."

She wanted to argue. Wanted to tell everyone that the victory was hollow, that the artifacts hadn't returned, that someone had played them all for fools and was still out there, still watching, still moving pieces on a board they couldn't see.

Instead, she let herself be swept into the celebration. Let the compound's medical team examine her wounds while voices cheered and hands clasped her good shoulder and people she barely knew thanked her for saving them.

She'd earned that much, at least. One night of pretending everything was fine.

* * * *

The truth came the next morning, as truths always did.

After she'd spent the first hour free last night healing herself. She had taken more damage than even she realized. But, thanks to the gift of revitalization and healing that nearly every Scion had, before she fell asleep in Keats's arms, she was able to get herself back to normal. Somewhat.

Alexis found Aaron in the war room, hunched over his workstation with the intensity of someone who hadn't slept since she'd left for the Arena. Screens surrounded him, displaying data streams and communication logs and patterns that made her head ache looking at them.

The room smelled of cold coffee and the particular staleness of recycled air that had been breathed too many times. Aaron's desk was littered with empty cups and crumpled notes, evidence of the obsessive focus that had kept him here while everyone else celebrated.

"You should be resting," she said.

"So should you." He didn't look up from his work. "But here we both are, because rest is for people who don't have security breaches eating through their networks."

The word hit her like cold water. "Breaches? Plural?"

"I've been tracking this for weeks. Ever since we started seeing patterns in the artifact thefts that suggested inside information."

Aaron finally turned to face her, and the exhaustion in his eyes was matched by grim certainty. "Someone's been feeding data to the other side, Alexis. Access codes, patrol schedules, communication frequencies. Everything we've done to protect ourselves, they've known about it in advance."

"The mole."

"Not a mole. A sophisticated infiltration that goes back months, maybe longer. Whoever this is, they didn't stumble into our systems. They were placed here. Deliberately. With access levels that suggest…"

He trailed off, but Alexis could finish the thought.

"Inner circle," she said. Someone with high-level clearance. "Someone we trust."

"Someone who's been watching everything we do and reporting it to whoever orchestrated this whole mess." Aaron's jaw tightened. He pulled up a display showing data flow patterns, lines of information branching out from the compound like veins. Some of those veins led to destinations that shouldn't exist, to recipients who had no business receiving their communications. "I don't have a name yet. The infiltration is too clean, too careful. But I'm close. Another few days, maybe a week, and I'll be able to trace the data flow back to its source."

Alexis thought of all the people she'd trusted over the past months. Rose, coordinating operations with quiet efficiency, she'd been with the Network off and on for years, due to her mental and psychological fragility? Makelo, ancient and alien but seemingly loyal, what did three thousand years do to a person's loyalties? Ellie, compassionate and eager, always ready to help, was her helpfulness genuine or a cover for something darker? Cerval, competent and invisible, doing the technical work that kept them all connected, the perfect position for someone who wanted to watch without being watched.

One of them was a traitor. One of them had been feeding information to whoever was behind the artifact thefts, the divine destabilization, the entire crisis that had nearly destroyed everything they'd built.

The thought made her want to vomit.

* * * *

Lily found them an hour later, her expression carrying the same grim weight that Alexis felt settling into her own chest.

"I've been checking with our divine contacts," she said without preamble. "The artifacts haven't returned. Not a single one. Whatever the binding terms were supposed to accomplish…"

"They accomplished exactly what they were designed to." Alexis's voice came out flat, hollowed by the realization she'd been avoiding since the Arena. "Kieran complied with the letter of my terms. He ceased all artifact thefts, because he wasn't the one doing the stealing. He returned what he had stolen, which was nothing, because his 'associates' handled the actual thefts."

Lily stared at her. "A loophole."

"He accepted my terms too quickly. I felt it at the time, something wrong about how easily he agreed. I should have known. Should have demanded better wording, more comprehensive conditions."

"You were fighting for your life in a cosmic arena against the son of Hades." Lily's voice cut through her spiral. "You did what you had to do. The loophole isn't your failure, it's evidence that someone planned this entire confrontation with an escape route built in."

"Planned by who?"

No one answered. The question hung in the air like a blade waiting to fall.

Lily moved to the window, staring out at the mountains she could no longer run through at the speed of thought. Her divine heritage was fading, the connection to Hermes weakening with every artifact that remained unreturned. Alexis could see it in the way she moved now, slower than before, more careful. The speed that had defined her was bleeding away, and there was nothing any of them could do to stop it.

"My father won't answer my prayers," Lily said quietly. "I've tried. Every day since the thefts began. He either can't hear me or won't respond. And I can't tell which is worse."

* * * *

Keats found them on the observation deck as evening painted the White Mountains in shades of rose and gold. The observation deck had been added after the compound's conversion, a wooden platform built onto the main lodge's roof, accessible through a trapdoor in the attic. It offered an unobstructed view of the White Mountains stretching north toward Canada, peaks that had stood for millions of years and would stand for millions more. On clear nights, the stars were overwhelming, no light pollution for miles, just the ancient dark and the even more ancient light. It was the closest thing to peace Alexis had found since her parents died.

He looked better than he had since before the Arena, the color had returned to his face, and his oracle sight no longer flickered with the desperate gold of someone pushing past his limits. But there was something in his expression that made Alexis's heart clench with familiar dread.

"You had a vision," she said. Not a question.

"Several. They've been coming more clearly since... since whatever was blocking them stopped. He moved to stand beside her at the railing, his shoulder brushing hers in the easy intimacy they'd rebuilt through fire and fear and the desperate certainty of almost losing each other. The interference that's been clouding my sight for months, it pulled back after the Arena. Not completely, but enough that I can see more than I could before."

"What did you see?"

He was quiet for a long moment, his gaze fixed on the distant peaks.

"Kieran wasn't the architect."

The words confirmed what Hades had mentioned and what she'd already suspected, but hearing them spoken aloud made them more real. More terrifying.

"He was a tool," Keats continued. "Shaped and pointed and used by someone else. Someone who's been planning this for longer than any of us realized. The artifact thefts, the divine destabilization, the challenge in the Arena, all of it was part of a larger design. And Kieran..."

He turned to look at her, and his oracle-touched eyes carried shadows that had nothing to do with the fading light.

"Kieran was supposed to lose. The whole confrontation was engineered to end exactly the way it did, with him defeated, with us thinking we'd won, with the real threat still hidden in the shadows."

Alexis felt the hollow feeling in her chest expand into something vast and cold.

"Then we haven't won anything."

"We've won time. We've won the chance to figure out what's happening before it's too late." Keats took her hand, interlacing their fingers the way they'd done since childhood. "Something greater is moving, Al. Something that's been working in the shadows for years, maybe centuries. I can't see it clearly, not yet, but I can feel it. Watching. Waiting. Planning its next move."

"Something ancient," Lily said quietly. She'd joined them at the railing, her expression fierce despite the fear underneath. "That's what you said before. Something ancient was blocking your visions."

"And it's still out there. Still working toward whatever goal it's set for itself." Keats squeezed Alexis's hand. "But at least now we know it exists. That's more than we knew before the Arena."

* * * *

The three of them stood together as darkness claimed the mountains, watching stars emerge in a sky that suddenly felt less like beauty and more like a reminder of how small they were against the vast machinery of cosmic power.

"We saved them," Alexis said finally. "The people here, the Scions who were counting on us, we bought them more time. That has to count for something."

"It counts for everything." Lily's voice carried conviction that Alexis wished she could feel. "You won the Arena. You proved that love is stronger than philosophy, that we have a right to exist, that someone will fight for us when the cosmos itself seems determined to see us erased."

"But the mole is still here," Aaron said. He'd followed them to the deck, his tablet clutched in his hands like a weapon. "Still watching. Still feeding information to whoever's pulling the strings."

"And the artifacts are still missing," Lily added. "Divine connections are still severing. Whatever the ultimate goal is…"

"We'll stop it." Alexis straightened, pulling strength from somewhere she didn't know she had left. "We'll find the mole. We'll recover the artifacts. We'll figure out who's behind this and we'll stop them before they can finish whatever they started."

"And if we can't?" Aaron's question carried no accusation, the practical concern of someone who dealt in data and probability rather than hope.

Alexis looked at her team, at Keats with his oracle visions and unwavering love, at Lily with her fading speed and fierce loyalty, at Aaron with his methodical determination and quiet courage. At the compound below them, full of Scions who'd trusted her to keep them safe.

"We will," she said. "Because the alternative is... unthinkable."

It wasn't a guarantee. It wasn't even a plan. But it was a promise, to herself, to everyone counting on her, to the memory of parents who'd died protecting her and friends who'd risked everything to stand beside her.

She'd made a deal with Chaos. She'd defeated the son of Hades in single combat. She'd proven that love could overcome philosophy, that belonging could triumph over ideology.

Whatever came next, she would face it the same way she'd faced everything else, with the people she loved at her side and the determination to protect them no matter the cost.

"The mole is in our inner circle," Lily said quietly. "Someone we trust. Someone who's been watching everything we do."

"Then we find them first." Alexis's voice carried steel that surprised even her. "Before they can do any more damage. Before whoever's pulling their strings can use them against us again."

She turned away from the mountains, away from the stars, away from the vast and terrifying questions that wouldn't be answered tonight.

"Tomorrow, we start hunting."

* * * *

Later, much later, Alexis stood alone in her quarters, staring at nothing while the compound settled into uneasy sleep around her.

The room was dark except for the faint glow of starlight through the window. She'd turned off the lights hours ago, preferring the shadows to the harsh clarity of illumination. In the darkness, she could pretend she was a girl standing in a room, not a champion who'd won a cosmic battle, not a granddaughter of Chaos who'd made promises she didn't understand.

The boon pressed against her consciousness like a stone she couldn't put down. That undefined favor she'd promised to Chaos, callable at any time, impossible to refuse. Zeus had recognized it. Had warned her about it. Had looked at her with the concern of someone who understood exactly what kind of entanglement she'd created.

She still hadn't told anyone. Not Keats, despite the love they'd rebuilt through fire and fear. Not Lily, despite the sisterhood that had grown between them. The secret sat in her chest like a second heartbeat, waiting for the moment when Chaos would call it in and she'd discover what price she'd agreed to pay.

You're fighting for people, Keats had said through the barrier. *That's not aberration. That's love.*

But she'd made a deal with a being who predated love. Who predated morality and meaning and all the things she'd told herself she was fighting for. And she'd told no one, because telling people meant trusting them, and trusting them meant admitting she wasn't strong enough to carry everything alone.

Old habits. The oldest ones were always the hardest to break.

She should tell them. Should share the burden the way she'd learned to share everything else. Should trust the people who'd proven they were worth trusting, over and over, through every crisis and revelation.

Tomorrow, she promised herself. *Tomorrow I'll tell Keats about the boon. Tomorrow I'll stop carrying this alone.*

It was the same promise she'd made yesterday. And the day before. And all the days stretching back to that desperate moment in Chaos's realm when she'd agreed to something without understanding its true weight.

But tonight, she let herself sit with the weight of everything that had happened and everything that was still coming. The victory that wasn't a victory. The secrets she still kept. The enemy she couldn't see, moving in shadows that hid from oracle sight.

Outside her window, the White Mountains stood silent and eternal. Somewhere beyond them, the world continued turning, unaware of how close it had come to losing the connection between divine and mortal. Somewhere in the compound below, a traitor breathed the same air as the people they'd betrayed.

And somewhere out there, somewhere in the vast darkness between stars, something ancient and patient continued to watch.

Something that had orchestrated all of this. Something that had shaped Kieran into a weapon and pointed him at everything she loved. Something that was still working toward goals none of them understood, still moving pieces on a board none of them could see.

The Chaos Arena was over.

But the real battle was beginning.

YOU FIND OUT FIRST.

Join the C.L. Stegall mailing list for release dates, exclusive short fiction from the world of the Scions, the Valensi, and the occasional dispatch from the warped mind of C.L., himself.

www.CLStegall.com/subscribe

Your email stays as secret as the Darkness.

The Chaos Arena

ABOUT THE AUTHOR

C.L. Stegall is a multi-genre fiction author who writes stories where nobody is simply wrong. His fiction — spanning urban fantasy, psychological thriller, and literary — is built on the conviction that the most interesting conflicts are the ones where the opposing side has a real argument, where extraordinary ability isolates more than it empowers, and where loyalty means something because it was chosen under pressure, not assigned by circumstance. He doesn't write clean moral universes. He writes the ones that look like the one we actually live in.

He is the author of The Valensi Chronicles — a three-book urban fantasy series following ancient, morally complicated beings navigating survival, identity, and the weight of centuries — and The New Scions, a two-book series reimagining Greek mythology as tragedy dressed in modern clothes. His standalone work includes Blood and Amber, The Black Stair, and others. The psychological thriller serial Warlocks: Dark Horse is forthcoming on Substack. Before writing fiction full-time, he spent nearly six years as President and Senior Editor of Dark Red Press, and a decade before that as a U.S. Army Spanish linguist with Military Intelligence — both of which left him with a world-builder's eye for detail and a permanent suspicion of anyone who seems too certain they're right.

He lives in Texas with his irrepressible wife of more than twenty-five years, Mona, and their cat Shoyu — most likely in his office, working on the next chapter of something nobody sees coming.

The Chaos Arena

www.ingramcontent.com/pod-product-compliance
Ingram Content Group UK Ltd.
Pitfield, Milton Keynes, MK11 3LW, UK
UKHW042005230426
12048UKWH00009B/558